Eden Bradley is a best-selling and award-winning author and writes dark, edgy erotic fiction. Her work has been called 'elegant, intelligent and sensual'.

She lives in L.A.

Praise for Eden Bradley

'Intelligent, haunting and sexy as hell…for you people who like story and heart with your erotica, I'd definitely recommend any of Eden's books, but particularly… *Forbidden Fruit*'
Maya Banks

'People are constantly looking for books similar to Fifty… well look no further, I have what you need! … Eden Bradley writes the most sensual books I have ever read'
My Secret Romance

Also by Eden Bradley:

The Dark Garden

Forbidden Fruit

Eden Bradley

**BLACK
LACE**

1 3 5 7 9 10 8 6 4 2

First published in the United States of America in 2008 by Bantam Dell
A Division of Random House, Inc.
Published in the UK in 2012 by Virgin Books, an imprint of Ebury Publishing
A Random House Group Company

The Random House Group Limited Reg. No. 954009

Addresses for companies within the Random House Group can be found at
www.randomhouse.co.uk

A CIP catalogue record for this book is available from the British Library

The Random House Group Limited supports The Forest Stewardship Council
(FSC®), the leading international forest certification organisation. Our books
carrying the FSC label are printed on FSC® certified paper. FSC is the only forest
certification scheme endorsed by the leading environmental organisations,
including Greenpeace. Our paper procurement policy can be found at:
www.randomhouse.co.uk/environment

Printed and bound by CPI Group (UK) Ltd, Croydon, CR0 4YY

ISBN 9780753541357

To buy books by your favourite authors and register for offers visit
www.randomhouse.co.uk

acknowledgments

To my fellow Smutkateers: Crystal Jordan, Lillian Feisty, and R. G. Alexander, for brainstorming through my issues with this story, and for those two-hour telephone conversations I could not live without.

To Lee Koenig, chef extraordinaire, my food and recipe consultant, for his fabulous recipes and his inspirational love of food. You must keep your eyes open for his upcoming cookbook and dating guide for men, . . . *And He Can Cook.*

I know I've said it before, but the chat-room challenge Divas are a constant inspiration—a long list of wonderful, supportive writers who cheer each other on every single day. You guys are truly amazing—thank you!

And always, to my critique partner, Gemma Halliday, for her constant willingness to read everything I write, and for knowing and trusting my voice.

chapter ✐ one

MIA ROSE CURRY LOOKED UP AT THE CROWDED CLASSROOM, at the rows of seats, full of expectant faces, at the others crowding in the door.

"This class is full," she told them. "If you're not already registered and you'd like to fill out a card to be put on the waiting list, please go to the registration office."

"This class is always full," a voice muttered from somewhere in the vicinity of the door.

Mia smiled. It was true. The Alternative Sexuality class she taught at San Francisco State was in high demand each semester. The students mostly came in looking for a cheap thrill and an easy grade, but she made them work for it. Made them do research, write papers. Tried to teach them something about the sociological effects of culture on sexuality. A few of them even learned something. And she always learned from watching them. From watching how they responded to the things they talked about in class, to the demonstrations, the films she showed them. She studied her students as much as they studied the class assignments. She couldn't help it. As a sociology professor, people were endlessly fascinating to her. Her whole life was about studying people, trying to understand them. Especially herself.

She looked over her classroom, making a quick assessment of each new student. She could usually tell which of them would work hard, participate in discussions. Who would hide in the back of the room and sneer. Who would leave as soon as any really controversial material came up.

Her eyes moved across the front row, drifting from face to face, and stopped cold.

God, he was too beautiful, this young man. Her student, she had to remind herself. A bit older than most of the others, maybe, but still . . .

Tawny skin the color of coffee with plenty of cream, dark, curling hair tipped with gold, as though he'd been in the sun. A close-cropped goatee framing a full, lush mouth. And the most startling eyes, a clear, crystal gray that contrasted with his dusky skin. Oh yes, too beautiful to be believed. And he was looking right at her, those clear gray eyes intense, focused. She shivered.

Your student.

She tore her gaze away, but not before she caught his quick smile. Every bit as shockingly beautiful as the rest of him.

Pulling in a deep breath, she forced herself to concentrate on her job: evaluating her classroom, putting her notes in order. She had to command herself not to look at him so she could begin her opening lecture, but even knowing he was there, at the edge of her vision, made the back of her neck heat up, her entire body, despite the winter chill in the air.

She took a sip from her water bottle and began. "Welcome, everyone, to Alternative Sexuality. In this class we'll study the various avenues of sexuality that differ from what many might consider to be 'the norm.' We will be covering some controversial material. Some of you may even find it offensive."

She moved to the front of her desk and leaned back against it, watching the students as she spoke. "We'll discuss a variety of fetishes and alternative practices, including foot fetishes, cross-dressing, bondage and mummification, domination and submission, pain and sensation play, leather, rubber and latex fetishes, food fetishes, sploshing, which is a fetish involving various kinds of liquids, bestiality, amputee fetish, exhibitionism, voyeurism, infantilism, and perhaps a few more."

There were some requisite snickers from the back of the room. Certainly nothing she hadn't dealt with before. And she was entirely comfortable with her subject here in the classroom.

"Many of you might think of the people who practice these forms of sexuality as freaks, and I'll admit I find some of these practices repulsive, even harmful, and we'll discuss that, as well. But I'm going to ask you to keep an open mind. To put aside any prejudice you may feel and consider these subjects from an objective, scientific perspective. To view these practices as a response to the person's environment." She put her notes down and looked at her students, trying to catch an eye here and there. "This is what we're going to really focus on. What causes people to have these yearnings? And are fetishes a healthy response to certain stimuli? Or are they a psychological defect?"

"What do you think, Professor Curry?"

Ah, God, it was him. The beautiful one. And he was watching her again, so intently. Was it possible she was imagining it? She had to draw in a breath, pretend he was just any other student. She would question why he had such an effect on her later.

"I think . . . what's your name?"

"Jagger. Jagger James."

"I think, Jagger, that it depends on the person, the fetish, and what caused this response in their lives. We'll talk more about this, but you should all know that fetishes can often develop through an almost innocent event, one moment in which an object becomes sexualized. For instance, a common fetish for men is panty hose. Very often this one comes about because a boy in his sexually formative years, anywhere from ages eight through twelve, sees his mother's panty hose slung over the shower curtain after she's washed them. The boy is curious, so he tries them on or even sometimes simply touches them, and has a spontaneous erection. He may never touch them again. Or he may touch them every week. It's different in each case. But in the boy's mind, the panty hose are now an object connected with sexual arousal. This may manifest later in life in the sort of fetish where he wants to wear panty hose. Or he may simply love to see and feel them on a partner. He may even become aroused browsing through the hosiery department in a store.

"I interviewed a man for my master's thesis, a perfectly ordinary guy. Tall, masculine. He loved football, camping.

But he also loved flowers. The scent, the sight, of them, a woman in a floral print dress or in floral lingerie was incredibly arousing. And this is how it started."

She moved across the room, watching her students, watching for their reactions to what she was telling them. Except for one. No, better to avoid his gaze.

"He took a bath when he was eleven years old. He liked to use Mr. Bubble, but the bottle was empty, so he tried his older sister's lavender bath salts, not knowing they wouldn't bubble up. During his bath, he masturbated to orgasm, surrounded by the strong scent of lavender. Now, in this particular case, he did it again and again, and developed a very strong fetish, which he has pursued into adulthood. But the same thing could have happened to another boy after only one incident. Or to another without any effect at all. There is only so much researchers understand about how these things work. But what we do know is that each situation must be evaluated on an individual basis."

Jagger spoke up again. "So you don't assume fetishes are a neurotic or even psychosocial tendency, necessarily?"

If they were, she was in very deep trouble.

"Not necessarily, no."

He smiled, and her legs felt as though they were suffused with a warm liquid. Melting. Yes, like melted chocolate. Milk chocolate. The shade of his skin.

Stop it!

She tucked a strand of her dark hair behind her ear. "This is exactly the kind of idea I want you to throw out the window until we explore the subject in detail. Here, we're going to stop making the usual snap judgments, rid ourselves of preconceived notions, and explore what truly goes on in a person's mind." She pushed off her desk and strolled across the front of the room, avoiding his gaze. Still, a small shiver raced over her skin when she walked past him. "We'll do research, assess data, witness certain events here in class, discuss others. And we'll have an opportunity to talk with some of the people who practice these things in their everyday lives. Please take a look at the class syllabus now to review the in-class activities. Then think about whether or not this is something you can handle. But I want you all to push yourselves a bit. To see these things, talk to these people, ask questions, and try to stretch your boundaries. To explore your own response to whatever the subject might be. To make yourself the subject of your own sociological study."

"Is that what you do, Professor Curry?"

Him again. Jagger. This time she looked him right in the eye. "Every day of my life."

It was the truth. Too bad she'd never been able to come up with any conclusive answers.

"Karalee, over here." Mia waved her friend to their usual table in the faculty lounge. She watched as Karalee crossed the room, graceful and lithe. Mia had always admired her elegant, willow-slender height, the way she carried herself.

"Hi. Sorry I'm late. A student had some questions after class." Karalee folded herself into the chair and opened a brown paper bag. "Tuna again. You'd think my mother packed my lunch."

"How was your class?" Mia asked her, spearing her salad.

Karalee pulled off her glasses, revealing blue, almond-shaped eyes, and tucked the glasses into her briefcase. With her height, her fine bone structure and exotic eyes, Mia had always thought she should have been a model rather than an English teacher.

"Class was fine. Good. I think I even have a few people who are actually interested in literature this semester. I like my night classes so much better. The students are older: people who really want to be there." Karalee paused, took a clip from her briefcase, and quickly twisted her shoulder-length, golden-brown hair into a neat bun. "But you don't have that problem with your class, do you?"

"With my regular sociology classes, yes. With the Alternative class, no. Never."

Karalee bit into her sandwich, chewed for a moment. "So, good group this semester?"

"Um...yes. They're fine."

"What was that?"

"What was what?" Mia stuffed a lettuce leaf into her mouth, but found it hard to swallow as her skin heated up.

"Did I just see you blush?"

Mia shrugged. "It's nothing."

"It's something, Mia Rose. Tell me."

"Okay. Okay. It's just...there's this guy in my class... God, I sound like I'm in high school. But he's no kid. An older student."

"How old?"

"Mid-, maybe late twenties." She took a sip from her water bottle, shook her head. "You would not believe how beautiful this man is. He has the most gorgeous skin, and his eyes...the way he looks at me..."

Karalee set her sandwich down, covered one of Mia's hands with her own. "Mia, this is one of your students you're talking about."

"I know. Don't you think I know that?" She paused, immediately remorseful. "I'm sorry, Karalee. I didn't mean to snap at you."

"It's okay. I just . . . you're really attracted to this guy. I can see it all over your face. And if I can, someone else might be able to see it, too. Be careful."

"I will be. And it's not as if anything would ever happen with him. I'm just his professor."

"You're a young, gorgeous professor. You're only thirty-three, for heaven's sake. He certainly wouldn't be the first student to find you attractive. Stranger things have happened, Mia."

"Well, nothing's going to happen. He's my student, I'm his teacher, end of story."

But her head was full of other stories, and there was nothing innocent about any of them. Quick images of his mouth coming down on hers, his hands all over her . . .

She really had to put a stop to this insane attraction. Because that's exactly what it was: insane. Jagger James was off-limits.

She had a feeling she'd have to remind herself of that every single day until the end of the semester. And then she could go off on her summer vacation and not see him anymore, think about him anymore.

If only she knew what the hell she was going to do in the meantime.

Of course he was the only thing on her mind that evening, after her night class and a quick dinner with a few coworkers. The fog was rolling in when she pulled up to her cozy little house across the street from Stern Grove in Golden Gate Park, pulled her briefcase and her laptop out of the car, and went inside. Her shoes scuffed softly across the hardwood floors as she went to turn on the lights.

She'd always loved this house; it had been her grandmother's. She'd inherited it two years ago, and had moved right in, happily leaving her apartment in the Richmond District behind. It was small but neat, with the old stucco walls so common in the homes built around the park in the twenties. And it had a working fireplace with gorgeous tile work her grandfather had added before she was born. The tiny back garden, with its small patch of lawn bordered by her grandmother's lovely roses, was just enough to let her enjoy a bit of gardening without it being a burden.

It was January now, and miraculously, a few sparse roses still bloomed. Something about the magic of her grandmother's garden. And like her grandmother, Mia loved this time of year. She swore she could smell the tang of the nearby ocean better in winter.

She tossed her briefcase and her purse onto the pale, overstuffed damask sofa and flicked on the heat as she went down the hall to her bedroom. She quickly changed into her usual loungewear: vintage satin pajamas and a matching robe in a soft shade of peach that made her feel like a forties film starlet. She loved the feel of the silk against her skin, so smooth it was almost like liquid, like honey.

Oh God, don't think about that now.

But her body had been alive all day. And Jagger James'

image was continually lurking behind her eyes, making her hot and trembly all over when she indulged herself for a moment, letting her mind wander.

She walked back down the hall and into the all-white kitchen, with its smooth, painted cupboards and white-tiled counters. This room she'd had redone last year, updating the appliances in order to indulge her passion for cooking.

Passion was one word for it, she supposed, her body giving a quick shiver at the thought. There was definitely passion where food was involved, much of which she'd never really allowed herself to think about, not consciously, anyway. She'd never found a partner whose interests lay in the same area, not since those early explorations with Ben. At least, that was the excuse she'd been giving herself for years.

She pushed the idea away before she had a chance to really examine it, opened the refrigerator, and took out a chilled bottle of Chardonnay, a nice white from the Napa Valley. She poured herself a glass and took it into the bedroom. Her big, antique brass bed looked all too inviting, with its fluffy, white down quilt and piles of pillows. Slipping out of her robe, she climbed in, intending to read. She sifted through the small pile of books on her nightstand; she tended to read several simultaneously. But nothing held her interest tonight. Instead, she found the remote and clicked on the television, flipped through the channels. No news, no talk shows. She wanted something peaceful, relaxing. She left it on the Food Channel with the sound down, idly watching a man sautéing vegetables. He had strong-looking hands as he stirred them, chopped a handful of chives, and added them to the pan. Nice. Even better when he started a sauce. Her body went warm, watching the sensual glide of the liquid as the disembodied hands stirred it in the pan, imagined they were Jagger's hands.

Her sex gave a sharp squeeze.

Why was she thinking of him? But then again, why not? She wasn't in the classroom now. Surely there couldn't be any harm in allowing herself to picture his face, his mouth . . .

Yes, his mouth, those full lips. What would they feel like on her skin?

She ran her hands over her breasts. Not enough. Unbuttoning her pajama top, she let the silk slide away, and smoothed her hands over her bare skin. Her nipples went hard as she imagined his mouth there, licking, sucking.

Yes.

Suddenly her body was swarming with need. Her skin went hot, her sex clenched hungrily. She needed more.

Leaning over, she took her vibrator from the nightstand drawer, switched it on. The pink, textured phallus buzzed to life. She pulled off her pajama bottoms, lowered the vibrator between her thighs, and touched it gently to her damp cleft.

Oh, yes.

With Jagger's face in her mind, she pressed a little harder, teased one hard nipple with the other hand.

Not enough, not enough . . .

She focused once more on the glow of the television, on the strong male hands stirring the sauce, pouring it over a dish.

Yes. Better.

Her body filled up with pleasure that quickly became an urgent stab of desire as she imagined it was Jagger's hands pouring the silky sauce over her skin. Him licking it off.

Yes!

Her breasts ached, her sex ached. She moved both hands down between her legs, spread the lips of her sex, and circled her clitoris with the vibrator, then moved it to dip inside. Pleasure shivered through her system, building and building. She pressed the vibe a little harder, closed her eyes, and saw Jagger's face hovering over hers. In her mind, it was his hands doing these lovely things to her. His mouth, yes, licking that sauce from her flesh.

Jagger, not Ben.

She'd always fantasized to the food images while thinking of Ben. Never anyone else. Never any other man until now.

She pushed all thoughts of Ben from her mind, feeling a little guilty. But her body needed Jagger now.

Needed him. *Jagger.*

Her body hovered on the edge, then she pressed the vibe hard against her clit, sending her tumbling over the edge.

She cried out as she came. And in her mind was a blur of hands and mouths, rubbing, sucking, licking, the flavors sweet and salty and pure sex. But it was all him. All Jagger.

And it felt too good for her to care.

Mia stuffed her notes into her brown leather briefcase after her Friday night Beginning Sociology class. She was looking forward to the weekend. It was always a bit of a shock to her system, the start of every semester. She'd need the weekend to shift gears in her head. And there was one subject she was really going to have to work on shifting: Jagger James.

She had to stop thinking about him. She'd come to class today, unsure as to how she could even look at him. Especially after he'd starred in her vivid, lustful fantasy the night before, driving her to such an intense climax she was left shaking and weak. But he'd been missing from class.

Her body was heating up again just thinking about the previous night, how sharp her pleasure had been. How devastating.

She tucked a strand of hair behind her ear and straightened up. Her nipples were hard, stimulated even by the caress of her sweater through the thin lace of her bra.

Yes, get home, get back into bed, and do it again.

"Hi."

She turned around. "Oh. Hi."

She could not believe he was standing there.

"Jagger. Um . . . what can I help you with?"

"I had to miss class today and I wanted to see if there was a reading assignment."

"You can find out by looking at your syllabus." She didn't mean to sound so cold. A defensive gesture, she supposed. She was burning up inside, with embarrassment, the shock of finding him there when she'd just been imagining him doing lewd and lovely things to her body.

Christ, Mia, get a grip!

"Ah, yes. I suppose I could." He had a deep voice, deep and husky. Like wood smoke and honey. "But I wanted to talk to you."

"About what?"

She could swear her sex was going damp, just being this close to him. He was even better up close. His skin really was as smooth as milk chocolate.

"I wanted to know if we could have coffee sometime."

Her breath stalled for a moment. "Coffee?"

"Coffee." He shrugged. "And talk."

"Jagger, I . . . you're my student. It's not a good idea. If you have questions about the class, I have office hours every Tuesday evening."

"I do have questions, but they're more . . . personal." He smiled down at her, that stunning flash of strong, white teeth that went through her like a small shock. Her fingers tightened around the handle of her briefcase.

"We shouldn't be having personal conversations."

He leaned into the doorway, a casual pose. "I disagree. Why don't we try it and find out?"

"You're very confident, aren't you?"

"I always thought confidence was a positive trait."

"It is. It's just . . ."

She couldn't even carry on a conversation with him! What on earth was wrong with her?

He reached out then, laid his fingertips on her forearm. "Think about it. I'll ask again."

Heat shivered through her, and her mind blurred. She shook her head.

"I can't. I'm your teacher."

"Yes, I know." He leaned in, until he was only inches from her. She should back up, she knew, put some distance between them. But she couldn't do it. "But we're both adults," he went on. "Think about it, Professor Curry. Mia Rose."

He said her name softly. She couldn't help that she loved the sound of it. She shook her head again.

"You should go now."

"Alright. But I'll be back."

He smiled at her, turned, and walked away, leaving her dizzy with confusion. He would come back, she understood that. What she wasn't clear about was whether or not she wanted him to.

He was too smooth, too charming. And so beautiful up close her fingers itched to touch him, just to brush her fingertips over his mouth.

God.

She was making it worse, letting herself think about things like this. But she couldn't help herself. She was all twisted up inside where he was concerned, totally out of control.

Dangerous.

Why did that idea make her shiver inside?

That night she went home and went to bed, ordered herself to go to sleep. But later she woke in the dark, tangled in the sheets, dream images of him flickering still in front of her eyes. And her hand went between her legs. She rubbed her wet cleft, pressing the heel of her hand hard onto her clit, sinking two fingers deep inside her. And with Jagger's face once more in her mind's eye, she came into her hand, calling his name into the night.

Jagger paced the length of his loft apartment. He couldn't seem to settle down, and it was well after midnight. He paused by one of the enormous windows and stared out over the city. San Francisco's Mission District had a long history as the home to drug dealers, flophouses, and prostitutes, but buildings like his all over the downtown area were being bought and remodeled, old warehouses converted into loft apartments.

He'd been lucky to get this place. It was big, and it had a

great view. He'd spent his entire savings buying the top-floor apartment and remodeling the kitchen. It had seemed important at the time, to have the dream kitchen. Even though after working in the restaurant business for too long, he'd lost the pleasure cooking had once given him. Too many long hours in the heat and the steam, cooking at such a frantic pace he didn't have a moment to really think about what he was doing. Simply working like some sort of automaton. Like a trained dog. And there was nothing left at the end of the night but the hard scents of oil and garlic on his clothes. No real satisfaction. But it had seemed right to have a chef's kitchen, anyway.

Mostly he ignored the kitchen these days, preferring to eat at one of the dozens of great local hole-in-the-wall restaurants or with his downstairs neighbors, Jean and her partner, Leilani, who was a phenomenal cook. But he never tired of the view from every window in the apartment. He loved the lights of the city below him, even the neon of the club signs. It seemed like magic to him, the mood and the energy of the city caught in a colorful splash of light.

But tonight the view brought him no peace. His mind was too busy, full of images of Mia Rose Curry's face. Her voice. Her scent.

Hell, he'd almost lost it earlier tonight standing next to her in the classroom. Her scent had hit him like a blow to the gut. Vanilla, but with an edge of some exotic spice. Good enough to eat.

He wanted her. Had to have her. He understood her concerns about the taboo nature of a relationship with him. But it didn't have to be a relationship. He wasn't in the market for a new relationship. Not anymore. Not after the last few disasters.

After Dana, he'd been able to bounce back. He'd fallen hard for her when he was starting college. Love at eighteen was excruciating. Especially when she'd left to go to another school across the country a year later. The hardest part had been that she didn't seem all that upset over leaving him behind.

Elena had been harder. She'd been furious that he'd decided to give up his career. They'd had plans, and those plans hadn't included him going back to school to get his master's. What it had come down to was that she wasn't willing to wait. A year later and he still had the ring in its velvet box in his dresser drawer.

No, he needed some time off. But that didn't mean he had to go without female companionship entirely, did it?

A night, maybe two, a few weeks together. He was sure they could keep it under wraps. And the blast of energy coming off her, the heat rolling off her skin tonight, told him she wanted this as much as he did.

He had to feel her skin under his hands. Had to kiss that lush, little red mouth of hers. Red as ripe cherries, without a trace of lipstick on. And the green of her eyes against all those midnight-black curls, her skin pale as any Irish rose should be.

He loved the idea of the contrast of their skin, couldn't get that image out of his mind. What would she feel like beneath his hands? What would it take to break through that cool veneer she wore like armor?

The ringing of the telephone startled him, and he shook his head as he flipped his cell open.

"Speak."

"Hey, Jagger, it's Jean." Jean and Leilani lived in one of

the ground-floor apartments. They'd been together for years. And they'd been his best friends since he'd moved into the building just over a year ago. Right after his breakup with Elena.

"You still there, Jagger?"

"What? Yeah, I'm here. What's up?"

"Leilani is doing one of her Hawaiian pig roasts tonight. Come on down and eat. We're having a few people over."

"I don't know, Jean. I think I'm staying in tonight."

"It's Friday night."

"Yeah. I have a few things to take care of. I'm just gonna lay low."

"Is everything okay? You sound a little out of it."

He ran a hand over his jaw. Was he okay? He wasn't sure. "Yeah, I'm fine."

"Okay. Maybe you'll come by tomorrow for leftovers?"

"Sure, I might do that."

"Good. Then you can tell us what's up with you, because I can tell it's something."

"Come on, Jean. Everything's fine."

"Yeah, yeah, Jagger. Have a good night."

They hung up, and he tossed his cell phone on the couch. He was a little taken aback that Jean had heard something in his voice. That this thing with Mia Rose was affecting him so much. Enough to make him want to hide in his apartment. To make him think about his past relationships.

What the hell was wrong with him?

Restless, he moved across the wood plank floors, pausing to turn on the stereo. The soulful sounds of Miles Davis filled the air, the old jazz his father, a musician himself, had taught him to appreciate during his summers in New

Orleans. Those summers with his father had been all about music. Music and the food that was unique to the Big Easy.

He paused a moment to appreciate a few sultry notes, then turned toward the bathroom, the only room in the apartment with full walls. He'd done the tile work himself, using gray slate on the floors and stone in the shower, on the counters. He loved the natural look of it, yet it had a stark, urban feel at the same time. Serenity and energy. Balanced.

He reached into the shower and turned the hot water on full blast, stripped down, then stepped in. He wanted the water, the warmth, to relax him. Instead, the heat of it only made him burn more inside. And all he could think of was having *her* in there with him, her naked skin pale against him. Even better, her wet flesh beneath the translucent fabric of a white cotton T-shirt.

Yeah.

His cock went hard, gave a jerk, and his hand went there, pressed on the shaft.

He leaned back against the wall, let the water fall over him. The shower had always been sensual to him. He loved to shower with a woman, couldn't do it without the sex. He had a real thing for water, for seeing and feeling a woman wet all over.

Get Mia Rose in here. Get her naked and wet.

He wrapped his fingers around his cock and stroked, then turned so the showerhead sprayed right onto him, hot and needle-sharp.

Oh yeah.

He stroked faster, letting the water do its work on him, his body heating up, buzzing with lust, with pleasure. And in his head he saw Mia Rose there with him, imagined what her bare breasts would look like with the hot water cascading over them. He would go down on his knees, worship her wet body. Spread her thighs...

He groaned, his cock hardening even more.

What would she taste like?

He thrust his hips, pumping his cock into his hand.

Had to have her, had to have her...

He *would* have her.

His climax came down on him hard and fast, shaking him to the core. Pleasure coursed through his cock, his body, his limbs. And all he saw was *her*.

Mia Rose.

Yes, he would have her. Had to find a way. He'd do whatever he had to. Because this woman he'd seen only a few times was already becoming an obsession.

He would have her, get her out of his system, then move on. Hadn't he spent this last year learning how to do exactly that?

He leaned into the cool tiles behind him, letting the water wash away his seed. It would take more than stroking himself to climax in the shower to get her out of his mind. He knew that. He'd have to find a way to get past that cool reserve of hers. To get beyond the restrictions of a student-teacher relationship.

Fuck it. He'd figure it out. Had to.

Had to.

Because he was pretty damn sure he'd lose his mind if he didn't.

chapter ✐ two

MONDAY AFTERNOON AND MIA'S CLASSROOM WAS STI-
fling. It was one of those rare warm days in San Francisco
that always came at the oddest times of year, and whoever
had used the room last had turned off the air. She flipped the
thermostat as she passed it, moving to the front of the classroom. She took her light sweater off, laying it over the back
of the chair behind her desk, then pulled some papers from
her briefcase and set them on the podium.

Monday had come all too quickly. She'd spent the weekend doing what she always did: gardening, firming up the
coming week's lesson plans, drinking a steaming latte from
the espresso cart as she wandered the local farmers' market
Sunday morning, admiring the rows of gorgeously colored
produce. On Sunday night she went home and made herself
a fairly superb ratatouille, took a good book to bed, then

quickly tossed it aside to watch the Food Network while she brought herself to orgasm over and over. With her pink vibrator, with her hands, driven by the scent of her dinner in the air.

Jagger James' face hadn't left her mind for one moment.

The first day of a new week. It had passed slowly. She had spent the day agonizing over seeing him in class. God, she was behaving like some twelve-year-old with her first crush.

But she had to admit, Jagger was the first man she'd felt any sparks for in a very long time. Too long. Although Mia had always prided herself on being a sexual sophisticate of sorts—she did teach the subject, after all, and had experimented with a number of things—it had been half a year since she'd had sex with anyone. Her little pink vibrator had become her best friend, and she hadn't minded at all.

Until now.

She wanted him. Wanted him so desperately her breath caught simply imagining his face. Those amazing eyes, like two pieces of clear gray quartz, set off by his smooth coffee-with-cream skin. He was almost too beautiful for a man, too exotic. Except that he was so tall, so intrinsically masculine, carried himself with such utter confidence.

Students began to file in and take their seats. Mia pretended to read from a piece of paper, but she really had no idea what was on it. She was keeping an eye out for Jagger, her pulse thrumming with anticipation.

Stop it!

But that was impossible. She wanted to see him too badly.

It really was too damn hot in the room.

Even hotter when Jagger walked in. His long-legged

stride was loose, relaxed, as he moved down the aisle and took a seat at the front of the room, only a few feet from her.

Her body surged with lust.

God.

How was she ever going to get through this class? This semester? Pure torture.

She began the lecture, doing her best to make eye contact with the other students, her gaze passing over him. She did manage eventually to find her rhythm in the familiar lecture, but only as long as she didn't look at him, just kept talking.

"Freud tells us that the unconscious mind is the source of our motivations, the desires for sex, food, the inspiration for an artist or a scientist. From his perspective, anything you yearn for is natural and not something over which you have any control. You can only choose how—or if—to act on these urges. Freud used the German word *'trieb,'* which translates to 'instincts,' or 'drives,' for these motivational forces. He also called them 'wishes.'"

Jagger raised his hand and she nodded, her cheeks warming before he even spoke.

"I've read that when you ignore the urges, they can become even more powerful. Freud said it's the wish breaking from the unconscious into consciousness. So does that mean it's unhealthy to suppress these urges, Professor Curry?"

Her pulse stuttered and she had one brief moment of self-doubt about the fact that she had long ignored her own desires, her own secret "wishes."

"That depends on what your drives are. If you feel driven to molest young children, then I'd have to say suppressing the urge is healthy."

"What if it's something less...deviant?"

Yes, another course for this discussion. Anything to make her stop thinking about her evening spent with her vibrator and the Food Network, and Jagger's image in her mind. "Ah, perhaps we should discuss the definition of deviant. Who would like to give me their take on it?"

Another student, an attractive young woman, spoke up. "Deviant behavior is repulsive, abhorrent."

Jagger turned around in his seat. "You seem pretty certain of that, Lora."

She shrugged. "You're the one who used the word, Jagger. The professor asked us to define it. I did."

Mia ignored the tiny part of herself that was disturbed by the fact that Jagger obviously knew this young woman, knew her name. "Abhorrent is a strong term. The Latin root of 'ab-hor' means to detest, to shrink back in horror."

The girl shrugged once more. "That's what I think of deviant behavior."

Jagger was facing Mia again. "I think there are more positive connotations to the word."

Mia nodded, trying to ignore the unmistakable sultry undertone in his voice. "Why don't you tell us what you mean?"

"You must admit there's a certain mystery to the idea of deviant behavior. Something intriguing. And I'm not talking about things like molesting children. I'm talking about consenting behavior between adults. What one person might define as deviant could be nothing more than healthy sexual exploration for someone else. Don't you agree, Professor?"

She knew her skin was heating up. She couldn't do a thing about it. "Since I teach this class, I imagine you all already know the answer to that. It's all a matter of perspective, in most cases, again discounting such things as child molestation."

"So, where would you draw the line, then?"

Why did it seem as though it was just the two of them having a private conversation? But as soon as that thought crossed her mind, she became acutely aware of the other students, watching her, listening.

"I draw the line at consent. Children, animals, are unable to speak for themselves. And there are other practices I personally consider repugnant and perhaps not physically healthy, such as scat play, blood play."

Jagger nodded. "But other than that? You feel it's all fair game?"

"From an intellectual standpoint, yes."

What about those more personal perversions, Mia?

She had to grip the edge of the podium to prevent herself from shaking.

Focus.

Jagger was smiling at her, as though he'd won some point. Maybe he had.

"Why don't we move on and discuss what you read in chapter eight?"

Class seemed to last forever, although it was the usual two hours. Far too long. Maybe next time she'd show a film.

Yes, to be close to him in a darkened room, the flickering glow of the film on the wall...

Stuffing her papers into her briefcase, she grabbed her sweater and was about to follow her students out when he approached her desk. God, he smelled good. That bohemian edge of patchouli, mixed with something dark and smoky.

As exotic as he was. Before she could help herself, she pulled in a long breath.

"Interesting lecture tonight, Professor."

"Thank you."

"But I didn't want to talk about that."

"No?" She looked up at him. He really was something up close. She shivered, commanded herself to hold still. Before she did something completely foolish, like pull his head toward hers and kiss him.

Don't be an idiot, Mia.

"No." He stepped closer. "I'm going to ask you again to have coffee with me."

"And I'll have to say no again."

"Do you really have to?"

She stared at him, her gaze meeting his. "Yes, I really have to. It's not . . . appropriate."

"Coffee isn't appropriate?"

"Not the coffee . . . the . . . look, it's not appropriate for a professor to spend time with a student outside of the academic setting."

No matter how badly you want to.

She had sudden visions of him pushing her down on the desk, pulling her skirt up, driving into her in one shuddering thrust . . .

Stop it!

"Even if we're discussing the class?" he asked her.

"You don't give up easily, do you?" She picked up her briefcase and slung the strap over her shoulder, trying to catch her breath.

"I don't give up at all." He smiled then, a smile that

reached his eyes. Such a sweet smile on a face she wanted to do very dirty things to.

He took another step closer and she caught his scent again, dark and sexy. Her body went a little weak. It started in her stomach, then spread outward, down her legs, into her arms, through her breasts.

"Come on, Mia Rose. People do it all the time. I see them in the cafés all over this neighborhood. I'm sure you've seen it, too. And it's just coffee. Or maybe some dessert to go with it. Do you have a sweet tooth?"

She nodded, swallowed.

"There's this place only a few blocks from here. They make this beautiful fruit torte." His voice lowered and he leaned in a bit, just enough for his scent to carry to her on the air once more. "Now I know women usually go for the chocolate, but I'm telling you, this stuff is not to be missed."

Why did he have to talk food? She tried to shake her head, to refuse, but she couldn't make herself do it.

"Come with me, Mia Rose."

How much could it really hurt? Just a simple conversation, some coffee, dessert. They would be in a public place, with a table between them.

Don't do it, Mia.

"Alright. I'll go with you. Just . . . just for the torte."

"Great. I have my car, or we can walk."

"Let's walk."

Not safe to be alone in a car with him. Too dark, too close. Too much like a couple of high school kids going to park somewhere and make out.

God, what had made her think that? She really had to get herself under control. But she was going with him.

He smiled, dazzling her once more, then he waited while she turned the lights off, locked the room.

They walked through the dark campus, weaving between the buildings, passing other students and faculty on their way out, Mia keeping a safe distance from him.

"So, Mia Rose, how long have you been teaching here at San Francisco State?"

Small talk. She could deal with that. Even if the fact that he kept calling her by her full name was making her legs shake for some inexplicable reason. "I've been here my whole career. I like it. I didn't really want to move away from San Francisco."

"Ah, so this city is home for you?"

"Yes. It's the only home I've ever known, really. What about you?"

"It's home now. I have a converted loft downtown. But I grew up between Berkeley and New Orleans."

"New Orleans?"

"My dad lives there. He's a jazz musician. Plays a mean sax, among other things."

They left the university grounds and passed onto the sidewalk. A small breeze blew the scent of the ocean past them, cooling the muggy air.

She pushed her hair from her face. "I've always wanted to see New Orleans."

"You should. It's different from any other city in the world. Great music. And it's a real food town, if that's what you're into."

If he only knew . . .

But all she said was, "I love good food."

"Do you, now?"

She turned to look at him, the streetlights illuminating his face. He really was gorgeous. "Yes. I like to think of myself as something of a gourmet. Not that I can cook nearly that well myself, but I appreciate anyone who can. Why?"

"I was a chef. Before I decided to go back to school. I could cook for you sometime."

He is too perfect.

Except that he was completely off-limits.

"I don't know about that..."

"We can talk about it another time. Look, this is the place."

A warm hand at the small of her back and he ushered her through the door of a café she'd passed before but had never tried. It was called simply Java. Inside, the rich scent of coffee filled the air, which was a little warm and close. The place was all muted colors and overstuffed furniture. No tables to provide a safe barrier between them. But it was too late to turn back.

"I'll order the torte. What would you like to drink, Mia Rose?"

"Oh, I can get it." She was flustered again. Or still, maybe.

"I wouldn't think of it."

He was all old-world manners, this guy. Something she secretly loved, even in this age of feminism. And it was only coffee. "Alright, thanks. I usually have a latte."

"Coming right up. Why don't you find a place to sit?"

Mia looked around, hoping for a single chair, but the only free spots were on the sofas. She found an empty one and sat, dropping her purse and her briefcase on the floor, and watched Jagger order for them, saw the ease with which he held himself. Something sexy as hell about that sort of utter confidence, that total lack of self-consciousness. Her hands were sweating. She wiped them on the front of her slacks.

He carried two oversize ceramic mugs and set them down on the long table in front of the couch, sat down next to her. Half a foot away, but too close by far.

"He'll bring the torte in a minute."

"Thanks. For the coffee."

"You're welcome."

The young, gangly server came out from behind the counter and set a small plate with a lovely slice of fruit torte on the table before them. Sliced strawberries, blueberries, and kiwi glistened beneath a shining sugar glaze, piled on top of a layer of custard and a flaky crust. Her mouth watered. Just looking at this gorgeous concoction with Jagger sitting next to her was doing things to her head, to her body.

You are on very dangerous ground.

Yes, but right now she didn't want to be anywhere else.

"You have to taste this." He picked up a fork, and she noticed then how large his hands were, how smooth the brown skin on the back of them. He had long fingers. The hands of a musician, like his father. But he was a chef instead. Too good.

He cut into the torte, held the fork to her lips. She was flustered, with him trying to feed her. She looked at him, and he locked his gaze with hers. There was humor in his sultry gray eyes. And something that was totally about sex.

She was shivering all over. And before she had a chance to

think about it, he was whispering, "Come on, Mia Rose. Taste this." And she opened her mouth and let him slide the fork right in.

It was sweet and tart on her tongue; she couldn't suppress a small sigh of pleasure.

"I knew you'd like it. Have some more."

He fed her another piece, then took a bite himself, using the same fork. It seemed an intimate gesture, somehow. And she became momentarily obsessed with the fact that the fork had been in his mouth, then in hers as he fed her one more bite.

He stopped to take a sip of his coffee and she realized how utterly lost she was. Straightening up, she gave herself a mental shake, sipped her own coffee. She was being ridiculous.

"So, um, Jagger...you've spent some time in New Orleans?"

"Yeah, every summer growing up, sometimes at spring break. Sometimes at Christmas. I go back every chance I get. My dad still plays at this club in the French Quarter most weekends. Goes on tour once in a while with some of the big-name acts. I love it there. It's my second home."

He paused, picked up a dark, succulent berry, and popped it into his mouth, in between those lush lips. They seemed even more lush framed by the dark goatee, something she'd always loved on a man. Mia watched, fascinated, as he licked his thumb, his forefinger. She shivered, a small chill running over her skin.

He went on. "The rest of the time I was with my mother, in Berkeley. She's an artist, a painter. I guess I've had a pretty bohemian life. Mom took me to Paris when I was ten. I think she hoped I'd become an artist, like her. And my dad was always trying to get me to play an instrument. Sent me a drum set for my thirteenth birthday." He paused, grinned. "Mom was not thrilled. But I just never had it in me, I guess. I found my art in food."

Another shiver went through her. If he only had any idea what those words did to her . . .

"What about you?" he went on. "Where did you grow up?"

"Oh, I . . ." She never knew what to say when people asked her this sort of thing. She hadn't even told Karalee, her closest friend, the whole story. But then, she hadn't ever let anyone quite that close, had she? "Well, my mom and I moved around a lot until I was thirteen. Then I came to San Francisco to live with my grandmother."

"Are you close with her? Your grandmother?"

"I was." A small stab of pain went through her that never seemed to quite go away. "She's been gone for two years."

"I'm sorry."

She looked at him then. There was sincerity on his face. He reached out and laid his hand on her wrist. Heat shot through her like a small stroke of lightning. She shuddered. "Jagger . . ." She looked down at his hand touching her, back at his face.

"Oh, sorry." He pulled his hand back. "I'm being inappropriate again, am I?" But he was smiling at her.

She sipped her coffee, set it down on the table. "So, Jagger, if you're a chef, why are you in school now?"

"Good question." He picked up his cup, his fingers unexpectedly tense around the handle for a moment, his eyes on the table. Then he loosened all over and settled back into the sofa cushions, his pose casual, relaxed. Maybe she had imagined that moment of tension? "I worked in kitchens since I was fifteen. I'd always wanted to cook. I went to school for it, got my own kitchen in some really great restaurants. But after a while, doing it every day, *having* to cook, took all the joy out of it for me. Working in a professional kitchen is unbelievably fast-paced. Not that I mind working hard. But there wasn't one minute in the day where I could really stop and *taste* anything, you know? So about a year ago I decided to go back to school. Just a few classes at first. Then I quit cooking altogether and came back full-time."

"What are you studying?"

"I'm going for a psychology degree. This is my last semester at State, then I'll transfer to U.C. Berkeley to get my master's. In fact, I only have your class and one other I take on Thursday mornings to fulfill my requirements before I move ahead. I left some of my electives for last."

"I don't understand how you're old enough to have had one career already and be ready to move on to another."

He leaned toward her, moving closer. "I'm old enough, Mia Rose. For anything."

His tone was pure seduction. She couldn't help but respond to it, her skin going warm all over. And she couldn't help but ask as she avoided his gaze, "How old, Jagger?"

"Twenty-six." He paused, keeping quiet for a few moments. Then he said quietly, "I'm not some eighteen-year-old kid, if that's what you wanted to know."

Doesn't matter anyway.

"Okay. I mean, I knew you weren't eighteen," she stammered.

It did matter, damn it.

She was an idiot.

"It's just coffee, right, Mia Rose? Nothing inappropriate. Although I have to say, I'd like there to be."

"Jagger . . ."

"I won't lie. I think you're beautiful. Smart, obviously. I admire you. And I'm very, very attracted to you."

"Jagger, I'm seven years older than you are. And I'm your professor. We shouldn't even be having this conversation."

Her insides were absolutely melting. It took everything she had to push those images of him with his hands on her from her mind.

He leaned forward, took her hand in his. Heat swarmed over her skin. "What we're doing here right now is perfectly innocent. But I'd be lying if I said that's all I wanted."

She yanked her hand back, every alarm in her body, in her brain, clanging at full volume. She stood up, grabbing her purse and briefcase. "I have to go."

He stood up, too, towering over her. "Please don't. I don't mean to come off so strong. I just wanted to be honest with you—"

"Don't be. I have to go," she repeated.

She turned and made her way through the overstuffed couches, the low tables, and pushed through the door.

Outside it had grown cooler, but the air did nothing to calm her burning cheeks. She knew this was wrong; she never should have come. And her body was absolutely on fire.

She wanted him. Impossible to deny. And the longer she sat next to him, talked to him, the more intense that yearning had become.

You can't have him, so you might as well get over it.

But how could she, if she had to face him in class three nights a week? Three nights when she had to go home alone, his face fresh in her mind. So that when she touched herself in the dark, it was his image that tempted her, tortured her, until her body screamed with the need for release.

As it did right now.

No.

This was crazy, and it had to stop. And she wasn't entirely certain that if he invited her to spend time with him again, she would be able to resist.

Jagger James was irresistible. That was the only thing she was absolutely certain about.

He felt bad. He hadn't meant to chase her away.

Jagger picked up his coffee and sipped the last of it before he bent to pick up the nearly empty plate of torte. He paused, lifted the fork to his lips, licked the bit of sweet custard clinging to the tines, where her mouth had been only moments before. Lust surged through him. That mouth of hers, that pouting red mouth in an otherwise innocent face.

She'd been angry; he'd seen it in the flash of her green eyes. Looking back, he supposed he couldn't blame her. He'd come on a little strong, maybe. But he wasn't into playing games. And he wanted her like crazy. Jerking off hadn't helped, no matter how many times he did it, stroking himself until he came into his fisted hand. His cock hardened at the thought.

Fuck, have to get out of here. Go home and do it again.

It wouldn't help. He knew that. He was twenty-six years

old, for God's sake. He could have hard-on after hard-on, no problem. Except that it was getting to be a problem, with Mia Rose.

She was his professor, and the only way to get around that was to drop the class. But he didn't want to do that, especially this close to graduation, just because he was hot for his teacher.

Hot didn't even begin to describe it. He was fucking obsessed with her, and he knew it. He just didn't know why.

She had secrets, that woman. He could see it in the tight bow of her shoulders when he asked about her family. Fascinating. People always did fascinate him, hence his study of psychology. Her secrets only made her more tempting.

Not the kind of woman he really needed in his life right now. Not after the promises he'd made to himself when Elena had left. He always fell too damn easily, he knew that.

Not that he was falling for Mia Rose.

No, all he wanted was to sleep with her. Spend a little time with her. Nothing more. No expectations. No opening himself up to be fucking crushed again. He was done with that. That's how he'd been operating for the last year. Finally his father's son. Something for Dad to be proud of. Even if Jagger wasn't entirely proud of himself.

But he'd learned his lesson after Elena. He'd spent this year learning to protect himself. He wasn't falling for a woman again anytime soon. And definitely not a woman like Mia Rose. A woman with secrets.

Yeah, get what he needed from her, *needed*, damn it, then walk away. He knew what he had to do.

Why did he have a feeling he wasn't going to be able to walk away from Mia Rose Curry?

chapter ✍ three

KARALEE BRACED HER HAND ON A PIPE ABOVE HER HEAD, holding herself up as she rode Gideon, her legs wrapped around his waist. His hands were on her hips, digging into her flesh as he pistoned into her.

"God, Gideon, harder!"

Pleasure swam through her veins with every luscious thrust. The single lightbulb hanging overhead barely illuminated his strong features, just enough that she could see the desire on his face: his mouth soft, his brown eyes intense.

"Fuck, Karalee. I'm going to come."

His panting breath matched her own as he shoved her back harder into the wall. He slipped a hand between them, pressed hard onto her clitoris.

"Yes, just like that, Gideon ..."

She bucked her hips into his hand, her clit swollen and

pulsing with need. And his powerful cock drove into her, impaling her, over and over. The tension in her body built, crested, and in moments pleasure flooded her, centering in her throbbing clit, spreading through her sex, her breasts, her entire body as she came. Gideon clamped a hand over her mouth as she cried out. She loved it.

"Christ, Karalee, someone will hear you."

But she didn't care.

And in moments he was tensing, shivering, panting her name as he came inside her. Jesus, they hadn't even used a condom. What was she, some slutty teenager?

But she'd loved every second of it. Loved the way they'd passed in the hallway, stopping to talk for mere moments before he'd grabbed her and dragged her into the janitors' closet, kissed her breathless as he stripped her panties from beneath her skirt and plowed into her.

She was trying to catch her breath, Gideon's flesh softening inside her.

"Jesus, Gideon."

"Yeah."

He was still panting, his breath coming in soft gasps. And he was still standing, one hand braced against the wall behind her, the other under her ass, holding her up. He caught her gaze, his eyes that smoky, sexy brown that had caught her attention the moment she'd seen him, when he'd been introduced at the first staff meeting of the semester two weeks earlier. The new dean of the History Department. She'd loved his tall, lean form right away, those square, masculine features, even the bit of gray at his temples, in sharp contrast to his nearly black hair. He looked like some classic movie star to her. But mostly it was his eyes: dark, hooded, sexy as hell.

They were locked on her now. He reached up and stroked her cheek with his thumb, a surprisingly tender gesture. Her heart gave a sharp squeeze.

Come on, Karalee. This was nothing more than hot, spontaneous sex.

Dangerous sex, which only made it better. But she was as turned on as she'd ever been in her life. By him. By the taboo nature of what had just happened, the fact that at any moment, someone could have opened the closet door and found them. And it was even better that they'd hardly ever even spoken before, had never done more than exchange a few words, a few flirtatious glances. That he'd known in some mysterious way she wanted this, wanted him, simply seeing him in the hall today.

Lifting her, he pulled out of her, zipped his fly. Her legs were a little shaky, and she had to stand there and breathe for a moment as she pulled her skirt down. He handed her discarded panties to her and she stepped into them. She wished he'd say something.

Gideon smoothed back his dark hair with one hand. She noticed then the faint five o'clock shadow on his jaw. Sexy. Like everything else about him.

"So. I'll see you around campus, Karalee."

He straightened his shirt, flashed her a smile, opened the door to the closet, and walked out.

Jesus! He was just going to leave her standing there with that for a parting line?

Her heart was still thudding in her chest, her body still

buzzing with orgasm. She ran her hands over her hair, her face. She wished she had her purse with her. She was going to have to walk out of this closet with no idea of what she looked like.

What the hell had she just done?

But she was smiling as she shook her head, smoothed her skirt down, tucked in her blouse, and drew in a deep breath. This was ridiculous. Dangerous. And the most thrilling thing that had happened to her in a very long time.

Perhaps ever.

She wanted it to happen again. But the way he had simply left her there, without talking about what they'd done, she had no idea what would happen next, if anything. It was frustrating as hell. Yet some small part of her was as absolutely thrilled by the uncertainty of it as she was by everything else about him, about this experience.

She really ought to have her head examined.

Karalee cracked the door open and peered out into the hall. Empty, thank God. Slipping out, she headed for the ladies' room to wash her face, pull herself together. That was going to be a challenge, though. Because sex with Gideon Oliver had left her head in as much chaos as it had her body.

Mia pulled into the campus parking lot, cursing her luck. If she didn't get to school early enough, she always ended up here, at the lot farthest from her classroom.

She pulled her purse and her briefcase from the backseat and grabbed her coffee thermos before she locked the door. Dark and strong with plenty of milk and three sugars. The sweet coffee was a treat she used when she was nervous or bothered by something. Just like her mom had when she was a kid. Of course, the sugar load may have been more about the drugs her mother did than anything else; heroin addicts were famous for their sugar cravings. But she really didn't want to think about her mother right now. She sipped the hot liquid, willing her pulse rate to slow. Why was she so scattered today?

As she started the walk toward the humanities building, her cell phone rang. It took a moment to dig it out of her purse.

"Hello?"

"Hi, Mia, it's Karalee."

"Hi. How are you?"

As she skirted the edge of another parking lot, she noticed a construction crew working, muscular men in white tank tops, sweating in the muggy air, their arms and shoulders cording as they worked. Her nipples tightened as one of them leaned into a jackhammer, worn blue jeans pulling taut over muscled thighs.

Nice.

She closed her eyes for a moment, remembering Jagger's scent, the heat of him sitting next to her . . .

Why was she so man-crazy suddenly?

"Sorry, Karalee, what was that?"

"I said I had sex with Gideon Oliver the other night."

"The new dean? Do you even know him?"

"No, I don't." Karalee paused. "We had sex in a janitors' closet at school."

"Well, that makes my problems seem minor. How was it?"

"It was amazing. Probably the hottest sex I've ever had.

We ran into each other in the hallway. And he just looked at me and it was this sort of surreal moment, and he said 'come with me,' and I did. He pulled me in there, stripped my underwear off, and shoved me up against the wall. We didn't talk about it. We didn't talk about anything. It just happened."

"Wow."

"I know. I had to tell someone, Mia."

"How did things end?"

"That's the strangest part. After, he just zipped up and left. Like it was no big deal."

"Maybe it wasn't, to him. I'm sorry, Karalee."

"No, it's fine." She lowered her voice. "Because, to be perfectly honest, I loved that. That we just did it without any working up to it first. But part of me wanted him to at least ask for my number. How juvenile is that?"

"It's not. I'd probably feel the same way."

"You know how I am about men. It's not that I want a relationship. But just to have him ask . . . but again, that part of it was hot, too. So, you're the sex expert. What does this say about me? That the best sex of my life was with a virtual stranger, in a place where we could have been caught? That even though I've always been the one in charge with a man, what I loved most about this thing with Gideon was the way he completely took over?"

"I'm sorry, Karalee. I can't even figure myself out right now."

"That guy again, Mia? Your student?"

"Again. Still." She shifted her purse and took a sip from her thermos. "I saw him. Jagger. I went to coffee with him."

"Jesus, Mia. Is that a good idea?"

"Of course it's not. But I couldn't not do it. I don't seem to have a lot of control where he's concerned."

"Why do you think that is?"

Mia shrugged. She really didn't want to get into it, even with Karalee, the first close friend she'd had in ages. It was too hard to open herself to people in that way. It always had been. With anyone but her grandmother, and she'd been gone for two years. She was out of practice.

"He's just . . . incredibly attractive."

"Mia, maybe I'm way off base here, but you're not the kind of woman to have her head completely turned by a guy just because he's attractive. You've always struck me as someone who operates on logic." Then, when Mia didn't answer, "Okay. We don't have to talk about it. But you might want to spend some time thinking about it."

"I will."

She had better think about it, figure it out. Because spending time with Jagger was taking a foolish risk with her career. And if she was going to take a risk, she had damn well better know what she was taking that risk for. A sexy smile just wasn't good enough.

But she knew there was more to him than that. So much more after spending time with him last night.

Dangerous.

Oh yes. He was dangerous. But just as it was for Karalee, the danger was part of the attraction.

"I don't think I'll see him again, Karalee. Other than in class."

"That's probably a good idea."

Mia nodded to herself.

No, she wouldn't see him again. Even though this sort of

thing really did happen all the time, professors sleeping with their students. Even though the mere idea of it made her shiver, lust surging through her system.

She would not risk her career over this good-looking boy. But she knew that was a lie she was using to placate her sense of guilt. Because Jagger was no boy. He was all man. He made every girlish part of her go soft and hot. Something she hadn't felt for far too long. And she had to admit, it felt good. Maybe too good to fight.

Mia could barely concentrate. Jagger sat in the front row, watching her. Thank God she planned to show a film.

She cleared her throat. "Today we're going to see a documentary piece about the primitive cultural practices which a number of fetishes are based on. I'm sure many of you have heard the term 'body manipulations.' For those of you who haven't, this term refers to piercing, implanting metal objects beneath the skin, stretching or binding certain body parts, any way in which the body is manipulated to appear different from its natural form. Today you'll see where these practices originate and also some of the people who practice these rituals, including Fakir Musafar, who is known as the master of body manipulations. We're going to see some extreme material: branding, skewering, the use of flesh hooks. Please try to keep an open mind, to let go of any preconceived notions. And when comparing the primitive practices to the modern, remember some of the things you read in this week's chapters about trance states, because that state of mind applies to both the modern and ancient practices."

She let her gaze range over the classroom, careful not to

catch Jagger's eye. But he was there at the edge of her sight. She could *feel* him.

"I don't happen to have any footage of it, but studies have been done in which the brain waves of meditating Buddhist monks were measured and compared against people practicing these sorts of body manipulations. The results were shockingly similar. The brain responds in the same way, whether that state of nirvana is produced through hours of meditation or by being pierced and hung from hooks embedded in the skin. As I've mentioned before, and will reiterate over and over during the semester, it's all about what goes on in people's heads, how our minds work."

"So, you're saying that sexuality is a mental process?" Jagger asked. "What about chemistry, Professor?"

She willed the heat from her skin, willed herself not to be shaken by his words, by the sound of his voice.

"Of course chemistry plays an enormous role in sexual attraction. But I'm talking about how people endure certain practices."

"If a person is turned on, then, they can do things they might not do otherwise?"

God, yes.

Her fingers gripped the edge of the wooden podium. "Yes, I would have to agree with that. Though most people have enough good judgment not to simply follow their urges without any thought for the consequences."

What the hell was she talking about?

Get back on track.

"Why don't we start the film? We can discuss this more later. Alex, will you please turn off the lights?"

The room went dark and she moved her chair to one side

of the room. Not nearly far enough away from him. As the narrator's voice began to drone, she lost all focus on what was happening on-screen. All she could think about was *him* sitting a few feet away in the dark, his silhouette in the flickering half-light. Hyperaware of his presence, there was too much time to let her mind drift into dangerous territory. To imagine his hands on her, his mouth. To imagine him cooking for her, feeding her as he had at the café . . .

Her body began to heat. Even worse when she looked up to see him glancing over at her. When he smiled, her thighs grew damp, her breasts aching. She looked away, shifted in her chair, desperately thirsty suddenly.

Keeping her eyes on the film, she watched as hundreds of people in Malaysia marched toward the temple caves of Kuala Lumpur during the annual festival of Thaipusam, a sinuous, surging trail of humanity. Many of their bodies and faces were pierced by long skewers called *vels,* decorated with peacock feathers, beads, colorful bits of cloth, an act of sacrifice to the gods. She'd seen this film dozens of times before, but now the writhing mass of bodies seemed utterly sensual to her.

Suddenly she was feeling things she hadn't felt in years. Oh, she'd *thought* about it all, spent years studying alternative sexuality, but she realized she hadn't really *felt* anything for a very long time. She hadn't allowed herself to.

But it was too much to grasp, sitting there in the darkened classroom, surrounded by her students. No, she had to pull herself together; the film was nearly over. She would deal with it later.

She'd been telling herself the same thing for longer than she cared to remember. But she meant it this time.

A few more excruciating minutes and the film ended, the lights came back on. Mia went back to the podium.

"Okay," she said, tucking her hair behind her ear, shuffling her notes. "Read pages one twenty through one forty-two, and we'll discuss the material on Friday. And don't forget to start thinking about your midterm papers. Anyone who's having a difficult time with a topic or has other questions can see me during office hours on Tuesdays. Have a good night."

Everyone stood up and moved out the door as she went behind her desk and began to gather a few scattered papers together. Everyone but Jagger.

Damn it.

She picked up her water bottle and took a sip. He was making this too hard.

She could smell him when he was still several feet away, that sex-scent of patchouli and *him*.

God.

"Hi, Mia Rose."

"Hi. What can I do for you?" She kept both hands wrapped around the water bottle.

"Look, I'm sorry I overstepped the boundaries the other night. I didn't mean to run you off like that."

"It's okay." She shrugged, but there were tremors of heat running over her skin.

"Let me make it up to you."

"What do you mean?"

He moved in closer, until he was right up against the desk. She swore she could almost feel the pressure of his body against the wood. But that was ridiculous.

"You did say you love good food, Mia Rose?"

She nodded warily.

"I'd like to cook for you."

She started to shake her head but he interrupted her, holding a hand up in front of him. "Before you say no, just hear me out. I told you I gave up cooking professionally because I was burned out. And I was. I still am, on that level. But cooking for someone, well, that's different for me. That's when I love it again. And I have a feeling you're the kind of person who would appreciate it. So, there's something in it for both of us, right?"

He looked so sincere. She couldn't figure out suddenly if the shaking she felt on the inside was about the food or him or the fact that she knew damn well she shouldn't do this.

But she was going to.

"What . . . what do you have in mind?"

"How about Cajun pan-seared sea scallops I get fresh off the wharf, with this great sauce that has a little spice to it? It's a special New Orleans recipe. I can't tell you what's in it; you'll just have to taste it yourself. And for dessert, a chocolate mousse unlike anything you've ever had before, with a fresh raspberry coulis. I guarantee your mouth will be in heaven."

Did he have any idea what his words were doing to her? Was he even aware that as he spoke, his voice had lowered, until it was a deep, dusky tone that reverberated through her body?

She nodded, hardly able to speak. "Okay. That . . . that sounds good."

Too good.

"It'll be great. I promise." He was looking right at her, a

small, crooked smile on his face. She could not get over how beautiful he was.

"How about Friday night? Here." He pulled a scrap of paper from his pocket and handed it to her. She felt the heat of his hand as his fingers grazed hers. His address and telephone number were written on it. Bold print done with a green Sharpie. Why did that seem to say something about him?

"You came prepared." She tried to smile, but she was still too tight with nerves, with heat.

"I knew you wouldn't be able to resist." His smile turned into a cocky grin for a moment, but she couldn't find it within herself to mind. "Eight o'clock. Come hungry."

Oh, she would. In more ways than one. She understood that she couldn't completely trust herself with him. What she didn't quite get was why she was willing to do this anyway. But she was going. To his apartment, where he would cook for her.

You have lost your mind.

"I'll be there. With my appetite."

He flashed another grin at her. Then he took her hand and brushed his lips across the back of it. So soft, his lips. She shivered.

"You won't regret it."

She did already. But he would make it worth her while. Her guilt. For once, she was letting go of her rigid self-control, the control that had held her together her entire life, but which also held her back from ever having what she truly wanted. And this man seemed to be the key, somehow.

She hadn't allowed herself to connect food and sex, other than those lonely nights in front of her television, watching disembodied hands stir sauces on the screen. Never with another person. Not since Ben, anyway. But that connection had been made the moment Jagger told her he was a chef. Despite the alarm bells going off in her head, she was going to Jagger's apartment.

Maybe she was a fool. But it was just food. Just a meal.

When had food been "just" anything for her?

Oh, she would regret this. No question about it. But she would damn well enjoy herself a bit first.

"I'll see you Friday, Mia Rose."

He dropped her hand, turned, and left. And damn her if she didn't check out the sinuous movement of his tight ass beneath fitted jeans as he went.

Karalee sat in her favorite chair in the university library, the lights dim this late in the evening. She loved to come here, to sit in the quiet corners and read. The classics, mostly. Jane Austen, Walt Whitman, even a little Shakespeare. She loved the near silence of this place, with nothing more than the white hum of the air system, the soft turning of pages, the cool slide of books from the shelves in the air, that quiet murmur of hushed voices. This was a sacred place to her, of sorts.

She glanced at her watch. It was just after nine. She hadn't realized how long she'd been here after her last class let out. She closed her book and stood, stretching. Time to go home.

"Karalee."

She knew that soft, deep voice. Knew the scent of him even better.

"Gideon. What are you doing here?"

"I came to look something up, then got lost in research." He smiled, that movie star smile of his. He really was the handsomest man she'd ever seen outside of Hollywood. It was easy to forget he was a history teacher. That position didn't seem nearly glamorous enough for him.

She smiled back at him. "What were you looking for?"

"It doesn't matter now."

He stepped toward her, and she felt the heat coming off him. Her mouth went dry. Her pulse thrummed, a deep keening that reached her sex and throbbed there, all heat and need and insistence.

Jesus Christ.

He curled a hand around her waist, pulled her in possessively. It didn't occur to her to protest.

He leaned in, his mouth right next to her ear, his breath warm in her hair. "Did you know that the security guard makes his rounds every hour, on the hour?"

"No. But why . . . why are you telling me this?"

She was breathless already.

"Because I just saw him go by. And that means we'll have this little corner of the library all to ourselves for approximately another fifty-five minutes. There's hardly anyone else here."

She swallowed. Her muscles were going loose all over, melting into him as he pulled her closer, until she could feel the solid ridge of his hardened cock against her thigh.

"Jesus, Gideon."

"You don't want to say no to me, Karalee. I can tell. I can smell your need."

Lust swam hot in her veins. She didn't say a word.

"Ah, I thought so." He paused, snaked a hand up into her

hair, pulled tight. Just enough to leave no doubt as to who was in command of the situation. "So nice that you wear these skirts. Almost as though you're waiting for me. Ready for me."

He slid a hand between their bodies, grasped her nipple through her blouse, her lace bra, and squeezed. She moaned, low in her throat.

"Are you ready for me, Karalee?"

"Gideon..." Her hands gripped his shoulders, digging into his flesh beneath his blue oxford shirt.

His voice lowered even more. "If I slipped my hand between your legs, would you be wet? I think you would be."

"Yes," she whispered. It was true.

"Come here."

He backed her up, farther in between the tall shelves, until her spine was pressed into the protruding edges of the books. She could smell the paper, the ink on the pages, the starchy bindings, and his skin. He moved his hand beneath the hem of her skirt. She gasped when he slid his fingers under her panties and right into the wet, aching heat of her.

"Gideon!"

"Shh. You don't want anyone to catch us like this. Do you?"

She was shaking all over. "No. No."

He plunged his fingers deeper. Pleasure shot through her, a lightning flash of need.

"I want to fuck you again, Karalee. You have no idea how badly. But this is not the place for that. So damn tempting, but even I have some control. No, now I'm just going to get you off. Right here, where anyone could walk by at any moment. But they won't. Or will they? Of course, that's what makes it so good, isn't it?"

He moved his thumb over her clit and pressed, circling the hardened nub of flesh. Karalee tilted her hips into his hand, hardly believing she was doing it.

"You like that, don't you? Tell me."

"Yes. I like it. Need it. Oh!"

He pumped his fingers deep inside her as her climax came bearing down on her. She shivered, tensed, bit her lip to keep from crying out. He moved his head in and kissed her, his lips pressing onto hers. And she was still coming when he opened her mouth with his tongue, slid inside. So wet and warm, driving her orgasm on.

She was shaking when he pulled his fingers from her.

"Beautiful," he said quietly. "Perfect, Karalee."

She grabbed his wrist. "Are you going to leave again?"

He brushed her hair from her face with a gentle hand, leaned in to kiss her once more. Lord, the man could kiss! She opened her mouth, let him in. His tongue twined with hers, and she wanted to come again suddenly. *Needed* to. Needed him to fuck her as he had in the janitors' closet. Oh yes, hard and fast and all animal.

He pulled away.

"I'm going now, Karalee."

"What?" She could barely think straight.

"You should have dinner with me this weekend. Leave your number on my office line."

"Oh . . . yes. Okay."

That smile again, then he touched his fingertips briefly to her lips, just long enough for her to catch her own ocean scent there, then he turned and left.

She watched him go, moving gracefully between the stacks, before she collapsed into a chair. Jesus, what this man did to her! She loved every minute of it, even that small sense of humiliation he always left her with.

Her sex was still throbbing. Oh yes, she loved it all. Loved that she had no idea what might come next. So, dinner with him this weekend? Their first real date. What would he ask of her? What would she do for him?

She knew she'd do anything, anything at all. Because just thinking about it was making her wet all over again. She couldn't wait.

chapter ✏ four

JAGGER CHOPPED A HEAD OF BUTTER LETTUCE, THE KNIFE coming down in a hard, staccato beat on the enormous butcher block built into the counter in his kitchen.

Take it easy, buddy.

Why the hell was he so wound up? You'd think this was his first date. How many times had he cooked for a woman? But tonight it was Mia Rose, and that was different.

His body was as wound up as a clock, his mind full of images of her: her heart-shaped face, those startling green eyes, the swell of her breasts beneath her blouse. And most of all that soft, lush mouth that begged to be kissed.

Slow down.

Oh yeah, he'd have to take things damn slow with her if he wasn't going to run her off again. She had that deerlike flight response down. He'd have to find a way to break through that. Because he planned on kissing that hot little mouth of hers. That, and every inch of her pale skin. He could almost imagine what she might taste like . . .

Shit! He yelped as he nicked his finger. Not a good idea to be so damn distracted with a knife in his hand. But she did that to him.

He had to get it together, to keep it under control. There was no reason why this woman should throw him off balance. No, he'd learned his lessons well, and although he'd dated a lot these last months, he'd kept his guard up, kept the promise he'd made to himself after Elena had left. Just like Dad, finally. Just keep it cool. It was simple enough.

But no one had ever made him feel the way Mia Rose did.

He hardly knew her. He was being an idiot.

He tossed the lettuce into a large wooden bowl and grabbed a handful of Roma tomatoes, chopped them up, going a little hard with the knife again. It didn't help to dissipate the edginess in his body. He threw the tomatoes in, crumbled some Gorgonzola cheese over them, added a handful of pecans he'd toasted earlier, then put the bowl in the refrigerator. It was a huge, brushed steel piece of equipment he'd had to have. You could fit food for twenty in there. He loved it. Just as he loved his Wolf range, the smooth, modern concrete counters, the dark wooden cabinetry he'd had custom built.

He'd used most of his inheritance from his great-aunt Glenda to do it. But she'd been a helluva cook herself; she wouldn't have minded. His father's family was all from New Orleans, a real food town. It was in his blood, he figured. Too bad he hadn't inherited the music gene. That would have made his father a lot happier than his becoming a chef.

A small pang went through him, but he pushed it away. He'd always strived to please his old man in other ways, but it had never worked out. They were too different. Dad could fall in and out of a different woman's bed every night, while Jagger just fell in love.

Not anymore.

He jammed the tip of the chopping knife into the butcher block, wiped his hands on a towel. Done with the food prep, he didn't know what to do with himself. He could not get Mia Rose out of his mind. She wouldn't be there for another hour. What was he supposed to do until then?

His cock gave a twitch.

Oh no. He'd been doing enough of that for a team of adolescent boys lately. He pressed down on his hardening member.

Down, boy.

This was ridiculous.

He grabbed the bottle of Cabernet he always kept on the counter and poured himself a glass. He needed something to take the edge off, and he was not going to masturbate again. Not this close to her being in his house. Christ, he would see her in an hour; he could manage to hold off that long.

Couldn't he?

But there it was again, her face, her mouth, that hot, gorgeous mouth. He knew exactly what it would taste like. Sweet, but not too sweet. Oh no, Mia Rose Curry was a little hard on the outside. He'd have to work his way past that before her lips went soft and let him in. But once he got past that edge of reserve, she'd be all pliant and loose. He could imagine what her body would feel like pressed up against his.

Her hips would be at that perfect height where he could fit his thigh in between them and rub right up against her hot little mound. And she would grind into him . . . yeah . . .

Christ.

He pressed his hand against his aching cock. He was hard as steel. And the wine was not going to help unless he drank enough to render him senseless.

He shed his clothes as he stalked across the open wood floor of his loft to the bathroom, kept his hand on his swollen member as he waited for the shower to heat up.

The water came down on him, slid over his naked skin, a sensation he loved. He always jerked off in the shower; it added to the thrill for some reason. Didn't matter why. Just picture her face, imagine what her body looked like, felt like, tasted like . . . and knowing she would be there with him in only an hour, close enough to touch that pale skin, oh yeah . . .

He gave himself over to the images flashing through his mind, his hand stroking and pumping his cock, until he was reeling, shuddering with pleasure. Lost.

His come was hot, slipping between his fingers. He had to close his eyes, give himself a moment to shake it off, that after-burn of climax that completely clouded his mind.

Yeah, he was losing it over this woman. He didn't know why. All he knew was that Mia Rose was a total mind-fuck for him. But he could handle it. Despite that small voice whispering doubts in the back of his mind. That familiar voice telling him he was falling again already.

At eight o'clock sharp Mia stood outside the converted warehouse where Jagger lived. The door was corrugated metal, big enough to fit a car through. She put her finger out toward the buzzer, pulled it back.

If she rang the buzzer, she would have to actually go up, see him.

Eat with him.

Just do it.

Silly of her. She'd made it here, and now she was afraid to ring the doorbell? But it wasn't the bell she was afraid of, or even him. It was herself.

Just do it, Mia.

She drew in a deep breath, the scent of damp sidewalk and exhaust from the cars passing by on Sixth Street, then pressed the button.

His disembodied voice came from a speaker over the door. "Hi. Come on up. Freight elevator to your right when you get into the building. I'm on the top floor."

A shrill buzzing and she pulled the heavy steel door open, slipped into the dim foyer, closed the door behind her. She found the cagelike elevator, got in, and pushed the button. The elevator slid upward, shaking a little as the old cables moved through the pulleys. She was shaking, too, a small trembling all over. She was nearly breathless by the time she stepped out into a small hallway, and Jagger opened the door.

God, he looked good, in a pair of worn jeans and a fitted white V-neck T-shirt with some band logo on the front that contrasted with his brown skin. She noticed for the first time the tribal bands tattooed around both biceps peeking out from beneath his sleeves. She had a thing for certain kinds of tattoos on a man, and this was her favorite.

The perfect man.

"Come on in. Did you find the place okay?" Jagger took her hand and pulled her gently inside. He smelled like that patchouli oil he wore; that and a faint whiff of soap. Clean and a little exotic at the same time.

"I'm familiar with the area, so it was easy. Oh my God, this place is amazing."

One large, open space, with the battered, wide plank wood floors so common in these old warehouses, and huge windows everywhere. He'd laid the place out into roomlike areas marked off with colorful ethnic woven rugs. The living room held two large couches in a dusky sage green, flanking a rectangular brushed-steel fireplace. An enormous slab of old, dark wood made a coffee table. And everywhere were pieces of art: pottery, abstract paintings, baskets, primitive musical instruments from all over the world. One wall was lined with towering shelves full of books. Old Ella Fitzgerald played, just loud enough to set a mood.

The man had great taste.

Her gaze wandered to one end of the loft where a low bed was set beneath a skylight. It was simple, Zen-like, with its charcoal gray duvet and wood platform. But it was piled with pillows in gray, black, and white. Starkly luxurious and masculine, but sexy.

Everything about Jagger James was pure sex to her.

She tore her gaze away and looked to the opposite end of the apartment. And saw the kitchen.

She moved toward it silently.

"So, what do you think, Mia Rose?" he asked her.

"This is . . . this is beautiful. Look at that stove! You could cook anything on there."

"Yes I can."

She turned her head and caught his pleased smile. Pleased, seductive.

God.

"How about a glass of wine? I'm serving a white with dinner, but I have this great Cabernet from Chile."

"Sure. Yes. I'd love some wine. Anything is fine."

She was still overwhelmed by his kitchen, by the lovely aesthetic of his living space. By this glimpse into who he was.

Jagger was no ordinary college student. But that much had been obvious from the start. And she realized she was probably in more trouble than she'd thought. He was too smart, too hot, too everything. And she was too unsure of her own motives in being here. But she didn't want to think about that now.

Jagger gestured to a pair of padded iron bar stools at the high counter that separated the kitchen space from the dining area. "Come and sit at the bar while I cook, talk to me. I love to have company in the kitchen."

Mia slid onto one of the stools as Jagger poured her wine, handed it to her. While he pulled ingredients from the commercial-size refrigerator, she glanced around the kitchen, a huge space with the same vaulted ceilings she'd seen everywhere in the apartment. The counters were the poured concrete becoming so popular in modern homes, the cabinets a dark, rich wood, the appliances all brushed steel. The overall effect was clean, masculine. And seemed to fit him perfectly.

She watched him work in his kitchen, the way he moved with utter efficiency, total confidence, as he set colorful, heavy pottery bowls out on the counters, pulled out bottles with oils and spices. She was beginning to feel a little weak and loose all over, just from seeing him handling the food.

She took a sip of the deep red wine, swallowed, sipped some more. The wine was either going to calm her down or make it worse.

"I hope you like spicy, Mia Rose."

Why did that sound sexual? She simply nodded.

He went on while he rinsed the tiny bay scallops at the sink. "I like to cook with spices, love that small bite of flavor. Spices need to be subtle. Use too much and it overwhelms the dish. Too little and it's bland. It's all about striking that perfect balance. Tell me what you like to cook."

"Oh, well, I like Italian cuisine, and I cook a lot of Asian dishes."

"Ah, then you know something about spices."

He smiled at her. And once more, she had that sense of sexual insinuation. She couldn't tell at this point if it was him or her overactive imagination. She was too stirred up, every nerve in her body coming awake, heating.

He was concentrating on what he was doing for a few minutes: seasoning and searing the scallops in a sputtering pan, steaming a pot of fresh asparagus spears. But she really lost it when he began the sauce.

It had always been that sort of thing for her, those fragrant liquids. Her sex gave a squeeze as he browned butter, whisked ingredients into a pan. She focused on his hands, his long fingers moving quickly. And her body surged with lust.

"You're going to love this, Mia Rose."

Oh yes, she would.

His hands were a blur of motion while the scent of the food surrounded her, filled her mind. Her breasts began to ache, her sex to fill with need. She could barely manage to sit still.

"Jagger, do you mind if I look around a little?"

"Sure, go ahead."

She slipped off the stool and wandered into the living area, went to stand in front of the shelves and pulled in deep breath after deep breath. When she'd calmed a little she searched the titles of the books there, which she'd been itching to do since she walked into the apartment. Plenty of classical literature, books on music, history, art, dozens and dozens of cookbooks, of course. And on a bottom shelf, a copy of the Kama Sutra next to a row of classic erotica: *Story of O, Lady Chatterley's Lover,* collections of erotic poetry.

She shivered, bit down on her lip.

"Are you a fan of reading, Mia Rose?"

His voice startled her. "What? Yes. I love to read. You have an interesting collection. Eclectic."

"Everything interests me. Literally everything. One of my favorite ways to spend a weekend is in bed with a stack of books. Just being lazy and reading for hours. What do you like to read?"

"I love reading everything, too. Books were a luxury when I was growing up." She moved down the shelves, running her fingers over the bindings. "Precious. I'll read anything I can get my hands on."

"I can't imagine books being a luxury. They were a necessity in my mother's house, and my father's."

"You were lucky." She moved back to the counter, lifted her wineglass, and drank.

"Yeah, I guess I was. So, were your parents just not into reading?"

"My mother and I moved around a lot." She really did

not want to get into this. She needed to change the subject. "When did you learn to cook?"

Not that food was any safer a subject, when she got right down to it. Her gaze was drawn back to Jagger at the stove. The mere sight of him stirring a pot, checking the asparagus for tenderness, made her weak all over. Her fingers tightened on the stem of her glass as she told herself it was simply a programmed response. One that had been programmed into her long ago. She could ignore it, if she chose.

"I always cooked. My mom is an amazing cook. She has really great instincts, and she taught me everything. My dad's a lousy cook, but he's always loved to eat, so I cooked for him whenever I went to visit him, even as a kid. It made him happy. Not as happy as he would have been if I'd turned out to be a musician, like him." He let out a hollow laugh, and Mia realized there was some deeper issue there. But she wasn't going to push his buttons; she certainly didn't want her own pushed.

"Did you have any formal training?" she asked instead.

"I went to the culinary academy here in San Francisco when I was eighteen, right out of high school."

"Ah." She couldn't think of anything more to say. She was too fascinated watching his hands as he spooned rice onto a pair of Japanese stoneware plates glazed in a deep red. When he ladled the scallops over the rice, poured the sauce over them, Mia bit back a groan. He crossed the asparagus spears over the top, picked the plates up, and gestured with his chin.

"Come on, let's eat."

She followed him into the dining area, which was partly hidden behind folding Japanese Shoji screens, where a sleek, modern wood table topped a large block-print rug in shades of orange, gold, and black. Jagger set the plates down on woven grass mats, then moved around to hold her chair for her.

She slid into her seat. Jagger pushed her chair in, brushed his hand over her shoulder, letting it linger there for one lovely, excruciating moment. She could swear the heat of his hand worked right through her cashmere sweater.

"Be right back." He went to the kitchen, returned with a new bottle of white wine and two fresh glasses, opened and poured the wine before seating himself. "Take a bite, Mia Rose, and tell me what you think."

"Alright." She picked up her fork, her hand a little shaky. What on earth was wrong with her? She managed to spear one of the small scallops and bring it to her mouth. "It smells wonderful." She bit into the delicate meat, and flavor filled her mouth. "This is incredible. Such layered flavors. Did you use a little balsamic vinegar in there somewhere? It has that rich edge to it."

"Ah, you do know food, don't you?" Jagger smiled before taking a bite himself. "Pretty damn good, if I do say so myself."

She smiled back, took another bite. He really was an easy person to be with. Why was she so nervous?

Maybe because she was keenly aware of the fact that she wanted to do a lot more than talk to him, eat with him. Although eating with him was lovely, sensual, intimate.

They ate in silence for several minutes, simply enjoying the food. And Mia let herself enjoy the tightness in her body, her sensitized skin.

"So, Mia Rose. Tell me what all that moving around with your mom was about."

Her stomach immediately formed a small knot, the sensual haze fading fast. "You really don't want to hear it."

"I *do* want to hear it." He leaned closer, his gray eyes on hers. "Whatever you want to tell me."

She shrugged, trying not to let the whirl of emotions inside her show on the outside. Emotions having to do with her past, but also what was happening right here, right now. Because she found herself wanting to tell Jagger about her childhood, something she rarely discussed with anyone. Maybe it was the expression on his face that told her he really was interested. Maybe it was the hint of command in his voice, the assumption that she would simply answer him. But she still struggled with the idea of telling him, of talking about it to anyone.

"It's an ugly story, Jagger," she said softly, picking up her glass to take a drink.

"Life can be ugly. The important pieces often are. That's just part of it."

"Why do you want to know?" A little anger was boiling beneath the surface suddenly, and she knew it showed on her face.

"I want to get to know you. Who you are, where you've been. I don't know why. I just do."

If he had touched her at that point, reached out to take her hand, she would have turned away, found some excuse to change the subject. But he sat perfectly still and waited for her.

"My mother was . . . a mess. An addict, if you want to know the truth."

She looked at him and he just nodded his head. There was no judgment in his expression. And no pity.

Her shoulders loosened a little; she hadn't even realized how tightly she'd been holding them. She went on. "She worked sometimes. But she didn't spend her money on the rent. She'd wake me up in the middle of the night and we'd pack up our clothes and go. That was when we were lucky enough to have a place to live. Sometimes it was just her car."

His voice was soft. "Shit, Mia Rose."

But there was no shock in the way he said it. Just honest sympathy. It made her want to cry. It made her want to tell him more.

"It ended when I was thirteen. She took me to my grandmother's house, a woman I'd never met before. But she took us in, as though my mother had never left. As though she hadn't taken off at eighteen. As though we weren't filthy dirty and Mom all strung out." She sipped her wine, watched her fingers stroke the stem of the glass. "Mom was gone in the morning. That's the last time I saw her."

"And your grandmother?"

"She raised me, helped me. She was an amazing person. I couldn't figure out why my mother would ever have left home, how she could have been the kind of kid who turned to drugs, being raised by this woman. I didn't know that Mom's younger sister, Colleen, had been killed in a car accident right before she left home. I didn't know my mother had ever had a sister. Grandma said my mom never got over it. I guess she didn't."

"At least she gave you over to your grandmother eventually. It sounds like that was the best thing that could've happened to you."

"It was. It was a gift."

"But you mentioned she's gone now, your grandmother."

"Yes."

"That's got to be hard on you."

Mia nodded. "I still miss her every day. But she left me her house, her roses. I suppose I like to think of her as still being there with me. Silly of me, I guess."

"Not at all. You feel closer to her there."

"Yes, exactly."

"We're all sentimentalists, inside, when it comes to that kind of thing."

"Do you think so? What are you sentimental about?"

"If you're done eating, I'll show you."

She nodded, and he got up, came around to hold her chair for her as she stood. He took her hand and led her into the living room. Next to the fireplace were wide wooden shelves, deep, like shadow boxes. She'd noticed them earlier, the collection of pottery, small sculptures, and art books there. And on one shelf was a guitar. It was art in itself, done in light and dark wood, the frets inlaid with mother-of-pearl.

"It's beautiful."

"My dad gave it to me when I was eight years old. I was still young enough that he had hopes I'd follow him into music. It's an incredible instrument. Too much for a child. But he wanted me to have it. I never even wanted to play the thing, but just knowing he'd given it to me was huge. Even at that age, I knew what it meant to him. It represented his hopes and dreams for me, you know?"

She wanted to touch it. To feel that satiny wood beneath her fingertips. And she wanted to touch him. But that was nothing new. What was new was this side of him, all cockiness gone, just Jagger being himself, opening up to her.

"You never wanted to play," she said quietly, "and yet

you've held on to this. I understand that. How it's important."

Jagger nodded, his face somber as he ran a hand over the curve of the guitar, gently, as though it were a woman's body he was caressing. Mia shivered. He turned to her, the mood breaking when he smiled.

"Come on. You're going to love dessert."

He walked back toward the kitchen, calling over his shoulder, "Go ahead and sit down again and I'll bring it out."

She went back to her place at the table. It was only a few moments later when he came back with a covered plate and set it down in front of her, stood beside her chair.

"Close your eyes, Mia Rose."

"What? Why?"

"Because I want you to really taste this."

She started to shake her head.

"Come on. Just do it."

His tone was teasing, yet still held that air of command that made her insides feel like liquid heat. He was smiling at her now.

"Do it, Mia Rose. You know you want to."

She laughed a little self-consciously, but she closed her eyes for him.

For him.

Stop it.

She heard a little rustling, then Jagger told her, "Open your mouth."

She did, feeling a bit foolish. Then he touched the tip of a fork to her lips, and she let him slide it in.

Chocolate mousse, rich and cool against her tongue,

followed by something tart and sweet at the same time.
Whatever it was, she wanted more. Wanted it all over her
skin. And it was him feeding this to her. As though they were
lovers.

God.

She let the chocolate melt on her tongue, squeezed her
thighs together, trying to ease the ache there. She did not
want to admit that the lust raging through her was as much
about the food as it was about her attraction to him. That it
was the combination that made her want to explode.

"Jagger—"

"Shh. Keep tasting. One bite isn't enough."

The fork against her lips again, and this time she opened
right up, trying not to groan aloud. Sugar suffused her
mouth, desire suffused her body. And then he touched her
lips with his fingertip.

"You have a little of the raspberry here . . ."

She opened her eyes and looked up at him. He was bent
over her, his face only a few inches from hers, his gray eyes
gone dark and hazy. He pulled his hand away, licked the
drop of sweet red sauce from his fingertip.

She was shaking. Her gaze went from his mouth to his
hand, to his eyes and back again. She was absolutely flooded
with need, with heat.

He leaned in, a fraction of an inch. Her sex gave a sharp
squeeze. She bit her lip.

"Jesus, Mia Rose," he muttered before he moved in to kiss
her.

chapter ✍ five

LIPS LIKE CHERRIES. WHAT SONG WAS THAT? JAGGER HAD heard it so many times. But now he knew exactly what it meant. Mia's mouth was soft and sweet, with chocolate and the tangy raspberry coulis. With *her*.

She was tentative at first, shy almost, but he kept kissing her, just a soft press of lips against lips, over and over. In moments she opened for him. He slipped inside, and it was like a shock, that wet warmth, the tangle of her tongue against his, the way she immediately gave herself over to him. He'd never felt anything like it.

He took her face in his hands and went down on his knees beside her chair. He had to do it. There was no way to kiss this woman and stay on his feet.

Jesus Christ.

When she sighed into his mouth he just about came

apart. And she went even looser, melting right into him. His cock was as hard as it had ever been in his life. He could barely breathe. But he wasn't going to stop.

He was nearly panting by the time she pulled back. She looked dazed, her pupils enormous, her cheeks flushed.

"Jagger..." She pulled his hands from her face and looked away.

"Ah, don't."

She shook her head. "This isn't right."

"It feels right."

It's just the sex, man. You don't need it to be anything else.

"That doesn't make it so, Jagger."

"Fuck. You're right. I'm sorry." He stood up. So did she.

"I have to go." She pushed her dark hair from her face.

"Look, you don't have to leave. Stay and finish your dessert."

"I can't." She moved to the console table by the door and picked up her purse. "I . . . thank you for the dinner, and . . . I really have to go. I'm sorry."

"I'm not. I'm not sorry I kissed you, Mia Rose."

She shook her head again. "I'm going," she said quietly, but he knew there was nothing he could do to stop her.

She pulled the door open and slipped through.

Damn it. The last thing he'd wanted was to chase her away again. But he'd had to kiss her. And he'd told her the truth. He wasn't sorry he'd done it.

That kiss had gone through him like heat lightning. Like a jolt of electricity. And now he was burning.

Fuck.

He pressed a hand to his aching cock, willing his erection to go away. But if it had been bad earlier, simply thinking about her, it was a hundred times worse now. Now that he'd kissed her, tasted her mouth.

He ripped his shirt over his head, yanked his pants down as he practically ran to the shower, jerked the handles, running the hot water. Steam quickly filled the room as he stepped under the sting of the spray. He grabbed the soap right away and lathered his cock, began to pump. He bit his lip, could almost taste her there still.

Mia Rose.

Pleasure shot through him, seemed to weigh him down, crushing him, until he could barely stand. He leaned against the wall of the shower, let his head fall back, thrust his hips into his fist.

Yeah, wet and slippery, just like she'd be inside. He knew it, knew it from the silk of her mouth, the slide of her tongue on his.

Mia Rose.

His climax bore down on him. Sharp and hot, his come spurting between his fingers. He was panting hard, his hips still pumping even after it was over. It wasn't enough. Not by far. Because his cock wasn't the only part of him obsessed with Mia Rose. And it wasn't only her body he wanted.

The woman had really spun his head. This endless need to come and come and come was only the beginning of it. He couldn't even think about the rest.

He leaned into the cool wall of the shower, let the water wash him clean as he tried to catch his breath.

Maybe once he fucked her he'd be able to work her out of his system. That's what he was telling himself anyway. Because the idea that there was something more was not acceptable. Not good for him, not good for her.

He'd made a deal with himself, damn it. That's what had gotten him over Elena. And it had been working. Nothing long-term. No emotions involved. Never give a woman the chance to get to him again.

The problem was, with Mia Rose, it might already be too late.

～

Karalee pulled up in front of Il Fornaio, just as Gideon had told her to. Yes, told her. He'd been very specific. She was to arrive at eight o'clock, wearing a black skirt and nothing underneath it. She'd trembled all the way there, feeling the cool leather of the car seat beneath her thighs. And there was something about knowing she was doing exactly what he'd asked of her that was frankly thrilling as hell.

The valet opened her door and she stepped out. The air was cool and damp this close to the bay. The strong scent of salt was replaced by garlic and baking bread when she opened the door to the restaurant and went inside. She looked around the crowded room, took in the black and cream striped wallpaper, the red leather booths, the starched white tablecloth. The murmur of voices layered against the music, broken by the occasional burst of laughter. She'd eaten here before, but she'd never arrived in this state of anxious arousal. Not here, not anywhere.

"Karalee."

His voice at her ear, deep, reverberating through her body. She turned to him.

"Gideon. Hi."

How strange, suddenly, to see him here, in a public place. To be on an actual date, rather than hiding in some corner, being fervently fucked by him. Not that she'd minded. She wouldn't mind now.

"We're ready for our table," he told the hostess. "Gideon Oliver, reservation for two."

The woman nodded and led them to a small booth in the corner. Gideon gestured her in. Karalee slid across the smooth vinyl, acutely aware of how naked she was beneath her skirt. Gideon slid in beside her, until his thigh pressed against hers.

"I see you came dressed as I asked, Karalee."

She nodded, her throat dry. He smelled too good.

"Did you do everything I asked?"

"Yes," she said, her voice catching. Then, more strongly, "Yes, I did."

He smiled at her, that Hollywood smile, all flashing white teeth and old-school charm. He really did look like an actor, handsome as hell, sculpted features, strong chin, dark, deep-set eyes. She went warm and liquid inside when he slipped an arm around her and leaned in.

"The pasta primavera is excellent here. We'll have some wine."

She nodded. She didn't know what to say to this man. Wasn't sure if this relationship, if one could call it that, was going to be about more than sex. But they were on a date, weren't they?

The waitress approached with menus, but Gideon waved a hand. "We'll both have the house salad. The pasta primavera for her. The tagliolini with prosciutto for me. And a bottle of Dolcetto d'Alba."

Gideon turned to Karalee as the waitress nodded and left. "You'll like this wine. It's a red, but more subtle than most."

"That's the first subtle thing that's happened between us," Karalee said. She couldn't help it.

Gideon grinned. "So it is. But I think you like that about me."

She laughed. "You're right. I do."

Her shoulders loosened. Maybe this could be a normal date after all.

His hand on her thigh made her jump a little. She watched his face as his hand slid up, right into the already damp V between her thighs.

"Spread for me," he told her, locking his gaze on hers.

Maybe not an entirely normal date.

Her breath escaped in a long, quiet sigh. Her lashes fluttered closed for a moment.

"Open your eyes, Karalee. Look as though nothing unusual is happening."

"You must be joking," she muttered through clenched teeth as he drove his fingers into her, pleasure flashing through her body.

"Your wine, sir." The waitress opened the bottle.

Gideon pressed his thumb onto Karalee's clit just as the waitress pulled the cork free. She ground her teeth hard to keep from crying out.

The waitress poured a small glass for Gideon. He lifted it to his nose, took in the scent, his other hand momentarily stilling between Karalee's legs. He sipped, nodded to the waitress. "Very good."

The woman filled both glasses and left. Gideon handed one to Karalee. "Here, try this. It's quite nice."

She lifted the glass with a shaking hand, while he went

back to work on her. She took a small sip of the deep red wine. It flowed smoothly down her throat, the flavor light and subtle, as he'd said. But she was having difficulty swallowing as Gideon continued his assault, circling her clit, pressing his fingers deeper inside her.

"Gideon . . ."

"Yes?"

His face was perfectly calm. How could this not be affecting him? But when she looked more closely, she saw the fever in his dark brown gaze, caught the heaviness in his breathing.

"Jesus, Gideon. I think . . . I'm going to come right here."

"Yes, that's exactly what I want you to do."

"But . . . I can't."

"You will. For me."

She started to shake her head, but he only pressed harder on her clit, drove his fingers in and out of her in a steady rhythm.

He leaned in another inch, until his breath was warm on her cheek. "You won't be able to help yourself in a minute, will you?"

What was he doing to her?

"No," she breathed.

And in the next moment it hit, like a wall of pleasure coming down on her. Pleasure and heat in a shivering surge that made her gasp, made her bite down hard on her lip to keep from whimpering.

"Jesus, Gideon," she murmured when it was over and he'd pulled his fingers from her. She wanted to lay her head on his shoulder, but she was too uncertain as to what this was, going on between them. Instead, she blinked hard, pulled in a deep breath, sat up a little straighter. When she looked at him again he was staring at her, smiling.

"What?"

"That was beautiful."

That wasn't what she'd expected him to say. She didn't know what she had expected. She hardly knew what to think herself. Picking up her glass, she sipped her wine, then quickly sipped again.

Gideon leaned in and whispered into her hair, "Did you enjoy that, Karalee?"

She pushed down the uncertainty seeping into her system, lifted her chin, looked directly at him, and smiled. "Yes. I did."

"Good. Because that's only the beginning of what I hope will be a very interesting evening."

"Is that so?"

"Surely you didn't think we'd have dinner tonight, then go our separate ways?"

"I hoped not."

A wicked grin lit his dark eyes. "I like that about you, Karalee. But I wanted us to get to know each other tonight, too. Otherwise I would have just taken you to some dark corner again."

"I like the dark corners. But I like it here, too. And I have to admit I'm curious about you."

"What do you want to know?"

Their salads arrived and she lifted her fork. She was starving suddenly. She speared a bit of lettuce and chewed for a moment, thinking. She was thoroughly relaxed after her lovely little orgasm. "I want to know where you came from, where you were before you came to San Francisco. You're something of a mystery at school, you know."

"Am I?"

"Are you telling me you don't do it on purpose?" she teased.

He laughed. "I'm not so mysterious. I've actually lived most of my life in San Francisco. I taught at U.C. Santa Barbara for eight years before coming to San Francisco State. But I grew up here. I always come back."

"What made you go to Santa Barbara? You don't strike me as the beach bum type."

He shrugged, a casual move, but she saw his features harden, his eyes going flat. "I needed a change. Needed to be somewhere different." He picked up his glass, drank the rest of his wine in one swallow, poured some more.

He didn't say any more. But his face had said it all. She'd hit a sore spot. One he obviously had no intention of talking about. But then, this was the first real conversation they'd had; she didn't expect him to bare his soul to her. Not that she needed him to. She decided to change the subject.

"How do you like your new job?"

"The staff is great. The students are great. They seem very interested in learning. A more sophisticated group than at some other schools."

"I agree. I'm not sure what it is. They're very focused."

He nodded, started in on his salad. She was glad to have distracted him from whatever had made him so uncomfortable.

"Do you miss Santa Barbara at all, Gideon?"

"No. I like the pace in San Francisco more. The lifestyle is a little too laid-back for me in Santa Barbara. And I'm glad to be back in my house here."

"You have a house in the city?"

"It's over on Potrero Hill. An older house. It needs some work now, after renting it out these last years. But there's a great view of the bay. And I opened the attic up to make a master suite when I first bought it. I put in these enormous windows, a couple of skylights. You can see most of the city from up there. It's like sleeping right under the sky."

"It sounds unusual."

"It is. It's incredible. And it's home for me. At least, it's getting to be again. I've only been back in the house for a month. What about you?"

"I'm one of those Midwest imports."

"Ah. Where do you hail from?"

"Indiana. I came to California for college and never left."

"So, you're one of those innocent small-town girls?"

"A small town, yes. Not so innocent, though."

He grinned. "No, I suppose I wouldn't call you innocent, Karalee."

"But I am a preacher's daughter."

"Seriously?"

"Oh yes. My father's a minister. If my parents had any idea what Chico State's reputation for partying was, they'd never have let me leave the house, never mind cross state lines to go to college."

"But you managed to get an education, to become a teacher."

She shrugged. "It was what I wanted to do, and it makes them happy, although they hate that I live so far away. Not that we're particularly close. But they have this archaic idea that a woman can't survive alone in the world. I think that's what's kept them together all these years. But that kind of thinking is one of the reasons why I couldn't ever go back, once I'd left. This city is my home now. It's so dynamic. I love it here. My father calls San Francisco a city of sin. I suppose it is. Maybe that's what I like most about it."

He grinned at her and lifted his wineglass. "Ah, Karalee, you're really something."

How strange to sit here, talking with him as though nothing had happened; simply two people having dinner. But even now her sex throbbed, wanting more. Wanting him.

"So." She leaned in, her wineglass in her hand, her fingers caressing the stem. She lowered her voice. "Do you always have sex in the janitors' closet?"

"Only with you. But it may become a habit."

She went warm inside. Something about the way he was looking at her, as though he might eat her alive. She'd like that. Love it, really. "I hope so."

He pushed his salad plate aside, reached over, and stroked the back of her hand with his fingers. She shivered, desire dancing over her skin. The man had great hands.

"I have plans for you later, Karalee. They don't involve a closet. But I think you'll enjoy what I have in mind."

God, even hearing him say these things was an incredible turn-on. She squeezed her thighs together.

"I can't wait to find out."

He smiled at her. She smiled back, lust surging through her system. Dinner couldn't be over soon enough.

🌿

Mia stood and wiped her gloved hand over her cheek. The sun filtered through the scattered clouds, touching her little garden with bits of gold. She'd been working there since sunrise, unable to sleep after her evening with Jagger.

She should never have let him kiss her last night. Should never have gone to his apartment for dinner. The only smart thing she'd done was to leave before things went any further. But she wanted to go back, wanted him to kiss her again.

She wanted him to do more than kiss her.

Why was she being such a prude suddenly, if even only in her own head? Why was she unable to be honest with herself about what she really wanted from Jagger? Because what she wanted was for him to put his hands on her, to touch her naked skin. She wanted to strip his clothes off, to see his body, to feel his skin against hers. She wanted his mouth all over her, to feel those lush lips, his wet tongue on her flesh . . .

She wanted him to fuck her. Oh yes. And she wanted him to feed her again, to take that lovely raspberry sauce he'd made and cover her in it, lick it from her skin in long, lovely strokes . . .

She shook her head and commanded her body to calm as she went back to work, pulling weeds, snipping the blown and browned roses from their stems, focusing on her task, on the pale winter sun warm on her back.

She hadn't experienced that sensual—sexual—connection between a man and food since Ben. Yes, she watched the cooking shows with her vibrator in hand. But she knew her physical response was nothing more than a reaction that had been built into her. She'd spent years learning about fetishes, trying to understand what motivated her own desires. She understood why she sexualized food. She knew exactly what Freud had to say on the subject, understood the chemical responses in the brain. But that was about her own history, not a specific person.

So why was it all coming up again now, with Jagger? Just because the man could cook, obviously understood something about the sensual nature of food. It meant nothing.

Or at least, it *should* mean nothing.

She worked for another hour. Then, her garden in order, she picked up her basket full of cuttings and dead roses. The scent of the roses came to her, along with the ever-present scent of the ocean.

She loved these smells. They reminded her of when she'd first come here, when she was thirteen years old. More than old enough to understand what her mother was, the things she did. She'd loved this house the moment she'd seen it. Loved her grandmother the moment they'd finally met. And she always felt guilty that she'd been so relieved when her mother had taken off in the middle of the night, leaving her there. Guilty that she never missed her, that she was simply glad to have a normal life, finally.

Moving to the back corner of the garden, she emptied the basket into the compost pile, took it to the small shed, and set it inside on a shelf along with her gloves, then headed into the house. In the kitchen, she washed her hands, poured herself a glass of iced tea, and drank it in long gulps standing over the sink.

She was good at guilt, that was for sure. She felt guilty as hell now over that kiss last night. Over the cravings that pulled so strongly at her insides she could barely stand not to pick up the phone and call him. Such intense yearning for him, driven by the whole food thing...it was all tied together, wasn't it?

No, no, no.

What was she going to do with herself? This was pure torture, to want him so badly and not be able to have him. So much worse after that teasing kiss last night. The man could kiss. She was pretty damn sure he could do a few other things. But she wasn't supposed to be thinking about this!

But she couldn't forget the feel of his lips, the taste of him, the scent of raspberries and chocolate in the air...

She was a mess over this guy, and she had no idea how it had even happened. This internal battle was making her crazy. *Jagger* was making her crazy. Another good reason to stay away from him.

She knew damn well what she *should* do: keep her distance, never allow herself to be alone with him. Never allow him to touch her again, to kiss her. But she also knew damn well she couldn't do it.

Jagger walked along Mission Street, the rich scents of garlic and spices wafting from the restaurants he passed, along with that sharp smell of damp pavement the San Francisco fog always seemed to bring out and the odor of sour booze from the bars and clubs where the crowds were beginning to gather for the night's activities. The streetlights illuminated the dark sidewalk; neon signs cast colorful shadows at his feet, blue and yellow and hot pink pooling in the small puddles as he moved down the street.

He'd been out at a bar with Jean and Leilani, but he hadn't been able to sit still. He'd drank a beer, then made his excuses and left. Shoving his hands deeper into the pockets of his jacket, he slowed his pace. He really didn't want to go home yet. Not that he knew where he wanted to go. But at home, all he'd do was sit around and think about Mia Rose.

Not that he wasn't thinking of her now.

He really did not want to call her. She obviously didn't want him to. And he didn't want to be that guy, not anymore. That guy who chased after a woman. Who couldn't stop thinking about her.

Not again. And not with a woman like Mia Rose, who obviously did not want to get involved. He'd be setting himself up for disaster.

Fuck.

Images of Mia flashed in his mind, one after another. And it wasn't only her mouth, the way her breasts moved beneath her clothing, the way her cheeks, her neck, flushed when he touched her. It was her hands in motion, the sound of her voice. And her scent was in his head all the damn time. He was almost getting hard now just remembering the way she smelled.

He stepped up his pace.

Have to get home, damn it. Have to call her. Have to see her. Have to touch her again.

He shook his head at how ridiculous he was being. But there was nothing he could do about it.

He took a right onto Sixth Street, moving quickly past the storefronts and apartment buildings until he reached his door. Inside, he punched the button for the elevator. Punched it again after a moment, jamming his thumb. Finally it came, and he got in and swung the gate shut with a rough clang. He paced as the car rode up to the top floor. He was already pulling his jacket off when he stepped out and keyed open his front door.

Tossing his jacket on the floor, he stalked to the phone sitting on the table next to the sofa. He stopped, stared at it.

Lord, what was he—twelve? He'd never had trouble calling a girl in his fucking life.

But Mia Rose was no girl.

No, there was something different about her. Something that made him feel like some kid. Lust-crazed. Needy. His hand was actually shaking as he reached for the phone.

He nearly jumped out of his skin when it rang. Yanking his hand back, he stopped to laugh at himself, then picked up.

"Hello."

"Jagger?"

Jesus Christ.

Pull it together.

"Mia Rose. Hey." Yeah, that was it, calm and cool.

He was so full of crap.

"Hi, Jagger. Um . . . I just wanted to . . . to talk to you."

"I'm glad you called."

"I wanted to say I'm sorry about the way I ran out on you last night. I shouldn't have been so rude about it. And I should have called you this morning, but I was . . ." He heard a long sigh. "I don't know, honestly. I don't know what my problem is. I'm being an idiot. I'm sorry."

"You're not being an idiot. And I really am glad you called. I want to see you."

He hadn't meant to say it; it just slipped out, as easy as silk between his lips, as easy as water.

Her voice was soft, a little breathless. "Okay."

"Okay? That's it? No argument?"

She laughed, making him smile. "No argument."

"Let me cook for you again. Or no, let me take you somewhere. There's this old Spanish place here, right by my house. It's been here for forty years. It's sort of a dive, but you won't believe the food. And the music is the real thing. Say you'll come."

"I will. When?"

"Right now."

"Jagger, it's nine-thirty at night."

"They're open late. Are you hungry?"

"Yes. I am, actually. I haven't eaten yet."

"Then come."

"Okay. Okay." She laughed. "I'll be there in a little while."

They hung up and he sank down onto the sofa, into the cushions. His cock was beginning to throb, just from the sound of her voice. So was his chest. But he wasn't going to think about that.

She would be here soon. He didn't need to think of anything else right now.

chapter ✑ six

RIDING THE BIG FREIGHT ELEVATOR UP, STANDING BEFORE Jagger's front door, all felt like déjà vu to her. Mia cleared her throat, smoothed her hair, straightened the pale gray wraparound sweater she'd worn with her jeans. Her stomach was fluttering. So was her pulse. She felt absolutely overwhelmed by an exquisite sense of anticipation. She paused, simply enjoying it for a moment before knocking on the heavy door.

Jagger opened it, smiling. He was wearing a black sweater tonight, the collar of a white T-shirt peeking out at the neckline, and worn blue jeans. A standard urban outfit, but he looked really good. Great, actually. He always did. She was fairly certain he looked every bit as good first thing in the morning, right out of bed.

Don't even think about it.

Impossible not to, with him standing there in front of her, smiling. Heat rose in her cheeks.

"Hey there, Mia Rose." His voice was low and smooth. Sexy as hell. "Do you want to come in for a minute? Or just get going?"

"It's getting late. Maybe we should go."

He stepped out, pulled the door shut behind him. The elevator was still there. Swinging the gate aside, he motioned for her to pass before him, clanged it shut behind them. They were silent on the way down. But he was close enough that she could smell the lovely clean scent that was pure Jagger, making her body light up with need, making her tremble inside.

She was almost relieved when they got to the ground floor and he led her out, then onto the sidewalk. He took her arm as they walked. So nice, this protective gesture, to simply have him touch her.

"It's only a few blocks; we can walk. Do you know this part of the city well?" he asked her.

"A bit. I've been down here to eat, to go to clubs, although it's been a while since I've done that. It fascinates me, though. It's a little dirty, a little colorful."

"Yeah, and it's a little dark and dangerous, maybe. But there's such an interesting mix of people in the Mission District. It reminds me of certain areas of the French Quarter in New Orleans. And I like things a little dangerous."

He turned to smile at her once more, that beautiful smile, his mouth full and lush, his teeth so strong and white. Oh yes, he was every bit as dangerous to her as the city streets. The way he made her want to open up, explore that side of herself she'd kept shut down for so long, both physically and emotionally.

Maybe she should spend some time figuring out if that was part of the attraction. But she didn't want to do that now. Right now she wanted to enjoy being here with him. Eating with him. If he only knew what that did to her, watching him eat, handling the food, simply sitting with him while she ate herself, all the flavors and scents and textures in her mouth mixed with the sexual tension of Jagger's presence.

No, don't think, don't think. All you ever do is think.

"Here it is. El Oso."

He held the door open for her and she stepped into a small space with scarred linoleum floors and low lighting. It smelled wonderful, something sharp and tangy in the air. Her pulse was fluttering, humming.

A middle-aged woman with her dark hair in a pair of long braids showed them to a cramped table in one corner. Jagger held Mia's chair for her. Why was she so charmed by his manners? That sort of thing had never mattered to her before. But she was charmed by everything about him.

She watched as he chatted with the waitress in Spanish, ordered sangria for them both, ordered food. She had no idea what it was he asked for. She didn't care. The waitress came back in moments with two glasses of sangria, dark and shining like liquid jewels.

"There's only one place in this town with better sangria, an amazing Cuban tapas place up on Haight Street. But I wouldn't tell them that here," Jagger said, keeping his voice low, intimate. In the dim light, his eyes were a deeper gray than they'd looked to her before. His voice dropped even lower. "I'm glad you called, Mia Rose."

"So am I."

"Do you want to tell me what happened last night?"

She paused, drank some of her wine, letting the spicy-sweet concoction slide down her throat. "Not really. But I'll try. I guess I owe you that." She sipped again, set the glass down, left her fingers curled around it. "I'm sure you're every bit as aware as I am that it isn't considered ethical for me to spend private time with a student."

He nodded. "I know. But that doesn't stop other people from doing it."

"I'm not other people, Jagger."

"No. You're not. I like that about you."

A warm flush crept over her skin, making it hard to remember exactly what her argument was supposed to be.

"Look, Jagger, I just . . . I shouldn't even be here with you."

"But here you are." He leaned in, until she could smell the clean scent of him: soap and something else, something a little dark, exotic. "I understand the ramifications of you being caught seeing a student. But we're both adults here. I'm pretty sure we can handle this." He reached out, touched the back of her hand with his fingertips. "Don't try to tell me you don't want to be here right now. Or that you came tonight just to say these things to me."

She shook her head, the heat from his touch running up her arm in a series of small shocks. She swallowed hard. "No. No, I didn't. I came partly to apologize. And partly to . . . I don't know. I don't know exactly why."

"You don't have to analyze it. I get the feeling you do that a lot. I don't mean that as an insult."

"No, it's true. Maybe being in the academic world is part of that. But it's also part of who I am, how I operate. I know that. Sometimes it has its uses."

"Yes, but not right now. You don't need to do that with me. With me, what you see is what you get. Let's just enjoy the evening, the food. Each other's company. Can we do that, Mia Rose?"

"Yes. Of course."

He smiled at her and she smiled back. She couldn't help it. His fingers were stroking the back of her hand, crept up to run over her wrist.

She wasn't going anywhere.

"You're going to love the food. I can tell you're someone who appreciates food. Truly appreciates it."

Beneath the table her other hand curled into a fist, her fingers gripping the edge of her chair. "I . . . yes, I am."

He leaned in a few inches. "Are you blushing?"

"Oh, well, it's just that you . . . you seem to be able to read me fairly well."

Even though she'd used it as a cover, it was true. She hoped that only went so far.

He shrugged. "I pay attention."

"Yes, you do." She took a sip of her sangria.

He kept stroking her wrist, leaned even closer. "I think you're one of those people who appreciate the sensual nature of food. Am I wrong?" He paused, watching her face. "I don't think I am."

What was he saying? Was she that transparent? But would it be so awful if he knew this about her?

"I . . . you're right. I do appreciate food in that sense. I love to go to the farmers' market and just look at the piles of produce. The colors and the textures of everything."

Jagger nodded. "That's part of what makes a good palette. And when the food feels good on your tongue."

"Yes, exactly."

She looked away, her stomach knotting suddenly. There was so much more to it for her. Her body was burning with desire simply skirting the edges with this conversation.

"What is it? What just happened?" He lifted her chin with his hand.

Such a tender gesture. She searched his eyes but saw nothing other than true concern there. And she had to deal with this sooner or later. How many years had she spent intellectualizing it all, without ever really confronting the issue?

"Jagger, what if I told you there was more to it for me? To the food."

"I'd be intrigued." He smiled, and her shoulders loosened a little. "Why don't you tell me about it?"

She picked up her glass and sipped, then sipped some more. "This isn't easy. Even for me. Even considering my area of study, what I teach. It's . . . it's different when it's personal. God, I shouldn't be telling you these things!"

"Why not? Maybe I'm the perfect person to tell. I'm not a family member. Not your husband. There's not that much at risk. And I can tell you I'm pretty damn sure I won't be horrified. But I don't think that's the problem, is it?"

"No. It's more that I have to stop overthinking everything. To face certain things about myself."

Jagger nodded. "We all do, at one time or another. We all have to face our truths." He paused, then, "I didn't take your class by chance, Mia Rose. I'm there to do a little of my own self-exploration."

She caught his gaze, nodded. "There are two kinds of people who take the Alternative Sexuality class. Those who want to gawk, and those who have a personal stake in learning about fetishes. I never saw you as a gawker."

Maybe that's what had drawn her to him. Maybe that's why she was able to have this discussion with him now. And even though they were still addressing it in cerebral terms, her body was heating up, a tight curling fist of lust low in her belly, spreading outward.

"Do you want to know what my thing is, Mia Rose? My fetish?"

His voice was deep and smooth. She licked her lip, tasted the wine lingering there. "Only if you want to tell me."

"Water. It's almost too simple. Except that it's not when it's happening, when I crave it."

"Desire is never simple, no matter how much it may look that way on the surface."

"Yeah, but all that Freudian stuff, all that stuff about 'wishes,' it's too complex. Because it seems very natural to me. But I'm finding out that not everyone feels that way. You don't."

"Of course I think it's natural."

"No, you only think it's natural for other people."

She shook her head as his words sank in. He was right. But she wasn't ready to admit it. Maybe not even to herself.

"I think . . . I think it is natural, even when it's not pretty. I mean, certain fetishes are a bit silly, or even frightening."

Jagger was quiet, thoughtful as he sipped his wine. "I think that fears and desires can come from the same place. From some mysterious, primal place inside each of us."

"Yes. Even the more extreme forms of fear and desire, phobias and fetishes, it's all mysterious on the surface, but if you dig deep enough, there's always an explanation."

"So, you're breaking our sexual desires down to science?"

"Maybe. But really I'm breaking the human psyche down to science. That's what psychology is. That's what sociology, cultural anthropology, is."

"But you're saying there's a scientific explanation for everything," Jagger insisted, leaning forward in his chair, his gaze intense.

"Well, the science of the mind, yes."

Why was she feeling so confused, suddenly, about a subject she'd had so well thought out for years?

"I get the science part, Mia Rose. But what about the emotional content? When does that come into play?"

She felt the breath go right out of her. It was as though he'd reached inside her and yanked open a door she'd kept locked up tight, one full of rust, neglect. She sipped her wine, gulped it down, really, buying time until she could breathe again.

"Mia Rose? What did I say?"

She shook her head slowly, her heart pounding. "Nothing. No. That's not true. Everything. It's just that . . . you're right. God, you're right. It's why I've held myself back from really exploring this . . ."

"You don't have to explain anything to me. But you might want to spend some time asking yourself what that's all about for you. And then maybe we can talk about it again."

She smiled shakily. "You're very confident that I'll see you again."

"Yes, I am."

He lifted her hand, brushed his lips across her knuckles. She shivered.

The charm was back on. And she was falling for it. But she didn't care.

She felt better simply having said the words out loud, admitting to her food fetish, even if they'd been a bit vague about it. They both knew what it was they were talking about. It was freeing to know he didn't judge her. And frightening that he'd reached some place so deep within her. But maybe the end result was that she could learn to judge herself a little less?

Her pulse calmed as Jagger refilled her glass from the pitcher the waitress had brought to the table, smiled at her, sat silently while she drank her wine, giving her time to settle down.

The waitress came to their table and set down two large bowls of paella: a pile of saffron rice topped with shrimp and clams, peppers and onions.

"Time to eat. You're going to love this, Mia Rose. I guarantee it."

Mia inhaled the spicy scent. "It smells wonderful."

"It tastes even better. They do it the right way here, where they caramelize the bottom in the pan. It's called *socarrat*. You have to eat it down to the bottom to really get the full flavor. Did you know this dish was originally created by the servants of the Moorish kings? Although some believe it was the Romans who invented it, and others think it was actually an Arabic dish. Here, the shrimp is beautiful, try some."

He picked up a piece and held it in his fingers, fed it to her, the plump, succulent flesh sliding between her lips. She chewed, letting the exotic spices fill her mouth, trying to ignore the buzzing ache in her body, the almost-touch of his fingers on her lips.

"Wonderful," she said when she had swallowed, letting him assume she was referring only to the food.

Jagger smiled, then took a bite himself. He was utterly unselfconscious about sharing a meal with her in this way, yet it seemed so intimate to her. It made her think of sex. *He* made her think of sex, whether food was involved or not. But of course, the food made it even better.

"So, talk to me, Mia Rose."

"About what?" She took a sip of the cool sangria, letting it mix with the spicy burn on her tongue.

"About yourself."

"Haven't we already done that?"

"I'm pretty sure we've barely scratched the surface."

"I'd rather you tell me about your life. What was it like in New Orleans with your dad?"

"Ah, New Orleans is a magical place. It's like no other city in the world. It's steamy and dark and a little sad, even at Mardi Gras. But it's also colorful and beautiful. And being there with my dad was always exciting. As I said, he's a jazz musician, and his friends are all musicians and artists. The most fascinating people."

The waitress came back and set platters on the small table, crowding their plates; meat and vegetable dishes, sending scented steam wafting into the air.

"This is *alubias verdes con ajo,*" Jagger told her. "Basically green beans with a lot of garlic. And this is some *chorizo,* just sausage and peppers. It's spicy, so you have to drink plenty of wine."

"Are you sure you don't have an ulterior motive?" Mia asked, laughing.

"Would you mind too much if I did?" He grinned at her and she couldn't seem to argue with him, despite the alarm bells going off in her head. "Ah, here's our *patatas a la importancia*. You'll love these potatoes. They're fried. You're not one of those women who's always on a diet, are you? No, never mind, I don't think you are. You're more of a sensualist, like me."

"Jagger, I'll explode if I eat all of this."

"You have to try a little of everything, at least."

She shook her head while he spooned food onto her plate. "You were going to tell me about your father."

"Ah, well, he's an amazing musician. Plays sax and piano, mostly, but he can play a little percussion, too. He's a good man. He used to take me around to the clubs when he had a gig when I stayed with him in the summers, sometimes a few nights a week. I'd hang around backstage, or out in front if one of his friends was there to sit with me at a table. I remember that smell of cigarette smoke and beer, mixed with a little perfume." Jagger took a bite of the potatoes, chewed for a moment. "And the women. There were always women around. That's where the perfume came from, I guess. But I learned to appreciate a beautiful woman. Dad was always a killer with the ladies. Still is."

"That's where you get it from, I suppose."

Jagger's features tensed, went a little dark. What had she said? But just as quickly his expression cleared. He picked up his sangria, drank, smiled at her, if a little tightly. "I guess so."

"And your mother? You told me she was an artist."

"Yeah, she's still here, in Berkeley. Still painting. She travels a lot, has friends all over Europe. She's there right now."

"No siblings?"

"Dad had two daughters after he and my mom split up, but they're kind of spread around. Serena is in Miami, Celia's in New York. I don't really know them. Their choice. What about you?"

"No. I'm an only child. I always wanted a sister. When I was really young, I used to pretend that I had one, in the way small children imagine things. It would have been nice, especially now, with my grandmother gone."

He reached out and curled his fingers around hers. "Sorry, Mia Rose."

She shrugged. "It's okay."

He looked at her for several moments, his gray eyes dark, unreadable. Then he lifted her hand to his lips, brushed them over the back of her fingers. A warm chill ran through her. She wasn't sure what it meant: that look, him kissing her hand so gently. But it seemed to mean something. Or was she reading too much into it? She had no sense of objectivity where he was concerned.

The waitress stepped up to their table and cleared the platters away, refilled their glasses. They drank quietly for a few minutes, lingered over the rest of their meal, talked of inconsequential things.

"Why don't we walk some of this food off?" Jagger suggested.

He stood, held her chair for her, and they went out into the cool night air.

"That was an amazing meal, Jagger. Thank you."

"It was my pleasure. I have dessert back at my place."

"Oh, I don't . . . I don't think I should."

"You'll be ready for something sweet by the time we get there. Or we can sit and have some more wine first."

"No, I don't mean . . . Jagger, I shouldn't go back to your place. I don't think it's a good idea. I need to figure some things out before I . . ." She trailed off, too unsure of what she needed to say, what she needed to do.

"It's alright. I understand. I'll walk you to your car, then."

She nodded, half grateful he hadn't argued the point with her and half wishing he had.

God, you really are a mess.

They moved down the street, the night air cool on her face, but Jagger's presence was warm next to her. As they walked, he took her hand, just a gentle twining of fingers around hers. It felt good. Better than it should have, and the sensation wasn't entirely sexual. It was *more,* a different kind of heat that moved through her chest, loosened her up inside. Opened her up.

They reached her car, a silver Mini Cooper, parked only a few doors down from Jagger's building, a little too quickly.

"This is me." She tried to drop his hand, but he held on.

"Come upstairs with me, Mia Rose," Jagger said softly.

She wanted to. Every cell in her body wanted nothing more than to go upstairs with him, to let him kiss her again, touch her. She blew out a long breath, leaned back against the passenger door of her car.

"I can't, Jagger."

"Alright. But I'm not going to let you go without kissing you."

He leaned in, and she found herself lifting her face to his, her mind emptying even before his mouth met hers. Then it was just the cool, plush texture of his lips on hers, that soft press of flesh upon flesh. Her hands went around his neck, his skin so hot and smooth there, and he moved in closer, leaning in to her, the weight of his body pressing her into the car. When his tongue moved her lips apart, he slid inside. She went soft and loose all over, her breasts aching for more than the hard press of his chest against hers, with the layers of sweater between them.

In moments she was panting, wet. And he deepened the kiss, the heat of his mouth making her crazy. She wanted him. Wanted him to fuck her. Right there. Right *now*.

His hips were hard up against hers, and that solid ridge of flesh pushed against her belly.

God.

Her hips tilted, her sex filled, throbbed, wanting, wanting. But she wasn't supposed to be doing this.

She was *not* supposed to be doing this.

He kissed her harder, wet and hurting, bruising her lips. His hands gripped her waist, his fingers biting into her, and all she wanted was more. God, she could almost come if he only kissed her long enough, just kissed her like this.

He pulled back, brushed her hair with his lips, with his cheek. He was breathing as hard as she was. He still had her up against the car, his body pressing her against the cold steel. His hands slid down over her hips, dug in again. She couldn't have moved even if he hadn't been holding her so tightly. She could barely breathe. She didn't want to.

"Jagger . . ."

"Fuck. I'm sorry, Mia Rose."

"No. That's not it."

"What, then?" He looked down at her, his eyes glittering in the silvery light of the streetlamp a few feet away.

The words came out on a half-whisper.

"I don't want you to stop."

Karalee stood at the front of Gideon's car, leaning against the hood. It was a 1968 Mustang. Black and sleek. Fully restored. Not what she might have expected him to drive. No, he was more the BMW type. The man was a mystery.

Even more mysterious as he paced in front of her, his steps echoing in the nearly empty parking structure. The smell of motor oil was in the air, the faint scent of old exhaust. If she looked beyond him she could see the lights glinting on the tall buildings of the Embarcadero, the stark beauty of the Bay Bridge, the velvet dark of the sky. It was nearly eleven o'clock at night, but she could hear the muffled sounds of traffic moving below. And yet she felt safe here with him, even though she knew full well what he was asking her to do.

He wasn't impatient. No, he was pacing off the energy that made his dark eyes glitter, that gave him such a sense of immediacy, of energy. She was shaking just a little. But she'd known instantly what her answer would be. Her entire body had swarmed with lust the moment he'd suggested it. He was the one who insisted she take a moment to think about it.

"Gideon?"

"Yes?" He stopped in front of her, stepped closer. "Do you have your answer, Karalee?"

"Yes. I want this."

He smiled. "I thought you might."

"You knew I wouldn't say no."

He nodded silently, then before she could think anymore he gripped her waist with his big hands and spun her around. She steadied herself, the hood of the car cool and smooth beneath her palms. He didn't have to ask her to lean over the hood, to spread her legs for him. She simply did it, her body following his lead.

He moved in close behind her and lifted her narrow black skirt. Heat shuddered through her when she heard him unzip his slacks. She was soaking wet already.

There was no preamble, which was exactly what she wanted. Just him spreading her pussy lips before sliding inside.

She moaned as he pressed his cock deep inside her, spreading a little more for him. One last hard thrust and he was buried deep.

"Fuck, Karalee."

"Oh, yes . . ."

She pushed back against him, wanting more, wanting all of him. He pulled out, let just the tip of his cock rest inside her, and held himself there, until pleasure spread through her system like liquid heat, her sex aching with need.

"Gideon, please . . ."

He slammed into her, jarring her, pulled out, then rammed hard into her again. One sharp thrust after another, and she was panting, gasping, as her body thrummed with desire, with the need to come.

His hand went into her hair, gripping hard, yanking her

head up, and that moment of total command made her go weak all over. She would have fallen if not for his arm slipping around her waist, holding her right up against him.

"Jesus, Gideon. Just fuck me. Do it."

His hand moved down, pressed against her clitoris.

"Oh . . ."

He pushed into her again, ground against her mound with his hand. Her climax bore down on her, making her shiver all over, hot, intense. When he pinched her clit hard between his fingers she came apart, whimpering, panting, biting her lip to keep from crying out. Pleasure moved through her, shook her to the core. And still he pumped into her in long, devastating strokes, driving her orgasm on until she wasn't sure she could take it anymore.

And then he stiffened all over, pausing for one long moment before shoving into her harder than ever with a deep groan.

"Fuck, Karalee. Need to fuck you. Just fuck you . . ."

She collapsed onto the hood of the car, his arm still tight around her waist. She felt as limp as a rag doll, as entirely helpless. But she felt wonderful.

He was still inside her, still half hard.

His hand loosened its grip on her hair, slid down to caress the back of her neck, sending a chill down her spine. And it was only then she realized she hadn't thought for one moment since he'd bent her over his car that they might be caught, that someone could drive by, see what they were doing. Right now she hardly cared.

Finally he pulled out of her, tugged her skirt down, turned her around, and pulled her in for a brief kiss.

"Very good, Karalee."

She smiled, feeling dazed, sleepy, yet invigorated at the same time. She could have fucked him again right at that very moment if he'd wanted to.

The low groan of a motor sent a shiver through the pavement beneath their feet, and a car turned the corner, cruised past them. Gideon smiled down at her, a wicked, crooked grin, and a new wave of pleasure swept through her.

Oh yes, he was dangerous, this man. But he'd given her a taste for danger. And there would be no turning back.

chapter ∽ seven

MIA BROKE AWAY FROM JAGGER, HER BREATH COMING IN short, sharp pants.

"Jagger . . ."

"Tell me you're not changing your mind now, Mia Rose," he groaned, "because I don't think I can take it."

"Jagger, we're in the middle of the sidewalk."

"Yeah. Come on."

He grabbed her by the waist and pulled her the few feet to his building, took her inside, keeping their bodies pressed close together. The elevator was open and waiting, and they got in. The door was barely closed before his arms were wrapped around her, his mouth on hers, that wet, sensual mouth. He opened her lips with his tongue, plunged inside, backing her against the wall while the old elevator creaked upward. She could feel his erection against her belly again, wanted it, needed it, inside her.

His hands were in her hair, his tongue delving deeper, his hips pressing into her, seeming to push the pleasure through her in a warm rush.

The elevator reached the top floor, and he was still kissing her as he backed them both out and into the hallway. He pulled away long enough to mutter, "Where is my damn key?"

Then they were pushing through the door and into his apartment, and his mouth came down on hers again. His hands were on her, tracing the curves of her body, gentle for a few moments, then kneading her flesh: her shoulders, her waist, her hips. He pushed her back, up against the door with a heavy thud. She didn't care. All she knew was the hard planes of his body against hers, his hands moving beneath her sweater to cup her breasts through the sheer fabric of her bra as fire raged inside her, making her wet and weak with need.

When Jagger pulled his mouth from hers it was to draw her sweater over her head, then his own. She saw the smooth contours of his chest for the first time, the rounded muscles of his shoulders, those tattooed armbands really doing something to her. Beautiful. And his nipples were dark and dusky, succulent. Her own hardened. She licked her lips.

He pushed her aching breasts together in his hands, bent his head, and laid soft, moist kisses on the curve of flesh there. She moaned, her body quaking with desire. She could hardly believe she was there with him, that he was touching her in the way she'd fantasized about all too often.

"Take it off, Jagger. Just take it off."

He unsnapped the catch and her bra fell away.

"Lord, you're beautiful, Mia Rose. I knew you would be."

When he drew one nipple into his mouth, she cried out, desire lancing through her. She buried her hands in his hair, knew the texture of the silky curls as though she had touched him before, held on as he sucked her flesh into his mouth. Her sex went hot, absolutely burning. And her nipples were so damn hard they hurt.

Again he stopped, this time to draw her jeans down over her legs, leaving her in her damp lace panties while he tore his own jeans off.

She had one moment to see that he wore dark gray tight-fitting boxer briefs before he sank to his knees before her. With one hand he pressed against her stomach, holding her against the door. With the other he tore the scrap of lace down her legs, spread them apart.

"So beautiful," he murmured once more.

She shivered, watching him look at her, waiting for him to touch her, to kiss her there.

He moved closer, his breath warm against her curls. But he didn't touch her. Her sex was so hot, swollen. Needing him. A single drop of moisture trickled down the inside of one thigh.

Finally, he bent and brushed his lips across her mound.

"Ah! Jagger..."

So good already, she could hardly stand it. Absolute torture that he didn't just dive in, take her hard clit into his mouth.

Oh yes...

He blew on her skin, and her clitoris swelled impossibly.

She moaned, tilted her hips toward him, braced her hands against the smooth wood of the door behind her.

He used his fingers to open the lips of her sex, and even that gentle pressure was driving her crazy.

"I'm going to taste you now, Mia Rose," he said softly.

"Yes. Oh, please."

His mouth came down on her, warm and wet, and she pulled in one gasping breath as pleasure knifed into her body. She was shaking all over the moment his tongue darted out, shook even harder when he licked along her wet slit.

"God, Jagger."

She could come at any moment, but she didn't want it to be over so soon. Not with him, with this man she'd been wanting as she'd never wanted anyone before.

He licked her once more, that long stroke of his tongue teasing her swollen flesh. Then again, and again. She'd never been so wet in her life. When he put his fingers inside her, sliding right into her aching heat, she cried out.

God, so good...

And then he closed his mouth over her clitoris, drawing it into his mouth. Her fingers scratched against the wood, searching for something to hold on to.

"Jagger, please. I can't...oh God...don't stop."

He sucked on that hard nub of flesh, pleasure driving deep into her body. In moments she was on that verge, her hips thrusting into his mouth, his fingers plunging inside her. And he kept sucking, sucking, until she exploded in a fury of heat and desire. Her vision blurred, pleasure poured through her, drowning her, until she could barely breathe.

She slid down the door, and Jagger eased her onto the

floor. He was kissing her again: her neck, her face. Then his mouth was on hers once more and all she wanted was him inside her.

"Jagger, I need to feel you. I can't wait."

"Ah, Mia Rose."

He picked her up and carried her to his big bed, laid her down a little roughly. He moved around the bed, and she turned to watch him pull a condom from the nightstand drawer, watched as he stepped out of his briefs. Then he stood for a moment beside the bed, looking down at her, and she saw him fully for the first time.

His cock was so beautiful, it almost hurt to look at it. Large and swollen, she swore she could see it pulsing. And it was covered in the most beautiful brown skin. Her sex throbbed simply looking at it.

"Mia Rose, wait here."

"What? Jagger?"

But he was moving through the half-dark apartment toward the kitchen. Muted light shone in through the tall windows, casting red and gold shadows across the floor, but it was too dark at the kitchen end to see what he was doing. She didn't really care. She simply needed him to come back. *Now.*

When he did he held an open bottle of red wine in his hand. She pushed herself up on her elbows. "Jagger, I don't want to drink any more. I just want you."

He said, "You're not going to drink it. I am."

He placed one knee on the edge of the bed, held the bottle over her. And she realized suddenly what he was about to do.

Her sex squeezed and her mind went absolutely blank for

several moments. All she knew was the keen edge of anticipation, of the realization of her deepest desires.

And then he tipped the bottle, and a few drops of the wine flowed over her breasts. She moaned, almost wanted to cry. He bent over her, and she let her head fall back as he began to lick the wine from her skin. His tongue was so hot and smooth. The scent of the wine was dizzying. The combination was devastating.

She could not believe this was happening. And somewhere in the back of her mind was that memory of Ben, the sweet scent of the whipped cream, the flavor of it on his tongue when he kissed her after licking it off her body.

But this was Jagger she was here with now.

He poured again, and the slide of the liquid over her skin sent tremors of desire deep into her body, arrowing into her sex, as though his wet mouth were there once more. Her hips tilted, her sex clenching tight, her fingers gripping the bedcovers.

"Ah, Jagger."

He was sucking on her skin now, on the full flesh of her breasts, working the wine into her skin with his tongue. And all she could do was writhe beneath him.

He poured once more, this time down the length of her stomach, and followed with his lips, his tongue. She was shivering, needing to come again. She couldn't hold still, couldn't stop moaning. She didn't care.

He lifted his head. "I didn't think you could taste any better, Mia Rose. But you do."

This time he poured the wine directly into the folds of her sex.

"Oh! Please, please ... God ..."

She was coming even before he touched her, just the sensation of the wine, the awareness of this exquisite fulfillment of her fantasies. His tongue dove in, plunged into her, his mouth sucking and hot, driving her climax on.

"Jagger, Jagger, Jagger..." Pleasure shafted through her, overwhelmed her. Her mind was spinning, her body reeling.

Jagger raised his head, using his hand to gently massage her clit, the lips of her sex. Small ripples still coursed through her.

"Jesus, Mia Rose. You're shaking. You came so hard. I've never seen anything like it." He paused. "I want to make you come like that again."

She was still coming, tiny waves undulating through her body. She couldn't seem to stop.

When she glanced up at him, she caught his smile, his hooded, silvered eyes as he slipped a condom over his rock-hard cock. She reached out for him and he came to her, laid his body over hers. He felt so good, all lean, toned muscles and the hard ridge of his erection sliding down over her stomach and coming to rest between her thighs and, finally, at her wet opening.

She spread her thighs wider, wrapping her legs around his waist. But he took her legs in his strong hands, spread them as wide as they could go. "Hold them there for me, Mia Rose," he told her. She did it, feeling utterly open to him. Wanton. A little dirty.

Propped on his elbows, he kept his eyes on hers as he slipped just the tip of his cock inside her.

"Oh..."

Pleasure moved through her, a quiet wave. And she could

still smell the sweet, acrid scent of the wine, could still feel that lovely stickiness on her skin. But she wanted more.

She slid her hands over his muscled buttocks and pulled him deeper.

"Yeah..." His voice was husky, breathless. "You feel so good inside, baby."

His hands went to her breasts, his fingers taking her nipples and pinching and tugging on them. Oh, so good, desire flooding her body, her sex, her breasts. She arched into his hands. And then he pressed his hips into her, his cock sliding deeper.

"Jesus, Mia Rose. I don't want this to be over so soon. But you feel...ah...amazing."

Pleasure shafted into Jagger like a sweet-edged knife, like every titillating sensation he'd ever felt in his life. He was shivering, trying to hold his climax back. And she was so damn soft and hot under him. Her writhing, her panting breath, were making him crazy.

He pushed in, moving deeper. And she let out a long sigh, her legs trembling. His cock throbbed.

He pulled in a deep breath, held perfectly still for a moment while he regained some sense of control. Then he slid his hands under her buttocks, lifted her up until he was kneeling upright on the bed, with her laid out before him. Her lovely body open, her thighs still spread so wide he could see the nub of her hard little clit, pink and swollen and so damn succulent he wanted to take it in his mouth again. But there would be time for that later.

He pulled her in closer, buried his cock in her damp heat.

"Ah, Jagger. So good, just like this."

He loved that he could watch her: her red mouth, the flush on her cheeks, on her breasts. Lord, her breasts, like two perfect globes of pale flesh. And her nipples dark red, as succulent as her tempting little clit.

He slid his hand over her taut stomach, downward until he found that swollen nub of flesh, pressed onto it, smiled when she caught her breath in a gasp. Then he pumped into her, harder and harder. Pleasure moved through him: his cock, his entire body. It took everything he had to hold back. But he knew she was going to come again, into his hand, onto his cock.

Jesus.

He was shivering, his cock really about to explode, when her pussy clenched around him in a long, hard spasm. And his climax ripped through him, burning, blinding.

Even through his own orgasm, he watched her come as he plunged into her, her fingers digging into the bedcovers. And the hot clench of her around his cock, gripping him, milking him, was driving him on, emptying him.

"Jesus, Mia Rose."

They were both panting hard. And even though his climax had faded, small bursts of pleasure still surged through him, as though he'd come with his whole body.

She was so fucking beautiful.

Mia was watching him, her eyes glowing green even in the dim moonlight coming through the windows as he slid his hands over her. Her skin was as smooth as silk, pale and fine. He couldn't stop looking at her, didn't want to stop touching her.

Ever.

Where the hell had that come from?

He was not going there again.

She felt good, that was all. She felt fucking amazing. And after all her resistance, she was totally open in bed. Wild. And Lord, the way she responded when he'd poured the wine on her! He could watch her come all night, loved the way she just fell apart.

Her dark hair was everywhere, splayed out on the bed, a few strands across her face. He reached out and brushed it away. She blinked a few times but didn't move.

When he began to pull out of her, she grabbed his wrist.

"Don't. Not yet."

He nodded, leaned over her, kissed her lips. They were soft and swollen. He kissed her again. If only his tired cock would cooperate, he'd fuck her again. Later. Right now it was good enough that she was here, that he could touch her, kiss her. Such a romantic idea. He decided not to think about that.

Instead he shifted, laid his body over hers, kissed the sweet skin of her throat, her jaw.

Yeah, too romantic. Just think about fucking her again in a little while.

His cock gave a small throb.

"Gotta pull out, babe," he told her, then did just that, rolled over, got up, and went into the bathroom to pull the condom off. He stared at himself for a moment in the mirror.

"Don't be a fucking idiot," he told his frowning reflection before heading back to the bed.

She was sitting up, still looking a little dazed.

"Have you seen my clothes, Jagger?"

"You're not going anywhere."

He pushed her down onto the pillows, and she smiled at him.

"I'm not?"

"Give me about three minutes to recover and I'll show you why."

She reached down and wrapped her fingers around his already hardening cock. "I don't think you have to explain."

Lord, this woman! He couldn't wait to get inside her again. So damn good, everything about her. The sex, her beautiful body, her face. Everything.

Yeah, everything. But he didn't want to think about it all right now. Not the way his pulse hammered just looking at her. Just talking to her. No, right now all he had to know was that he would fuck her again. Again and again, as many times as his body would let him. There would be plenty of time to deal with these other ideas later, when he was too tired to do anything else. When she had gone and he wouldn't be as likely to say something stupid to her.

He didn't want her to leave.

Don't think about it now. Just touch her. Make her come again. Yeah.

For tonight, he could fool himself into thinking that was all that mattered, even if beneath all that he knew it was bullshit. There was a lot more to it than the sex. He was that kind of guy, even if Mia Rose wasn't that kind of woman.

But for now, she was right there, under his hands, her sweet thighs already spreading for him. He bent his head and buried his face in her body, lost himself there. It was morning before he thought about anything else.

Karalee unlocked the door to her house and Gideon wrapped his hands around her waist, pushing her inside, kicking the door shut behind him. She swore she could still smell the scents of motor oil and exhaust from their session in the parking structure earlier, could practically feel it all over her skin. It was even more apparent now, in the confines of her small house. Something incredibly sexy about that smell.

"Bedroom," he demanded.

Karalee smiled to herself as she took his hand and led him to her room. The man was insatiable. Lucky for her.

He was already pulling her clothes off, until she was completely naked, small, soft piles scattered across the dark blue and gold Persian rug on the floor.

"You're fucking beautiful, Karalee," he told her, his voice low, predatory in that way he had when he was about to do something dirty. "On the bed."

She sat down and started to slide toward the middle of the mattress, but he grabbed her and pulled her to the edge, pushing her onto her back with one hand between her breasts.

"Here. Right here." Then he spread her thighs roughly, went down on his knees, and buried his face between her legs.

He went to work right away, his tongue sweeping over her already hard clit, then sliding down her damp slit, pushing inside her. He was kneading the flesh of her hips, his hands hard and bruising. And she was panting, breathless, shivering with desire.

"Jesus, Gideon."

He slipped one hand between her thighs and pushed his

fingers inside her while he sucked hard on that swollen nub of flesh. Harder, rougher. In moments she was writhing, bucking, whimpering. He reached up with his other hand to twist one of her nipples. Sensation shot through her, from her breast to her sex, settling in the center of her body. Like fire, like liquid heat, blistering hot.

His hands, his mouth, were relentless, hurting her, driving her on. Pleasure crested, paused for one electric moment. And then she was plunging over that edge, coming, crying his name, crying in pain. But she loved every single moment. Every single sensation.

Before she had a chance to catch her breath, Gideon stood, unzipped his fly. He pulled a condom from the pocket of his jacket—he was still wearing his jacket!—and sheathed himself. She tried to sit up, but he pushed her back, wrenched her thighs apart even wider, and shoved his cock right into her.

Another shock of pleasure, nearly as powerful as her climax, ripped through her. He began to pump. Over and over, hard, driving thrusts. His hands were rough on her breasts, pinching and twisting her nipples, sending shocks of sensation through her system. But he was going too hard and fast for her to do more than lie helpless beneath him, lost in pleasure, in pain that was pleasure.

"Christ, Karalee."

"Yes, Gideon. Harder!"

"Fuck, yes . . ."

His hips plunging, fucking her, fucking her, and she was coming again, coming apart beneath the fury of his driving hips, his pummeling cock.

She was half out of her head. She didn't care. This was all she needed from him. All she'd ever needed.

You know damn well it's a hell of a lot more.

She pushed the idea away. Easy enough with him stiffening, shuddering, ramming into her as he came. Then his weight on top of her, the zipper of his jacket biting into her naked flesh. And the sweet relief, the serene knowledge that this man had taken her over completely.

This was what she needed. The thrill of being caught was obviously what drove Gideon. For her, it was all about allowing this man to take her over.

This man, who was the first one strong enough to do it.

Jagger woke to the sounds of traffic moving in the streets below, alone in his bed. He felt... empty. Something he'd never wanted to feel again.

He sat up, scrubbed a hand over the stubble on his chin. Jesus, he could still smell her on his hands. All over the bed.

Why had she left without saying anything? What the hell did that mean? And why was he being such a girl about it, anyway?

He was fucking losing it.

He threw back the covers and swung his legs over the side of the bed, went into the kitchen to get coffee going. The day stretched ahead, as empty as his bed was this morning.

This was ridiculous. He needed to get out of the apartment, distract himself. He put the coffee filters back in the cupboard. It was still early. He'd head down to the farmers' market, look at the produce, and buy his coffee there, pick up some mangoes for Leilani to make up for his flaky behavior lately. Maybe he'd get some flowers. Red roses for Mia Rose. Yeah. They'd look great against her pale skin.

Jesus. Flowers.

Flowers were for a relationship. Flowers were when a woman meant something to him.

He ran a hand over his hair, dug his fingers in, and gripped until it hurt. So, Mia Rose meant something to him. So what? That didn't mean he needed to get his heart stomped on again. He wasn't going in blind. He understood this woman was not relationship material, that she didn't want to be. He could handle it.

Shaking his head, he moved across the apartment to the bathroom. Maybe a long, hot shower would get his head back on straight. A cold shower would probably be more effective. He had to do something. Because he really was losing it over Mia Rose.

How the hell had this happened? And more important, what was he going to do about it?

He stood in front of the bathroom mirror, as he had the night before. He looked like the same person, if a little scruffier, a little bruised around the eyes from lack of sleep.

He should never see her again. It'd be the best thing for him. He had spent over a year learning to be the kind of guy who could shut his feelings off. He'd learned to protect himself. And who the hell did he think he was, anyway, getting Mia Rose to open herself up to him, when he wasn't willing to do the same in return? Not on that deep level, where it really mattered. He was not that sensitive guy anymore, the guy who could get hurt.

No, he should never see her again. But he knew damn well he wasn't going to do that. Because being with this woman, watching her change, watching her blossom, had changed him in some elemental way.

After being with Mia Rose, he wasn't the same person at all. He might never be again. And the scary part was, he wasn't sure it mattered anymore.

chapter ✿ eight

MIA PACED HER KITCHEN, HER ARMS WRAPPED AROUND HER body as though she could protect herself from the emotions pouring through her.

This was all wrong. Last night should never have happened. Bad enough that Jagger was her student, that she'd jeopardized her career. She'd also jeopardized her emotional well-being. She'd known it going in, known that what Jagger made her feel was more than a simple case of lust. But she'd done it anyway.

She was a fool.

The question was, what would she do now? Now that her body *knew* his. Now that his scent was so firmly ingrained in her mind she could never forget it, that blend of clean soap and dark patchouli. *Him.*

She paused in her pacing to put the kettle on the stove for

tea, pulled a mug and a tea bag from the cupboard. A long-standing source of comfort she'd picked up from her grandmother. Grandma had always thought almost any trouble could be soothed away with a good cup of tea. But Mia knew she was in deep trouble this time. Her situation with Jagger was going to require a lot more than tea.

Standing in front of the window, she looked at her little garden, at the dew clinging to the few remaining rose petals, gleaming drops reflecting shades of pink, yellow, red. The rest of the garden was lush green, except for the sky, which was as heavy and gray as she felt inside.

She could not see him again. He got under her skin too much. Made her open up. Open up to him, open up inside. He made her remember Ben, her first love. Her *only* love. The beginning of her obsession. And the intense pain of loss. She didn't want to remember how that felt. But she couldn't help it now.

Ever since she'd met Jagger, she was coming apart inside, in some beautiful and utterly terrifying way.

The kettle whistled, startling her out of her dark musing. She turned the stove off, poured the steaming water into her cup, and stood watching it steep, trying to get her mind to calm, her body, which was still buzzing with the aftereffects of orgasm after orgasm.

She shook her head in the empty room. She had to stop thinking about him, and she couldn't do it here. It was too quiet. She was too alone. She needed to get out, maybe walk in the park or go down to the beach and watch the cold, crashing waves. If she stayed in the house one more minute, she was going to pick up the phone, call him, ask to see him.

Taking her tea, she went into the bedroom to get dressed,

and only a few minutes later she was in her car, her tea mug cradled in the cup holder in the center console. She sipped as she drove, still unsure as to where she wanted to go, what she wanted to do with her day. And her heart was still beating at a million miles an hour.

There was a great bookstore down by the wharf. She could lose herself for hours in there. Maybe she'd try to find a new cookbook for her collection. She turned onto Van Ness, shifted as she climbed the hill and headed toward the bay.

She was surprised at how hard it was to find a parking space, then remembered there was a farmers' market around the corner on Sunday mornings. Maybe she'd wander through there before hitting the bookstore. Finally a spot opened up and she pulled in, slipped into her jacket, and grabbed her purse as she stepped out into the foggy morning air, heavy with salt this close to the ocean. She could hear the low murmur of the crowd two blocks away, the strumming of a guitar as she passed one of the local street musicians and threw a dollar into the cup at his feet.

She reached the rows of tented booths and wove between the throngs of people. There was color everywhere: piles of vegetables and fruits, stacks of homemade bread, jams, honey. And there were flowers at every stand, it seemed.

She stopped to buy some gorgeous purple Japanese eggplants, a bouquet of fresh basil tied with string, a small bunch of Roma tomatoes. Such a lovely distraction, the sights and smells, the people. She was beginning to calm down, her pulse slowing, even if Jagger's face was in the back of her mind the entire time.

She shook her head, trying to rid herself of his image, the

scent of him, the taste of his skin still lingering on her tongue . . .

"Mia Rose?"

Her heart slammed into her chest like a hammer blow.

God.

"Jagger. What are you doing here?"

He seemed momentarily stunned. Well, so was she.

"What am I doing here? What are you doing here? Is this where you went when you left this morning?"

"What? No, of course not. I just got here. I just . . ."

But what could she say? She'd crept away while he was sleeping. It had felt necessary at the time. She realized now it had been rude, at the very least.

"Jagger, I'm sorry. I couldn't . . . I had to leave."

He nodded his head, his face somber. Had she hurt him?

"Yeah, it's alright. No problem." He paused, ran a hand over his hair. "I was just wondering what happened to you."

"Well, I'm fine, as you can see."

What a lie that was.

He nodded. "Yeah."

They stood in an uncomfortable silence while her pulse fluttered in her veins.

Finally he asked, "Do you want to get some coffee?"

"I don't know if that's a good idea."

He was silent for a moment, his softening gray gaze on her face. Then he said quietly, "Come on, Mia Rose. I know why you left. I probably would have, too, if it hadn't been my house."

Her face went hot. "What are you saying?"

"That this is scaring the shit out of me, too."

She had to look away, to look at the ground. What he'd

said was all too true. And she felt like an absolute coward. Brave of him, to be so honest. He was a hell of a lot braver than she was. Maybe more grown-up about the whole thing, despite being so much younger.

"Mia Rose." He said her name softly. And it reminded her of the way he'd whispered to her in the middle of the night before pulling her into his arms, kissing her, pushing into her body. She shivered, gooseflesh rising on her skin.

Looking at him, she caught his gaze. God, his eyes were beautiful, like two pieces of quartz in the morning light.

"I don't want us to run away from each other, Mia Rose. Can we...just not do that? I understand why you left, at least on some level. I know why *I* want to run. And I want to talk to you about it. I don't know why." He paused, ran a hand over his hair once more. "Lord, I know I'm not making sense."

"No, you are. And you're right. I am scared, Jagger. Of a lot of things."

He took her hand, folded his fingers around hers, and squeezed. She wanted to cry suddenly. And when he pulled her in she didn't resist, didn't pull away when he bent his head and gently kissed her lips. Instead, she inhaled, took the scent of him into her body, leaned into him. Let it feel good.

His voice was low, as gentle as his kiss. "Come on. I could really use some coffee."

"Okay."

She let him lead her away, through the crowds of people, past the booths of produce. She left her hand in his, let them both have this moment of tentative connection that was so unfamiliar to her. She couldn't stop being afraid, not entirely.

But for now, she could simply let things *be* between them. Somehow Jagger admitting his fears made her own a little easier to handle. It was a revelation to her, that sharing her fears seemed to make them fade into the background.

Jagger was a revelation to her on several levels, and she had a feeling she'd only scratched the surface of who he was, what he had to offer. And for the first time in too many years, she gave herself permission to find out.

The telephone rang, waking Karalee from a deep, dreamless sleep. She rolled over onto her stomach, her arms and legs achy, but pleasantly so. She smiled to herself, remembering the night before with Gideon: in the parking lot, and then again here at her house. He was even rougher with her in bed than he was when they were in public, as though he needed that when the element of risk, of being discovered, wasn't there. Not that she minded.

She grinned to herself as she picked up the phone. "Hello?"

"Karalee."

Gideon.

Her sex gave an involuntary squeeze simply hearing his voice.

"Hi. Good morning." Oh yes, she could almost feel his hands on her again. She shivered.

"What are you doing?"

"I just woke up. You kept me up until after three. I didn't even hear you go, I was so tired."

"How soon can you be ready?"

"For what?"

A long pause, and then, "You don't really think I'm going to answer that, do you?"

She laughed. "Give me thirty minutes. Where shall I meet you?"

"I'll pick you up."

He hung up and she rolled onto her back, let her hands drift down her body, pausing to cup her breasts. They were heavy, wanting, her nipples two hard peaks beneath her own fingertips. Jesus, he'd turned her into a nymphomaniac.

Slipping her hands between her thighs, she brushed her mound. She was swollen and wet already. But she didn't have time to indulge her needs. Besides, she knew Gideon would take care of those later. He always did. How decadent to know she had that to look forward to.

With a sigh she got out of bed and headed for the shower. Almost too tempting to take the sprayer, aim it between her thighs, and make herself come. She'd done it many times before. That sprayer was a single woman's best friend. But it was also too tantalizing to force herself to wait for Gideon.

She got through her shower and dried her hair, pulled on a silk camisole and matching thong in a pale shade of blue that looked good against her skin, topped it with a pair of jeans and a sweater in the same shade as her lingerie. She wrapped a narrow, cream-colored scarf around her neck, slipped on a pair of brown leather boots, and at exactly the appointed time, her doorbell rang.

She opened the door, her wallet and her short tan leather trench coat already in hand.

Gideon looked great, as always. He was casually dressed today, in khaki cargo pants and a fisherman's sweater. But he still looked sophisticated, like something out of a Ralph Lauren ad.

"Good, Karalee, you're ready."

He smiled, that dashing smile. Such an old-fashioned word, but he really was dashing. Like some old-time film star.

"I wouldn't think of keeping you waiting." She smiled as she said it, but it was true. Gideon had an air of command about him she couldn't resist. She didn't want to.

He offered her his hand; she took it and let him lead her out to the car. He opened the door for her, handed her in, and she loved the gallant gesture, as she loved everything he did.

He got in and pulled into the street. She watched him as he drove, the way he handled the car with the same assurance with which he did everything else. The way he shifted gears seemed purely sexual to her. She could watch him all day if she didn't need so badly for him to touch her.

"So, not even a clue, Gideon?" she asked him.

He turned to her, smiled. He didn't say a word.

She sighed, shook her head at him. But she knew she'd find out soon enough.

They drove up Fulton Street alongside Golden Gate Park, then he made a turn into the park itself, wound between long expanses of green beneath the ancient eucalyptus trees. She rolled down the window a little so she could smell them, the pungent perfume that seemed to be released whenever the air was damp, which was much of the time in San Francisco.

"They smell good, don't they?"

She turned back to Gideon, surprised. "They do. I love them, their scent. I love the cool, damp air. It all seems to make for a certain mood about the entire city."

"That's one of the things I missed, the scent of this place, when I was away."

She couldn't figure him out. He was so mysterious, completely closed off to her in so many ways, and yet there were moments like this when he said something revealing, something that showed a more sensitive side, hidden away beneath his slick facade. And even though most of the time she was perfectly content with his air of mystery, when he let these deeper glimpses through, she found herself wanting to know more.

"Are you ever going to tell me why you moved away, Gideon?"

"Maybe someday. Why do you need to know?"

"It's not so much that I need to. I'm just...curious. People are interesting to me. I always want to know things. My mother couldn't stand that when I was growing up. I was always asking questions."

"Maybe the problem was that she didn't know how to answer them."

She wrapped her fingers around the shoulder strap of the seat belt. "Maybe."

"There aren't stock answers to every question, Karalee."

Suddenly she knew they were no longer talking about her mother. "Yes, you're right about that. Life isn't always clear. Sometimes I don't even understand my own reasons for doing certain things. Or not doing things, as the case may be."

"Here we are."

He pulled over and parked along the street, next to a long strip of grass leading to a tree-covered hillside.

"Where are we, exactly?"

"You'll see."

He got out of the car, came around, and helped her out. She knew enough already to wait for him rather than jump out herself.

He laid a hand lightly at her waist and they moved down the sidewalk, turned at the corner, and she saw across the street the big building that housed the Academy of Sciences behind the leafless fruit trees and the rows of wood benches that made up the music concourse in front of the band-stand, like an enormous open seashell.

A little farther up the sidewalk and he nodded at the high red-painted gates set between towering bamboo: the gates to the Japanese Tea Gardens.

"I didn't know you liked tea," she joked, but he just smiled, led her through, paid their fee at the small booth just inside the gates.

"I like it here," he said as they moved down the meander-ing paths set between small, beautiful bonsaied cypress trees and delicately leaning willows, the pools with their stone lanterns and painted wooden bridges, the orange and black koi fish darting between the water lilies. "The whole idea of this sort of Zen architectural design appeals to me, even if this place is a little over the top. I like it best early in the day, or off season, as it is now, when there aren't too many tourists around. When it's quiet."

They wound around to the back of the gardens and up several steep flights of stairs, then stepped down into the teahouse, which was really more of a long, roofed terrace overlooking the pools. A waitress in an embroidered silk kimono seated them on small stools at a long, lacquered wood table close to the railing. She set a fragrant pot of tea and a small plate of rice crackers and almond cookies on the table before Karalee had had a chance to unbelt her jacket and settle in. The place was nearly empty; one other couple took up a table at the opposite end of the terrace.

Gideon poured for Karalee, handed her a cup.

"It's peaceful here," she said, watching the koi move languidly through the water below.

"Yes." He drank from his teacup, played with a rice cracker, but he didn't put it in his mouth. "So," he said after a minute, "what about yourself don't you understand?"

"What?"

"You said in the car that you don't always understand your own reasons for doing things. Or for not doing things, which I find even more intriguing."

"Ah. Well . . ." The question caught her off guard, and she had to take a moment to organize her thoughts. "Well, for instance, I don't believe in love. I mean, I don't believe in it for me. And the permanence of it seems highly unlikely to me. For anyone. I don't really know where that comes from. I mean, I had a fairly normal family, average middle America. My parents have been together for nearly forty years. But I never got any sense of them loving each other. I understand different people express it in different ways, but I never saw it. I know a lot of couples are the same way. They exist together in some loveless, passionless void, and their kids grow up still hoping for love, believing in it. But for me, love is something I've always been sort of . . . indifferent about. I know that must make me sound cold, but I've just never experienced it, other than loving my family, or my friends. I mean romantic love.

"I honestly don't think I was traumatized by it. I simply developed a certain belief system. Or lack of belief, I suppose. And you see so many people getting divorced. The idea of that sort of love existing and lasting doesn't seem viable to me. We're all alone, in the end, whether we're in a relationship or not, don't you think?"

She looked at him, and it was as though a storm had settled over his features. His eyes were absolutely flat.

"Gideon? What did I say?"

He glanced away, stared into the gardens below the terraced teahouse. "Love does exist, Karalee," he said through gritted teeth.

That was the last thing she'd have thought to hear him say. It shocked her somehow. And it made her realize that beneath his smooth exterior was pain of some kind. Something he kept hidden away. It was several moments before she could manage to speak.

"I'm sorry, Gideon."

He shook his head, seemed to shake off the mood, all but for the tiny lines of tension around his eyes, his mouth. "Nothing to be sorry for. I didn't mean to be so terse with you."

"And I didn't mean to dismiss love so casually. Maybe I'm wrong to do that. I didn't mean to offend you."

He was quiet for another moment, then, "Let's not talk of it anymore."

He slid his hand over hers, turned her hand over, and stroked the inside of her wrist with one finger. She didn't know what had just happened, exactly, but she was happy enough to let it go. To enjoy the long, sweet shivers his touch was sending through her like a faint electric current.

They drank their tea, talked about work, ate the cookies. The fog never lifted, the sky a heavy, damp gray, but it made her feel as though they were cocooned in the teahouse. She almost didn't want to leave when he suggested they get up and walk around the gardens, but she was happy to be wherever he was.

What the hell did that mean?

But she didn't want to question anything today. Or Gideon. She wanted to simply enjoy it, to enjoy him.

They wandered along the paths, stopping to admire the giant bronze Buddha, to throw pennies into the wishing well. Everywhere was the scent of eucalyptus, of pine and juniper and new grass. They walked up the steep stairs to the pagoda at the highest point in the gardens, then down the narrow path that led behind it, where there was a secluded deck partially hidden by tree branches. Gideon pulled her into a corner of the deck, then had her step over the small wooden fence where the surrounding park had been left to grow wild.

"Where are we going?"

"Shh. Just come with me, Karalee."

"We're not supposed to be here, Gideon."

"I know."

When she looked up at him his eyes were dark, glowing, his crooked grin absolutely wicked.

"Oh . . ."

She smiled as he pushed her up against the rough bark of

a tall pine tree, that little bit of fear at being caught, his utter command over her making her hotter, wetter, immediately. She could feel the texture of the tree even through her coat. One fleeting thought about how crazy this was, then he kissed her and she stopped thinking altogether.

His mouth came down hard on hers, his tongue driving inside, hot and slippery and making her shudder with need. His hands were under her sweater, cupping her breasts, thumbing her nipples. His hips ground into hers and she could feel his cock, hard and ready against her thigh. She needed to have him inside her. When he slipped one hand into the front of her jeans, she stopped caring about anything else.

She angled her hips, spread her legs a little, wanting to let him in. Then he was undoing her jeans, sliding them down her legs. Her panties followed. She was panting already. He slid his hand between her thighs, his fingers sinking right into her wet cleft.

"Ah, always ready for me, Karalee. So damn wet for me."

"Yes . . ."

She heard his zipper, the sound of him tearing a foil packet open, then he spread her thighs wider with a rough hand. Lifting one leg, she wrapped it around him and he pushed into her.

"Gideon . . . ah!"

He moved deeper, pulled back a bit, then began a hard, pounding rhythm as he teased her clit with his hand between their bodies. Pleasure shafted through her. And the harder he fucked her, the deeper that pleasure went, burrowing into her. Yes, deeper and deeper. Her ass was slapping into the rough bark of the tree; it scratched her skin. Didn't matter. That small pain was all part of it, part of him fucking her, hard and fast and dangerous.

When she heard the voice of someone passing close by their half-hidden spot, the intensity soared, her body exploding, clenching hard around his pounding cock. He clamped a hand over her mouth as she groaned, and she came even harder. Pleasure, hot and clean, rushed through her, pulsing deep in her veins. She shivered in his firm grasp, her hips thrusting into him.

Then he was groaning in her ear, shoving his rock-hard cock deep into her, shaking all over.

"Karalee . . . fuck."

He buried his face in her hair, and she had one brief flash of . . . what? Something warm and lovely washing over her, centering in her chest. Then he pulled out of her, helped her pull her clothes back on. She was still buttoning her jeans when a man in a dark green gardener's uniform came to stand on the other side of the fence.

"Hey, you two. You're supposed to stay on the path."

"Yes, of course," Gideon answered smoothly, standing in front of her, his body shielding her from the other man's view. "My girlfriend wasn't feeling well. We're going home now."

She went all trembly inside, and told herself it was from nearly being caught rather than from hearing Gideon call her his girlfriend.

How juvenile. It wasn't as though she'd ever needed to be anyone's girlfriend.

The gardener nodded, stepped back while Gideon helped

her over the small fence. She could feel the man's eyes on her back as they walked back down the path.

"He wasn't happy with us," Karalee muttered.

"Do you really care?" Gideon asked her, smiling.

She laughed. "No, I really, really don't."

He pulled her into his side, one arm around her waist, his hand gripping her hip. "Why don't I take you back to your place, where I can fuck you properly?" he suggested in a low voice. "Where I can fuck you all day. Where I can fuck you right through the wall."

Impossibly, her body was heating up again hearing him say these things to her, her sex wet, hungry for more. All she could do was nod.

They went back to his car, got in, and took off, Gideon shifting smoothly as they sped back toward her house, some classic rock coming from the stereo. She kept replaying that sensation of nearly being caught, her pulse beating wildly. And that other sensation, the one she didn't quite understand but instinctively wanted to push away before she figured it out.

Not now.

She looked over at him; he turned and smiled at her, and a small tremor ran through her. No, now all she wanted was for him to take her home, to fuck her, as he'd said. Wasn't that all she'd ever needed from any man?

Yes, that had always been the way it was for her. Few men had really been able to understand that about her. Some had said she was more like a man when it came to dating, relationships. How ironic that something was shifting inside her now, with the one man who truly didn't seem to want anything more from her. Ironic and crazy and too sad, if she let herself follow this new feeling, this train of thought.

Don't even go there.

No, she'd stay in her comfort zone with him: a little detached, not too emotionally involved, just in it for a little fun. Because nothing more existed. She'd just said so, hadn't she? She didn't believe in love.

Did she?

chapter ✑ nine

JAGGER SPILLED A CRÊPE FROM THE PAN ONTO A SMALL PLAT-
ter, sprinkled it with a fine dusting of powdered sugar. His
mother had taught him to make crêpes, and they came out
perfectly every time.

"I'm glad we ran into each other at the farmers' market
this morning, Mia Rose."

"So am I. I'm sorry I'm so...stubborn sometimes.
Stubborn and neurotic."

"Maybe I like that about you."

He smiled at her and she laughed.

Wrapping his hand in a dish towel, he lifted the Pyrex
bowl of strawberry compote he'd just made from the pan of
hot water and spooned a bit over the crêpes, then set a few
fresh strawberries around the edge of the platter.

"This looks amazing." Mia Rose was perched on a bar

stool, leaning onto the counter, a look of pleasure on her face. Her beautiful face. Dazzling when she smiled, as she did now. Yeah, that was the word for it. Dazzling. And cooking for her felt damn good, better than it had in a long while.

He flipped the dish towel over his shoulder. "There's nothing like homemade crêpes. Most people don't realize how easy they are to make. I've been making them since I was ten years old." He set the platter down on the counter and sat on the stool beside her. "Here, you have to taste them while they're still hot."

He cut into one with a fork and lifted it, was surprised when she blushed. But she opened her mouth, let him slip the fork between her lips. Something sensual about watching her eat, about the way she savored the food. The way she took the food into her mouth, between those red lips . . .

He shifted to ease the ache in his groin.

Mia Rose moaned softly, her eyes closing as she chewed. "Oh, that's really good, Jagger."

She spoke as if she were talking about sex rather than food. His father had been the one to tell him that if he wanted to get a woman into bed, to give her chocolate. But he knew after talking with her the other night that food *was* sex to her. And suddenly, because of that, it was to him, too.

He smiled, took a bite himself. "Yeah, it is. I like to make these late at night. I don't know why. They taste better after midnight for some reason."

"Maybe I'll have to find out."

He caught her gaze. Her eyes were shining, an impossibly deep green. And a strange surge went through him, something sexual, yes, but also a sort of realization. That there was definitely more to this food thing for her than the usual sybaritic pleasure most food lovers took in the flavors and textures. It went even deeper than what she'd told him about her sexual desires and food. And something inside him connected with her on that level, so that her desires were suddenly his own.

Keeping his gaze on hers, he fed her another bite, watched as she closed her eyes once more, her dark lashes shadowing her high cheekbones. Heard the soft sigh of pleasure she made low in her throat when he fed her one of the ripe berries. She bit into it, and he watched the way her teeth came down on that delicate red flesh, the way her lips wrapped around it.

Oh yeah, pure sex. Sex and food.

He was getting hard. Even harder when he took another bite himself, letting the sweetness fill his mouth, and always watching her: her pouting red lips, her gleaming eyes. And without thinking too much about it, he set the fork down and dipped his fingers in the warm strawberry sauce, touched a fingertip to her lips. She opened right up, licked the tip with her tongue, then took his finger into her mouth. Pleasure moved through him, straight to his groin. And he saw the flush on her cheeks, felt the desire coming off her like some palpable thing, feeding his own.

"Here, try this," he murmured, reaching over the counter to pick up the container of powdered sugar.

He tapped some onto a spoon, held it to her lips, and didn't even need to tell her to open for him; she simply did it, the tip of her pink tongue waiting for him. He sprinkled a little there, watched her close her lips, smile.

"Oh, that's nice, Jagger."

There was no mistaking the smoky tone to her voice, the

flushed cheeks, the quickness of her breath. There was no mistaking his own excitement.

Her gaze was on his as he leaned in, pausing only inches from her mouth. He saw her small smile before moving in to kiss her. She was all sugar and strawberries and Mia Rose. The sweetest lips imaginable. Even sweeter when he opened her mouth with his tongue and slid inside.

He took her face in his hands, kissed her harder. And the taste of her, the feel of her, was making him crazy already, crazy with needing her, with images of the sugar on her lips. On her body. Oh yeah. Too good to resist. She would love it. And his cock was rock-hard, ready for her.

He stood, pushed his stool away with one foot, and started to undress her. She didn't resist as he slipped her sweater over her head. He wanted to see her naked breasts, but it was so good to take one moment to pull back and watch her nipples going hard beneath the sheer white lace of her bra. His mouth was actually watering.

He pulled his shirt off in one sweep, then reached out to cup her breasts through her bra. She leaned in to him, moaned softly. He could feel the heat of her in his hands, her hardening nipples. And when he undid the front clasp and let that smooth flesh fall into his hands, his cock gave a hard twitch. Lord, her skin was on fire, and her nipples were full and dark red. He wanted to touch them, to taste them.

He reached for the container of powdered sugar, tipped it, and let it fall in a shower of fine white dust onto her breasts. She gasped. And he smiled at her, at the shock and the lust on her face before he bent down and ran his tongue over her powdered skin. Sugar filled his mouth, along with her sweet, pliant flesh. His cock was throbbing. He pushed her breasts together with his hands, sucked the sugar off one hard nipple, then the other, before really going to work, licking the sugar from her skin, the curving mounds of her breasts, the tender flesh in between, while Mia moaned and writhed in her chair.

"God, Jagger . . . Oh . . ."

Her hands went into his hair, held him tight, her fingers burrowing. He could hardly stand it, to have her responding like this, to feel her shivering beneath his hands, his mouth.

He had to fuck her. No question about it. He pulled back.

"Promise me you won't move."

"Yes, I promise." Her voice was breathless, sexy.

He moved away with some effort, went to find a condom in his nightstand, came right back to her, his cock so damn hard he was barely able to walk. Once back at the counter, he kicked his way out of his pants, helped her wriggle out of hers, then handed her back onto the stool. So fucking gorgeous, sitting in his kitchen, naked except for the traces of powdered sugar on her breasts and a pair of silver hoop earrings.

So good, to look at her, to make himself wait. He smiled, watched her face as he dipped into the strawberry compote again, then spread it over her breasts, mixing it with the sugar.

"Jagger . . ."

"I know."

He knew the food added an element of excitement. That seeing how it affected her made it better for him, too. He didn't understand why. But it did.

He spread the red mixture over her skin, kneaded it into

her breasts, keeping his eyes on her face. She'd closed hers, her head back, her breath coming in hard pants already. Unbelievable. And he needed to fuck her so badly, to slide in between her thighs, bury himself inside her tight pussy. But not yet.

He bent in and started to lick, the sticky sweetness doing something to him he couldn't comprehend. Didn't matter. All that mattered was her slick flesh beneath his tongue, her hard nipples as he sucked on them, teased them. His cock impossibly hard, straining to get at her.

He lifted his head and kissed her, pushing his strawberry tongue into her mouth. So hot and wet, he couldn't hold back anymore. Taking the condom from where he'd set it on the counter, he quickly tore the foil and sheathed himself, his own hands on his cock almost too much for him. He spread her thighs and pushed right in between the swollen folds of her pussy lips, paused as pleasure washed over him.

"Mia Rose . . ."

"Yes, do it. Please, Jagger."

Her legs went around him and he grabbed her hips, thrust hard, impaling her, rocking the bar stool. Her sex clenched around him, like steel and velvet, like pure liquid heat. He was shivering in moments.

Hold it together.

He had to pause for a moment, close his eyes, catch his breath. And then he felt her hands on his chest, her fingers coated in the strawberries, smearing it onto his own hard nipples. And when she arched up and sucked one nipple into her mouth, he almost lost it. Pleasure shafted into him, straight to his pulsing cock. He groaned, pumped into her in long strokes. It was too good to stop: his cock inside her, her hot, wicked little mouth on him.

When she bit down a little on his nipple, he gasped, nearly came.

"Jesus, girl."

But he didn't pull away. She bit a little harder, sucking and biting. And her pussy clasping him, sending lust pulsing hard and hot through his cock, his belly. He couldn't stand it.

He wrapped one hand around the back of her head, twined his fingers in her hair, pulling her head back, and with his other hand on her hip he tilted her, drew her body in closer. Then he really started to fuck her. Driving into her hard and fast, their bodies pressed together, the strawberries and the sugar making a delicious friction against his chest while the legs of the stool clattered against the floor. He bent and took her mouth with his, tasted the sweetness there once more, and knew he was going to come any second.

He felt the tight clench of her sex around his cock even before he heard her cries. Then she was coming, trembling all over, moaning and panting. And he couldn't hold back, plunging into her as he came in a shivering rush of pleasure. Fire exploded behind his eyes as a blinding heat shot through his body. And all the time he could feel her, smell her, taste her. Pure sugar. Pure sex.

When it was over he simply stood there for a while. He didn't want to let her go. And he didn't want to question that right now. No, right now it was all good.

They were both panting, their bodies stuck together. Finally, her grip on him loosened and she slumped onto the high stool. She was covered in a red, sticky mess, but she'd never seemed more beautiful to him, with her hair mussed, her lips dark red and tender-looking. Too fucking beautiful.

"Mia, Mia Rose..." He couldn't stop smiling at her. Her eyes were completely glazed. He stroked her hair from her cheek. "You okay, girl?"

"Yes." She paused, bit her lip, closed her eyes for one brief moment before they fluttered open again. "Yes, I'm fine."

He could swear he saw something in her eyes, some sort of shadow. But he wasn't going to press her about it.

"We made a fine mess here. How about we go get cleaned up?"

"Okay."

He pulled out of her, slowly, smiled when she shivered. Then he took her hand and led her to the big bathroom, cranked up the hot water in the slate-tiled shower, and pulled her in with him.

The water fell all around them from the enormous rain-shower head he'd installed. He stood a few inches from her, where he could watch the water making wet trails over her skin. He felt a small pulse in his cock. If he hadn't come only moments ago, he'd have a raging hard-on just from seeing her like this. From watching her hair turn dark and wet, the remnants of the strawberry compote and the sugar washing off her body.

He reached out, stroked the stickiness on her skin, rubbed it away beneath the warm water. She was quiet, still, letting him do whatever he wanted.

"You sure you're okay, Mia Rose?"

"Yes. I really am. It's just that... God, I don't know if I should say this."

"Come on, girl, you have to tell me now."

She laughed a little, a hollow sound.

He slid a hand over her shoulder, pulled her in closer. "Hey. What is it?"

"Jagger . . . you know that alternative sex has been my life study. But I've never really . . . God, I'm about to sound really pathetic."

"We've talked about this. Skirted around the issue, anyway. I know you've never let yourself do what you really wanted to do, never gave in to your desires." He stroked a strand of dark, wet hair from her cheek. "I don't see you as pathetic because of that. That's the way it goes sometimes. We all have our stuff. I've got my own history, my own crap to deal with. I've had my heart broken a few too many times. I'm beginning to understand how that's affected my life, the choices I make. But I'm also learning to accept it."

"God, I'm sorry, Jagger."

"Yeah, so am I. But it's part of life. I've realized recently that we have to let the bad shit go eventually. It's like poison to hang on to it."

"I know," she said quietly. "I'm trying. Meanwhile, I can't . . . I can't quite get over this senseless . . . shame. And I'm embarrassed about even having this issue. Me, of all people!"

She turned away, but there was nowhere to hide, just the two of them naked in the shower.

"The only regret you should have is that you haven't explored this sooner." He stroked her damp cheek. "I'm sorry."

"For what?" He was being so nice, she almost couldn't stand it. His tenderness was making her weak and warm inside. A little out of control, in a way even the food and the sex hadn't.

"I'm sorry you feel you have to hide this part of yourself. And I swear you don't have to do that with me."

She shook her head. "I don't even get it myself. I can stand in front of a roomful of people and talk about anything: anal sex, sadomasochism, anything. I don't know why I'm struggling with this. Against it. Except while it's happening, of course. Then I'm just . . . helpless. Maybe that's part of the problem."

Had she just admitted that to him? To herself?

"You said it before: It's different when it's personal. When it means something." He paused, laid a small kiss on her forehead, then said quietly, "What does it mean to you, Mia Rose?"

She shook her head again. God, she couldn't tell him! Couldn't talk about Ben, about how this had all started.

"Do we have to go there right now, Jagger?"

"No. We don't have to talk about it at all. I just wanted to let you know you can, with me."

"Okay. Okay." She nodded, let her gaze fall to the shower floor, watching the pattern the water made as it hit the slate tiles. She pulled in a breath, waited for the familiar knot to form in her chest, was surprised when it was nothing more than a faint tightening sensation.

Maybe it was the soothing warmth of the falling water. Maybe it was Jagger's arms around her. Maybe she would tell him everything, at some point. But not now. It was too much to think about: Ben and what had happened to her body tonight. To her mind. Her heart.

She'd spent years learning to forgive Ben. And years hiding that part of herself that wanted food with her sex. She'd studied sex and fetishism, knew all about the body chemistry and the brain chemistry of sex. The psychological theories regarding fetishes. It all made sense, as long as she didn't apply it to herself. Jagger was right. That's when it all melded together and all she knew was what she *felt*. After all her years of collecting data, analyzing, she understood *why* she craved the things she did. But other than those empty nights with her cooking shows and her vibrator, she hadn't been able to go there with any man. She hadn't felt safe enough.

Until now. She could still hardly believe it had happened.

"Come on, Mia Rose. Let me wash your hair."

"No one has ever done that for me, other than my hairdresser."

"You don't know what you're missing. Here, turn around."

She did as he asked, stood quietly while he soaked her hair, squeezed some shampoo from a bottle, and began to work it in. It smelled a little like incense, but mostly just clean. It smelled like Jagger.

His hands on her hair were so lovely, his fingers massaging her scalp, the back of her neck, then down to her shoulders. There was something so intimate about being in the shower with him, something more than being naked anywhere else. She had a strange sensation of safety, with the warm water coming down, the scented, steamy air. And his hands working their magic on her, washing the tension from her body.

He moved in closer behind her, and lust shivered up her spine as his wet skin made contact with hers. His soapy hands slid around the front of her body, over her breasts. Her nipples hardened into his palms, her sex swelling, growing damp with need. Her mind let go, and she let herself be in the moment, enjoying his touch.

His hands were so slippery; it was the most amazing sensation. Almost as good as it had been with the strawberries and the sugar. She moaned.

He pressed in tighter, his cock hard against the small of her back.

"Have I told you about my fetish, Mia Rose? Really told you?" he asked quietly, right next to her ear.

"Yes . . . no. Maybe you haven't, not in detail," she murmured, hoping it had something to do with his soapy hands caressing her breasts, because she really didn't ever want him to stop.

"I have a thing for water. I've told you that. For seeing a woman wet. Feeling wet flesh. You feel ten times more naked to me, wet like this. But I don't think I've told you how crazy it makes me to see you this way. Totally out of my head." His fingers played over her nipples, rubbing, twisting.

"Oh . . ."

"Can you feel how hard I am? How much I need you?"

"God, Jagger."

He slid his hands down farther, over her belly. She arced into his touch, gasped when he slipped one hand between her thighs and over her aching cleft.

"Yeah, just like this, Mia Rose. So hot and slippery." He pressed his cock into her back until she could feel every ridge against her skin. "Do you see what this does to me? I could come just like this. I think I will. And you're going to come, too."

With one hand he spread the lips of her sex; with the other he rubbed against the tight nub of her clitoris. Pleasure shot into her system, hard and fast. And somehow the water made it better; she was hyperaware of it washing over her skin. Of the heat. Of that gliding sensation everywhere their bodies met.

Jagger shifted downward, his cock sliding, pumping in between her buttocks, then upward against the small of her back. His hand pressed into her hungry cleft. When two fingers dipped inside she cried out, tilted her hips into his hands. Something about the way he held her wide open made her feel raw, wanton. And his cock rubbing against her back, her buttocks, so hot and hard, driving the wicked heat deeper into her system. Lust, burning hot, flowed from his fingers pumping in her sex, pressing onto her clit, through her body. Soon she was shaking, needing to come.

"Jagger . . . don't stop."

"Ah, baby girl, I won't stop . . . can't stop."

His fingers worked her mercilessly, milking her for pleasure while his cock thrust hard against her back. And soon the sensation spiraled, flashing behind her eyes, filling her head, her body, and she was coming into his hands. Pleasure spread, her legs going weak. Then he shuddered, tensed, and cried out as his hot come flooded over her skin, making her come even harder.

"Jagger!"

He buried his head in the back of her neck, bit gently into the tender flesh there. She leaned her weight into him as she tried to catch her breath.

"Mia Rose."

"Mmm . . ."

"I want to do this again." His voice was low, sleepy. "Again and again and again."

"Yes . . ."

Sex with Jagger was so utterly sensual. The food, the shower, the way he touched her, spoke to her. Amazing. It had never been quite like this for her before. She felt so good at this moment, she didn't want to think about anything else. She couldn't even care that he knew that secret side of herself, the side she'd kept locked away for so long. But no, that wasn't true. It seemed important, him knowing.

Perhaps she would feel differently tomorrow, when this aura of sensuality wore off and she was alone, with time to think. But for now, she was content to be here, just like this. Their bodies pressed together, while all around them the water fell, the heat and the steam like a veil over their naked skin.

chapter ten

KARALEE GLANCED UP FROM THE PAPERS ON HER DESK AT the knock on her office door.

"Come in."

The door swung open and Gideon walked in, closing it behind him. He was dressed in black slacks today, a blue oxford shirt. He almost looked like the academic he was, except that she knew there was much more to him. That thoroughly wicked side her body was responding to already, simply seeing him walk through the door.

She smiled. "Hi."

"Hi."

He smiled back at her, that predatory smile of his that went through her like a hand stroking her naked skin. She shivered as he moved closer.

"I had to see you, Karalee."

"About what?"

He was right next to her now. He swung her chair around, grabbed her, and lifted her to her feet. She was wet with need before he even kissed her. And when his lips came down on hers, his tongue thrusting into her mouth, she started to shake. How could he do this to her so easily?

But she didn't have time to think about it. He turned her in his arms, hiked her skirt up around her waist, and was pulling her panties down a moment later.

"Gideon—"

"Shh." He bent her over the desk, and she heard the now-familiar sounds of his zipper sliding down, the tearing of a foil packet. Then he had his hand on the back of her neck, bending her forward, until she had to rest her hands on her desk, bracing herself.

"Spread, Karalee."

She did it, weak with lust, wanting to do whatever he asked of her.

Gideon gripped her hips and slid right into her wet heat. She felt herself clamp around the thick length of his cock, pleasure surging into her. He began to pump right away, fast and furious, his arm tightly clasped around her waist. She could barely breathe, stab after stab of sensation knifing into her body. It was too much, too fast. She started to come almost immediately, her system flooding with pleasure.

"Gideon!"

She was still shivering with her climax when he pulled out, spread her buttocks with his hands.

"Wha...? What are you doing, Gideon?"

"Quiet."

Then one hand was running over her jaw, his fingers sliding into her mouth. She took them in, sucked.

"Yes, that's it, Karalee," he murmured.

He pulled his fingers away, slipped his hand between her thighs from behind her. He swiped at her sex, rubbing over her wet slit, then moved back, to that other tight hole. A new surge of need went through her.

She'd had anal sex before, enjoyed it. But never had she wanted it like this.

"Yes, Gideon," she whispered. "Do it, please."

He slipped one fingertip in, using her own saliva, her own juices, as lubricant. Pleasure moved through her as he pushed it in a little farther. And with his other hand, he teased her clit, slid into the folds of her pussy. She was soaking wet everywhere, it seemed. Shaking. Backing into his hand.

"More, Gideon."

He pushed his finger deeper, and she took it right in. Her sex clenched hard as he plunged the fingers of his other hand inside her, impaling her from two directions at once.

"Oh my God..."

"Ah, you're too good, Karalee. You can take anything, can't you?"

"Yes. Please..."

He added a second finger to that tight hole. She was ready for it, forcing the muscles to relax, to take him in. And he was fucking her with his other hand, in and out. She moaned.

"More, Gideon."

He pulled his hands away, used them to spread her cheeks

wider. Then she felt the head of his latex-sheathed cock behind her.

"Oh, yes..."

"I'm going to fuck you now, Karalee."

"Yes!" She could hardly wait.

He used his finger to moisten that tight opening once more, then he slid the tip of his cock in. She took a deep breath, let her muscles relax to take more of him into her. He moved a little deeper, passing that tight ring of muscle.

When he reached around her and took her clitoris between his fingers, rolling, pinching, she shuddered, desire surging through her from every direction. It was all so damn good, his clever hand on her clit, his cock moving, inch by lovely inch, into her ass. It seemed to take forever before he was buried deep inside her, but every moment was exquisite. Lust, that anticipation of being filled in this way. And the sound of his deep, panting breath. Finally, when he was buried to the hilt, he paused.

"Tell me what you want, Karalee," he demanded.

"I want you to fuck me. Fuck me hard. I can take it. Just do it."

"You are something, Karalee."

He tangled a hand in her hair, grasping until it hurt, pulling her head back. But she loved it. And then he started to move, his cock slowly pumping in and out of her ass, his fingers sinking deep into her sex. She was filled in every way. Sensation, intense, nearly overwhelming, stabbed deeply into her body, made her shiver, made her whimper. Made her feel that sense of his utter command over her body. Over her.

The edge of the desk bit into her hands as she held on

tight. Didn't matter. Nothing mattered but Gideon's cock, filling her so completely, sliding in and out of her, while his fingers worked her sex mercilessly.

Soon she was coming again, harder this time, so damn hard she was sobbing, shaking. Gideon grunted and plunged deeper.

"Christ, Karalee."

He pulled out of her with a groan, let her hair go. She leaned against the desk, shivering, weak, her skirt still bunched around her waist.

She expected him to zip up, to walk out of her office. But instead she felt his hands on her skin, stroking gently: her buttocks, her thighs. Then he leaned over her, smoothed her hair aside, and kissed the back of her neck. Goose bumps moved over her skin. And that strange sensation she'd felt with him in the park came back once more, filling her chest with a gentle, seeping heat.

No.

She heard the soft whisper of his zipper and her chest tightened before he pulled her skirt down, turned her around in his arms, and kissed her mouth gently. She felt shocked by it, the tenderness of it after what they'd just done. Her heart was beating like mad.

His lips were so soft; he just kissed her, over and over. Then he stroked her hair from her face. She didn't understand. When he pulled away she looked up at him, into his dark eyes. And she found something open in them, something she'd never seen before. Something that made her chest tighten, pull.

"I have to go," he said quietly.

"Yes. Sure. I have to . . . I think I have a class soon."

He nodded, let her go, stepped back. He stood there for a moment, simply looking at her, making her pulse race even faster. Her head was spinning. Then he left, shutting her office door behind him.

She felt absolutely dazed. By the sex, yes, but even more by what she was feeling. By what she thought she'd seen in his eyes, in his touch.

Impossible.

Maybe. She wasn't built for this part of a relationship. She preferred things short and sweet, then to back away before anyone got serious. She knew damn well she wasn't the kind of woman to be tied down in a relationship. To spend years with someone, only to end up as miserable as her parents. She'd spent her life avoiding that sort of thing. But something was definitely different with Gideon. Different for her. And different for him suddenly, as well, unless she was imagining things. Something that was scaring the hell out of her.

She sat down in the chair behind the desk, smoothed her skirt down over her thighs, realized vaguely that her panties were still on the floor.

This man was really messing with her head.

Gideon was a player. She'd known it going in. The perfect partner for her: uninvolved, a little dirty. Just have their fun together, then part ways with a smile. The problem was, she wasn't sure she was ready to get rid of him. Not now.

Maybe not ever.

Don't be a fool.

She never had been before, not over a man. She wasn't like other women, always chasing after a commitment, and most men loved that about her. Maybe even Gideon, so this was a really bad time for her to change.

She shook her head, grabbed her purse from the floor beneath her desk, and dug for her hairbrush. She was being a fool. She was still herself. No man was going to change who she was on the inside, what she believed about relationships, about herself. Not even Gideon Oliver.

But some small part of her knew that if any man could change her, he could.

She ran the brush through her hair in hard strokes, pulling through the tiny snarls.

Don't be stupid!

She yanked through a knot in her hair while her heart hammered in her chest. With fear. With dread. Because she knew she was losing her head over Gideon Oliver. Her head, and maybe more.

🍃

Jagger had left his Monday night class early. Too awful, trying to watch Mia Rose up there talking, teaching. His concentration was totally blown. And he kept getting hard watching her, listening to her voice, remembering the way her breasts felt in his hands, how hot and tight she was inside. He'd actually gotten up and left the room before the class ended, which he never would have done if she hadn't said in the message she'd left for him earlier that she needed the night to herself to think, get her head straightened out.

He'd gone home, run the shower, stayed in there until the water went cold, stroking himself to one orgasm after another. He would have done it a fourth time if he'd been capable of getting hard again, if he hadn't run out of hot water.

He'd wanted to call her, even though it had been nearly midnight. She was probably asleep anyway, her cell phone turned off. But now it was Tuesday afternoon and he hadn't heard from her. And he was moping around his apartment like some lovesick kid, hardly daring to let his cell phone out of his sight.

He still couldn't concentrate on anything. He'd tried doing some homework, but that had been a bust. He'd tried watching a movie, but he couldn't focus even on that. Frustrated, his body too jacked up to sit still any longer, he got up off the couch and headed into the kitchen. Without thinking too much about it, he started pulling things out of the refrigerator, the pantry, lining everything up on the counter.

He wanted to make crêpes again. But only if Mia Rose was there with him to eat them. No, it would have to be something else or he'd have to cook with a raging hard-on. Hell, he'd had to do nearly everything with a hard-on ever since the weekend. Since he'd known what her body felt like, tasted like.

After talking with her so intimately, he almost felt guilty about the way his body was responding. It didn't seem appropriately sensitive. But even though he was totally out of his head over her, he was still a man. He couldn't help it.

"Fuck." He pressed a hand to his half-hard cock, took in a long breath, then turned to the sink, washed his hands in cold water.

He went back to the counter, opened up a package from the Cuban butcher shop down the street, took out his favorite knife and began to bone the chicken, then cut it up into pieces. With a small mallet, he hammered out the breasts until they made a pair of tender fillets. He breaded and seasoned them while he heated a sauté pan.

He started to get hard again while he was working on the

sauce. All he could think of was pouring it over Mia Rose's naked body, licking it from her skin. She would love it. And he'd love it: his mouth on her, hearing her moans.

Soon he had a small pile of chicken piccata waiting on a platter that he didn't want to eat. And he didn't feel any calmer than he had before.

He washed his hands again, grabbed his cell phone from his pocket, and dialed his neighbors. Leilani picked up after the first ring.

"Hello?"

"Leilani, it's Jagger. Are you hungry?"

"I'm always hungry. And you know you're the only person who can cook as well as I can. What are you making?"

"I have chicken piccata, and I was about to put on some rice."

"I made a nice minestrone last night. I'll bring it up. Jean should be home any minute. I'll leave her a note."

"Okay, great. See you in a few."

He flipped his phone shut, a little relieved. Company would get his mind off Mia Rose. Maybe.

Jesus, he was screwed up. Over a woman. Again.

His gut tightened.

It was too damn late, so why was he fighting it? He was in deep. All of this anxiety over it was ridiculous. He may as well give in to the inevitable.

He filled a pot with water, added a little salt, a pat of butter, poured the rice into a measuring cup. The kitchen windows were getting steamy, the air warm and soft, reminding him of Mia Rose in the shower. All that hot water coursing down her naked skin. The feel of her, slick and slippery, her breasts filling his hands . . .

He groaned as his cock came to life, filling, throbbing. He shook his head. He had to calm down before Leilani got there.

He poured a glass of wine for himself, took a long swig, then spent a few minutes wiping down the counters, putting away some of the ingredients he'd pulled out to cook with.

The doorbell buzzed and he found both Jean and Leilani at the door, dressed in their standard jeans, black T-shirts, and heavy black boots.

"Hey, come on in."

He stepped back. Jean let her partner go in first. Leilani, a petite Hawaiian woman with her black hair in two ponytails, carried a large pot in a pair of pot holders to the kitchen counter. Jean, a tall, athletic woman with a short crop of white-blond hair, followed her, giving Jagger a squeeze on the shoulder as she passed.

"What are you up to, babe? We've hardly seen you."

"Yeah, I know, Jean. I've just been . . . I don't know."

Leilani lifted the lid off the rice, sniffed, set it back on the pot. "When are you going to tell us what's wrong, Jagger?"

"Nothing's wrong." He rubbed at his jaw, went into the kitchen, poured some wine for the women.

Jean took her glass from him. "We've hardly seen you lately, after you've been like our adopted son since you moved in." Leilani rolled her eyes and Jean interjected, "Not that we're old enough for you to be our son. Happy, Leili?" She turned back to Jagger. "You're not going out anymore. And don't think we didn't notice that chick in your apartment last weekend."

"Yeah. Well . . ."

"Wow," Jean said.

"What?"

"You really like this woman."

He shrugged. She was right. There was no use denying it. He took another sip of his wine. "Yeah." He set his glass down on the counter, ran both hands over his hair. "Yeah, I do. And I don't know what the hell to do about it."

Leilani came to stand by him, put her hand on his arm. "Jagger, I've never seen you like this."

"I've never seen myself like this. I'm a fucking mess over this woman, if you want to know the truth. I can't stop thinking about her. You two know about Elena, what that did to me. I swore I was not going there again. Ever. But it's happening." He paused, shook his head. "No, it's even more, with this woman. With Mia Rose. And it makes me feel like . . . like I'm out of control. Like I'm rolling downhill at a hundred miles an hour without any brakes."

"I know that feeling." Leilani looked at Jean, her brown eyes going soft for a moment.

He shook his head, pushed off the counter, and turned the rice off. "Maybe I'm freaking out over nothing."

"It doesn't sound like nothing, Jagger," Leilani insisted.

"I'll get over it. I'll have to."

He started to spoon rice onto plates, laid the chicken on top, ladled the light sauce over it, watched it pool, and thought of Mia Rose. When he looked up, Leilani and Jean were both watching him carefully.

"What?"

"You don't look like you're getting over this woman any-time soon," Jean said quietly.

"I'll be fine. I don't know why I brought it up. Let's sit down and eat."

Lord, he was full of shit. He was lying to them. Lying to himself. His brain was ping-ponging between fighting what he knew was true and brief moments of acceptance. His mind struggling against his heart.

He was just as confused as Mia Rose.

What was really messing with his head, though, was that he *felt* different. He felt changed. And he wasn't sure if—or how—he could change back. He wasn't even sure he wanted to, because when he was with her, talking to her, touching her, everything felt absolutely right.

He was either about to reach nirvana, or he was going to hell.

It was eleven at night, but Mia couldn't sleep. She sat at the little table in her dark kitchen with a glass of wine. Wrapped in her satin robe, she gazed out the window at her rose garden, which was illuminated only by the faint amber glow of the back porch light. Beyond the few feet of the stone footpath visible in the dim light, the first few rosebushes, their buds closed tight against the night, was the deep, black sky, the slivered moon hanging like a charm. But she wasn't really seeing what she was looking at. She was seeing Jagger.

When she'd left early Monday morning he'd been so damn sexy, lying in bed on his stomach, the sheets rumpled around his waist, the brown expanse of his back bare. Beautiful. Like art to her, every lean muscle, the texture of his skin.

She crossed her legs against the pressure building there already, simply imagining the slope of his spine, the ripple of muscle across his shoulders. And those tattooed tribal bands encircling his biceps. So, so sexy.

She took a sip of wine, pushed her hair away from her face. Her own cheek felt hot to her. Her whole body was hot. She untied the old satin robe, letting it fall open. That was better, the air cooling her skin. Her nipples tightened, filled. She opened the robe wider, the sleek fabric sliding across her nipples, and they hardened even more.

God, what this man did to her! She couldn't seem to go even a few minutes without thinking about him, her body burning for him day and night. Pure torture to see him in her classroom, to see him and not be able to touch him.

She picked up her wine again, sipped, licked a stray drop from her lip. Thought of his lips, his tongue in her mouth.

The man could kiss. And he had great hands, hands that knew how to play her body like no other man ever had. And he was willing to explore her fascination with food, with liquids, was really getting into it himself.

Her sex clenched at the memory of him licking the sugar from her breasts, his mouth hot and wet on her flesh, and she moaned softly. Her hands went to her breasts, cupped the full, aching flesh. Brushing her nipples with her fingertips, she moaned again, her sex heating up. She slipped one hand between her thighs. She was wet, eager, Jagger's face, his hands, his clever mouth in her mind, right behind her eyes when she closed them.

Oh, yes . . .

She slid her fingers over her slick flesh, in between the folds, then over that hard, needy nub. Easing back in the chair, she spread her thighs. With one hand still playing with her nipple, rolling, tugging, she used the other hand to tease herself, stroking the plump lips of her sex. Pleasure coursed through her in long, slow surges, like heat, like his hands on her in the middle of the night. She tilted her hips and dipped her fingers inside, felt that velvet clench along with a wave of desire so strong she groaned aloud. But she needed more.

She reached for her wineglass, dipped her fingers in, and ran her wet fingertips over her breasts, dipped again and stroked that swollen flesh between her thighs.

Oh, God, yes...

She pushed two fingers deep inside, the stroking of her own wine-damp fingers on her breasts making her crazy, desperate. And in her mind's eye it was Jagger's hands on her. She was shivering all over, on the edge of climax already. Her hips rocked into her hand and she thrust deeper, harder, until she hit her G-spot. She squeezed her nipple hard between her fingers, and her whole body seized in pleasure.

Her cell phone went off, vibrating on the kitchen table. But she was still coming, long, fierce waves of pleasure rolling over her. And her vibrating phone seemed to draw it out of her, to feed the intensity. She was still shaking, her sex still clenching, when she picked up the phone and saw his name on the caller ID.

Jagger.

She flipped it open.

"Jagger?" She knew she was breathless. She didn't care. She wanted more than anything just to hear his voice now, with the desire still flashing like small electric shocks through her system.

"Mia Rose, hey."

"What are you . . . ? I mean, it's late. And I haven't heard from you."

She hadn't meant to sound accusatory. She was the one who had asked for time off to think, after all. But she felt suddenly desperate to talk to him, to see him.

Her sex gave another squeeze.

God.

"Yeah, look, I . . . I need to see you, Mia Rose."

"Okay."

She was still dizzy, disoriented. She couldn't quite figure out why he was calling her now, what he wanted. He sounded so odd, so distracted. She picked up the wineglass and took a sip.

"Now."

"What? What do you mean, 'now'? Jagger, is everything okay?"

"Yeah . . . no. I don't know. I'm coming over."

She heard a click and the line went dead.

He was coming over? Now? And what was the tension in his voice about? Her stomach knotted. Her sex went damp all over again.

God, she was a mess.

Pushing her hair from her face, she sat up. She felt a sudden sense of total displacement. What was she supposed to do? She looked around the dark kitchen, pulled her robe closed, and tied the sash. Her cell phone went off again.

"Hello?"

"I don't know where you live."

"What?" Why couldn't she think straight?

"Give me your address, Mia Rose."

He sounded a little breathless himself. Her body was buzzing all over.

She told him where she lived and he hung up once more. Standing, she went into the living room, taking her wine with her. She felt . . . she wasn't sure what she felt. Heavy with anticipation, yes, and with that lovely orgasm still. But there was something else going on, something that absolutely paralyzed her. She didn't know whether to change, to light some candles. To pour a glass of wine for him. To be afraid he was coming to tell her he didn't want to see her again.

Her stomach clenched.

No. Not that.

She didn't want to think about why that idea scared her more than anything. Yes, she was scared. And so damn excited she could barely breathe, every muscle strung tight with nerves and anticipation.

The room was dark other than the pale light coming in through the window from the streetlights outside. She sat on her overstuffed sofa, all white-on-white damask and covered in pillows in soothing, clean shades of white and ivory. And waited.

chapter ∽ eleven

IT SEEMED THAT ONLY A FEW MINUTES HAD PASSED WHEN there was a knock on her door; the sound reverberated in her belly. She got up and let him in. Jagger closed the door behind him, and she could see him staring at her, his eyes two dark orbs in the dim room, but luminous with heat. She could feel it coming off him, even though he stood a good three feet away from her.

He was dressed in a vintage T-shirt in some dark color, a band logo emblazoned across the front. And those worn jeans that fit him so well, with the heavy black boots she loved. She was going warm and weak all over simply at the sight of him, at knowing he was so close to her. And she could feel immediately that he wasn't there to tell her good-bye. Oh no. He was every bit as hot and edgy as she was.

She stood blinking at him, unable to think of anything to

say. A brief pause, and then he was on her, his mouth coming down hard on hers without a word said. She melted right into him, let him pull her in tight, until she could feel every plane and curve of his chest through his T-shirt, the cold press of his belt buckle against her belly, the hard ridge of his erection.

Oh, yes.

He opened her lips with his tongue, slipped his inside. Sweet and fast at the same time, thrusting into her mouth. And then he was opening her robe, filling his palms with her breasts. With a sigh she arched into his touch, pleasure driving into her, making her breasts, her sex, throb with need.

He pulled away from her mouth to fasten his lips on one nipple, to swirl his tongue over the hardened tip.

"Jagger, please . . ."

She didn't know what she was begging for. But he did.

He lifted his face to hers once more, murmured against her mouth between kisses, "Do you have any honey, Mia Rose?" He stroked her nipples with his fingertips.

"Honey? Um . . . oh, don't stop."

He grinned a little wickedly. "I have more in mind for you. The honey?"

"Yes. In the kitchen."

She was shaking all over already, imagining what he might do with it.

"Show me."

She moved on unsteady legs into the kitchen with Jagger trailing behind her. Her mind was as numb as her legs. But she found the squeeze bottle of honey in a cabinet and silently handed it to him.

"Now the bathroom."

She swallowed, nodded, then stepped into the hall, showed him the door. He smiled at her, moved past her, and turned the light on.

"Ah, this is perfect. I was thinking the shower, but this old tub. The claw feet. Oh, this'll be Victorian porn."

She laughed a little, but her entire body was steaming with lust. She could hardly wait for him to touch her.

He pulled his shirt over his head. His jeans went next, until he was standing naked in front of her. His cock was as beautiful as she remembered, hard and golden brown, the head swollen. She licked her lips as he slipped her robe from her shoulders. Ah, too good to be naked with him. She was soaking wet already.

He swept her hair from her face, picked up a clip from a basket she kept on the counter and piled her shoulder-length hair on top of her head. He leaned in to brush a kiss across her lips, whispered against them, "Now get in the tub, Mia Rose."

"Oh. Oh..."

She did as he asked, with Jagger holding her arm as she stepped over the edge of the old porcelain tub. She felt more naked than she ever had in her life, standing in the middle of the bathtub, her nipples hot and hard, the porcelain cold and smooth beneath her feet.

"Sit down, baby. Yeah, just like that. Stay right there."

He picked up the bottle of honey and licked his lips, watching her. She was absolutely dying for him to touch her, to put that slick, sticky honey on her skin. To do to her whatever he wanted.

"Do you know, Mia Rose," he said quietly, "that until I met you, I'd lost my passion for food. It was probably buried there, underneath the burnout. But you've brought it back for me. In ways I never expected. I wanted to tell you so you'd know this isn't just for you. It's for me, too."

She nodded, unable to speak, her chest, her sex, aching with such keen anticipation she could barely think. The porcelain of the old tub was cool against her bare bottom. But the cold hard surface all seemed part of it somehow.

Jagger leaned closer, raised the bottle, and squeezed a stream of golden honey onto her shoulder. She trembled as it hit her skin, dripped down in an endlessly slow track. And she felt suddenly as though everything were moving in slow motion: Jagger's sultry smile, her own breath, the honey sliding over her shoulder, her collarbone, the curve of her breast. And the heat moving languidly through her system.

"God, Jagger," she breathed.

He moved the bottle lower, squeezed it once more, and the honey flowed over her breasts while she watched, paralyzed by the current of desire shivering through her. Her sex swelled, pulsed, between her thighs.

Was this really happening?

When he moved lower, let the honey drip over her belly, her thighs, she could barely handle it. She wanted to spread her legs, to offer him her aching breasts, to beg him to touch her, to lick the honey from her skin. How exquisite to know he would in only a few moments.

And then he reached out a hand and began to smear the golden liquid over her: down her arm, which felt as sensual to her as if he'd slipped his hand between her thighs. Her mind was emptying at an alarming rate, and she struggled for a few moments as his fingers traced that stickiness along the undersides of her breasts. Finally, she gave herself over to the inevitable. Let her mind go, gave her body entirely to him.

"Ah, Jagger." This time it came out on a long sigh.

"Yeah, baby. You love this, don't you? I can see it. In the way you're breathing, in the way you hold your hands perfectly still. I'll taste you soon. Lick every inch of your skin. But not yet."

A tremor ran through her at his words, at knowing he would do everything he said he would.

Yes.

Then his hands were all over her, sliding in the honey, massaging it into her breasts. He played around her nipples, rubbing in circles, until the pure need for his touch made them hurt. But it was too good, the way he was touching her, torturing her, the waiting itself.

He spread the honey across her belly with his hands, and lower, into her dark curls. She shivered, moaned.

His voice was quiet, low, full of smoke. "Yeah, that's it."

Using his thumb, he pressed the stickiness into her clitoris. She groaned aloud, writhing, panting suddenly. And then he bent his head and slid his tongue over her throat, down to her breast, taking her nipple into his mouth and sucking.

"Jagger!"

Her hands went into his hair, into the dark, silky, gold-tipped curls. He sucked harder, paused to lick, to bite a little. Her body surged into his mouth, her hips arching. Desire moved through her, sharper now, making her swell, ache, all over. She was nothing but heat and need, dizzy with it all.

He moved his mouth over her breasts, and her sex pulsed hard, harder. The tension in her body rose, crested, and she felt herself at that lovely edge, sharp as a knife. An image of Ben flashed behind her closed eyes, doing this very thing so many years ago: the whipped cream on her breasts, him sucking on her nipples until she came.

She opened her eyes, looked down at Jagger's head, his beautiful brown skin, and knew it was *him* doing these things to her. Knew it was him she wanted.

Pleasure swarmed her, hot and dark, and she tensed, her sex flooding until her juices ran down her thigh. She held his head tight to her breast and he sucked harder, harder, his tongue swirling over the swollen tip. She was keenly aware of the honey on her skin, dripping in rivulets down her heated body. She could smell it. And it smelled like sex to her.

Jagger bit into her rigid flesh, and that was all it took. She went hurtling over the edge, pleasure pounding into her body like a hammering pulse-beat.

It began with a shivering low in her belly, her sex, moving outward, into her breasts, her arms, her legs. And she collapsed like a rag doll, Jagger catching her, lowering her against the side of the tub. The porcelain was cold and hard against her back. But his sucking, wet mouth never left her. Then he was in the tub with her, beautifully naked and kneeling between her spread thighs. And before she was even done coming, he was spreading her legs wide, diving in to lick the honey from her sex.

Pleasure shivered through her, making her keen, a long, panting cry, as he slid his tongue up the length of her slit, aching and sticky with the honey. He reached her clitoris and drew it into his mouth, sucked on it as he had her nipple. And impossibly, she was coming again, or maybe still. Didn't matter. All she knew was the pleasure rushing through her system, the fireworks going off in her head, the sound of her own voice calling his name.

"Jagger! Jagger . . ."

He kept working her with his tongue, his hands holding her hips, rocking her body into his mouth. She couldn't seem to stop coming, small shivers running through her, that lovely, endless aftermath making her weak, sleepy. But he wasn't done with her.

Jagger stroked her thighs, her belly, his hands hard on her flesh, demanding. Then he was straddling her body, squeezing the honey onto his cock.

"Yes, oh God . . ."

She leaned up and took him into her mouth. He was sweet and so damn hard. She took it all in, pulled back, paused to lick at the swollen tip, tasting the honey, tasting him. She moaned, wanting only to please him as he'd pleased her, and swallowed him deep, his cock hitting the back of her throat. Her eyes watered. She breathed in through her nose, commanded her throat to relax, took him deeper still. And now it was him moaning, panting, as she sucked him, using one hand to hold him in her mouth, to pump his rigid flesh.

"Mia Rose, Mia, Mia . . . yeah, baby girl."

Her body was heating up again, just the taste of him, the feel of him, in her mouth, the scent of honey everywhere, still sticky and sliding down her body. His hand was in her hair, and he brought his other hand to her face, slipped one honeyed finger into her mouth along with his cock. A sharp stab of pleasure went through her at that. She didn't know why. She didn't care. She just kept sucking on him, his lovely cock, his finger.

He thrust between her lips, filling her, sweet and a little rough. She wanted him to come in her mouth, to mix his seed with the honey. She wanted him to fuck her. She wanted everything.

"Baby, baby . . . gotta stop."

He pulled back, and she was so dazed with pleasure, with a deep, aching need, she could barely see straight. She was vaguely aware of him leaning over the side of the tub, pulling a condom from the pocket of his discarded jeans.

He was going to fuck her now. One hard clench of pleasure in her sex. Oh, yes. That was exactly what she wanted.

He picked her up, turned her around so that she was standing once more, bent over, her hands braced on the edge of the tub. He moved in behind her, and she spread her thighs for him. He went in with his fingers first, tracing the wet lips of her sex.

"Just do it, Jagger. Now. Please."

He held her lips wide with his fingers and guided the tip of his cock inside her. He paused there for one long, lovely moment, her body clenching in anticipation. Then he thrust home, driving deeply into her body.

She was going to come again.

And then his hand curved around her cheek, his fingers slipping into her mouth once more. Thick and sweet with honey, his fingers moved inside her mouth, pumping in time with his hips, feeding her. She sucked them in, surged back onto his cock, wanting to take all of him, any way she could get him. His flesh in her body, the honey. *Him.*

Jagger.

His body tensed behind her; she could feel his stomach tightening, felt the weight of him driving hard into her. And as he groaned, slamming into her, her own climax rolled over her, making her shudder, making her moan around his fingers still in her mouth.

His arm went around her waist, and together they shivered, panted. His body was pressed up against hers, the honey melding them together in some lovely way. She was shaking so hard she would have fallen if he hadn't been holding her up.

After a moment he pulled out of her, turned her around, and eased her down into the tub once more.

He could not believe this woman. Could not believe what she did to him. His heart was racing, pounding. And his cock was still throbbing, tremors of orgasm still pulsing through his body.

He reached behind him and turned the water on in the tub, waited for it to get hot before he put the plug in place. He watched her sitting there, dazed, so damn beautiful, covered in the golden honey, her hair half falling out of the clip, her eyes absolutely glowing. He could not get enough of her.

He could accept that. The sex was fucking amazing. Spectacular. What he couldn't wrap his mind around was the absolute *need* to take her in his arms, to hold her tight.

Maybe he shouldn't think about it. He wasn't able to think clearly right now, anyway. Maybe just do it. Think about it later. Yeah.

He got on his knees, pulled her in close. She smelled like sex, the earthy edge of honey making it sweeter. So soft and pliant in his arms, her breath still coming in small pants. He had to run his hands over her, every curve: her shoulders, her sides, her hips. Over her narrow back.

They were quiet while the tub filled. She leaned in to him

and dropped her head onto his shoulder. His chest knotted up tight, then his stomach. And even though he was half numb with his orgasm, his pulse was racing faster and faster, with Mia Rose so limp and yielding, so trusting, her hair soft on his skin. He couldn't deal with it. Too close. Too . . . something.

Fuck.

He turned her around again so her back was to him, then leaned back against the edge of the tub and laid her against the front of his body. She was still soft and pliant all over, silent. But it wasn't any better with her back to him. No easier than it had been to see her face, her lips red and swollen, bruised looking. He didn't want to kiss her any less. Didn't want to hold her any less.

He'd never felt anything like it in his life.

Fuck it.

He ran his hands over her sides, her smooth skin still covered in the sticky remains of the honey. He willed his cock back to life, but he was too depleted. He'd need a few minutes. He hated how desperate he was to feel something other than what he was feeling at that moment. To focus on the sex rather than on what else was happening to him.

He was fucking doomed.

He shut the water off, sank down another inch into the heat of it. Mia Rose still hadn't said a word. And when he tried to distract himself by sliding his hands over her breasts, she let out a small sigh. Oh yeah, he could handle this. He played with her nipples, teasing them into two hard points.

Finally she said, "Wash me, Jagger?"

She reached up and pulled a sea sponge and a bottle of liquid soap from the side of the tub, and he took them both.

The soap smelled like vanilla. Like her. He squeezed some onto the sponge, ran it over her body. And he was heating up again, low in his belly. Just being wet with her, seeing the shine of the water on her skin, feeling it like silk under his hands.

He ran the sponge over her breasts, felt her squirm against him. Jesus, her breasts were perfect. He'd never seen anything like them in his life. But the truth of it was, he'd love them even if they weren't perfect. It didn't matter.

He ran his free hand over her soapy skin. Oh yeah, even better like this, the water and the soap beneath his fingers. But she seemed to really love the touch of the sponge. He was getting hard again. Wanted to fuck her again. Or just rub up against her hot, wet skin, something he'd always loved to do. Just rub up against her, come all over her. Oh, yeah.

He moved the sponge lower, beneath the water, and ran it over her cleft. She sighed once more, spread her thighs, let her head fall back against him. And as he massaged her slick little pussy with the sponge, he teased her nipples with his free hand, loving the hardness of them under his fingertips. In only moments she was panting again. And his cock was rock-hard, pressing against her buttocks, between those tight cheeks.

Mia surged back against him.

"Yes, Jagger. Come onto me."

She got it. That this was what he wanted. Needed. He rubbed the sponge faster over her sex, loved the way she pumped her hips in the same rhythm. The friction was amazing on his cock, as it skimmed between those lovely cheeks, against her wet, slippery skin. Pleasure coursed through him, sliding like the water. Soon Mia Rose tensed, bucked her hips, whimpered as she came. And those low sounds of pleasure coming from her mouth made him explode. His cock went absolutely rigid, and he thrust faster. The pure power of his orgasm shattered him, like shards of glass, almost painful. And he came and came, into the water he loved so much, onto the skin he'd come to love.

The sharp thud in his chest only made him climax harder. And Mia Rose was panting and squirming against him. He couldn't stop, couldn't stop the tremors of postorgasm, couldn't stop the sensation deep in his chest that he didn't want to understand.

He was left shivering. His arms went around Mia Rose's body, held her tight.

Don't think about it, man.

Too late. Too fucking late.

And he was too weak with coming to fight it. Fuck it. There would be time to deal with it later. Right now it was all about her soft body, her curves pressed right up against him, the scent of her hair and the goddamned honey everywhere.

Mia woke in the predawn dark, her body loose all over, the sheets pushed to the foot of the bed, both of them naked. She could smell him even in the dark, like honey, very faintly. Like her own soap. Like Jagger. Lovely.

She lay there for a few moments, simply breathing him in.

She didn't want to question last night. Didn't dare ask herself, and certainly not him, what had happened. She'd felt a shift in him while they were in the tub. She could swear something changed . . .

Or was it some strange moment of girlishness? She wasn't used to having those kinds of moments. How could she possibly know?

Everything had changed for her in some subtle way since she'd been with Jagger. She felt different about herself as a woman. Better. Freer. Even her class felt different to her, as though she had a deeper insight into those things she'd been teaching for several years. All of her research, her years of study, seemed to have led up to this moment in time with him. And the two things seemed intrinsically linked, as though one could never have happened without the other.

A little scary, to know that this man was changing her, changing her life.

But there she was, the heat of his sleeping body beside her. And it was wonderful and frightening and comforting in a way she still didn't dare trust. She normally didn't like a man to stay the night. She liked her space. But right now, all she wanted was him here with her, just like this. She wanted to touch him, to curl into him.

She shook her head in the dark room. She must be losing her mind.

Looking at him, she was barely able to make out his quiet form. She reached out, stroked one finger over his bare shoulder, then up and over his jaw. Touched his mouth. And shivered with a longing so deep, so profound, it made her want to cry.

He stirred, whispered, "Hey," his voice rough with sleep.

"I'm sorry. I didn't mean to wake you."

"Mmm."

He slid an arm around her, pulled her down onto his chest. His heart beat in a slow, even rhythm beneath her ear. He was so steady, so calm. So unlike her, her own head always filled with one frantic thought after another, rushing around at a hundred miles an hour. Common among those with a genius IQ, she'd been told by her teachers. She'd been tested as soon as she'd entered the eighth grade; her grandmother had seen to that. And it had been such a relief when they'd put her into classes that had actually challenged her. It was the emotional stuff she couldn't handle. And she could never seem to turn her brain off. But Jagger knew how to unwind. Maybe he could teach her how to do that.

He was teaching her already. Something about how to let go. The way her body responded to him made her do it whether she wanted to or not. But she was pretty sure it was good for her. Just like her friendship with Karalee was opening her up, helping her learn to trust again. Maybe that's what it was with Jagger, too.

Don't take that too far.

No, she never did, did she? She wouldn't now. Not even with him.

She wouldn't.

Her heart gave a hard squeeze. And she knew she may have gone too far already. But all she wanted at that moment was to let it all go: the tension, the fear, the neurotic overthinking, and just be with him. To exist purely in the moment, as Jagger seemed to be able to do.

What had Scarlett O'Hara said? Tomorrow was another day.

For once, she was going to try to let it be.

chapter ⚬ twelve

KARALEE DREW IN A DEEP BREATH AS GIDEON THRUST INTO
her from behind, right into her wet, waiting sex. She didn't
know, after their last experience, if he'd want to fuck her
pussy or her ass. She didn't care. It was all good. Anything he
wanted.

She braced her hands on the marble wall of the bathroom
stall and surged back into him, wanting him deeper, already
shuddering with pleasure. And he had his fingers on her clit,
teasing, pinching, hitting all the right spots.

He thrust harder, deeper. He knew just how to do it, fast
and furious. All the better if they weren't going to get caught.
Yet she came every time. Came harder than she ever had in
her life.

Oh, yes . . .

She bit down on her lip. She knew to keep quiet. But she

let out a little mewling sound so that he clapped a hand over her mouth, held tight. God, she loved that. That sensation of really being commanded. Taken over.

The tension built, his hand and his cock working her. Hard. Merciless. Pleasure shafted deep into her body, spread, heating her skin all over.

He whispered into her hair, "I love to fuck you, Karalee. Up against the wall like this. I love to see your naked ass. And your pussy is so damn tight and wet." He drove his cock deeper. "I love to fuck you as hard as I can. Just. Like. This."

Each word was punctuated by a ramming thrust. She cried out behind the safety of his hand across her mouth as pleasure stabbed into her. Her body tensed, her sex clenching, and she came in long, shuddering waves. Behind her, Gideon drove into her, so hard she could barely stay upright. Then he grunted, and his hand fell away from her mouth.

It was only a moment later that she heard him zip up. She couldn't move, her legs still spread, her dress still up around her waist, her thighs aching. Gideon reached down and stroked a finger across the still-quivering lips of her sex.

"Clean up. Then meet me in the bar."

He left. It took her a few minutes to move. She lowered herself onto the toilet, her legs still shaky. When she was done she opened the stall door, peered out into the ladies' room. It was empty. Grabbing her purse from the hook on the back of the door, she slipped out, went to look at her reflection in the enormous bronze-framed mirror.

The bathroom at the Clift Hotel was almost ridiculously luxurious. With its red-lacquer paneled walls, everything accented in bronze and gold. The sleek pair of sofas covered in caramel suede in the lounge area. The little marble tables.

Even the red marble stall was beautiful. The feel of that sleek marble beneath her hands as Gideon rammed his cock into her . . .

Her sex clenched once more. The man could fuck, like some beautiful, wicked satyr. She couldn't get enough. And she was really learning to love these dirty little public encounters. It made them both even hotter, and by the time they made it back to her place, they were always ready for more. Hotter than if they hadn't touched each other all night.

She pulled a small brush from her purse, brushed her hair. Then, digging in her purse again, she found a tube of lipstick. Her mouth looked swollen, even though he hadn't spent more than a moment kissing her. Pink and swollen, like the lips of her sex. She squeezed her thighs together at the ache there.

She washed her hands, letting the cool water run over her heated skin. Finally, she smoothed the black knit wrap dress she'd worn with her high black stiletto-heeled boots, straightened the heavy strand of silver and pearl beads at her neck, and made her way back to the bar.

The Redwood Room was one of the most famous bars in San Francisco, with its polished redwood paneled walls, and the bar said to have been made from a single, massive redwood tree. It had been redone in recent years, the style a bit more modern, updated with sleek red leather couches, low tiled tables, the subtle custom-made lighting. But there was that air of old elegance that still spoke of the history of the place.

She joined Gideon at the bar.

"I ordered a martini for you," he told her.

She nodded. She would drink whatever he wanted her to.

It was part of the power play that ran like a not-so-subtle undercurrent between them. She wondered sometimes how much of her attraction to him was that power play doing things to her head and how much was real. Because she was beginning to feel something powerful for him, and she couldn't be sure how much of that was her infatuation with what was happening between them, the things he did to her, or if it was truly about *him*.

Gideon was so mysterious. So secretive. But that made him all the more attractive, while confusing her even more. And the fact that he kept her body, her head, buzzing with a constant series of orgasms wasn't helping her to think any more clearly about it.

She slid onto the high stool next to him, crossed her legs. Unexpectedly, he leaned over, brushed his lips across her cheek. "You really are spectacular, Karalee," he said quietly. "I'd like to fuck you right here. To slip my hand in between those crossed, ladylike thighs and get you off again."

Her sex gave a hard squeeze, going wet once more. He sat back, smiled at her as though they'd been having a perfectly normal conversation, sipped his own drink. Well, for them, this was a normal conversation.

She smiled at him. "I'd love for you to do that, Gideon. You know I would."

He laughed. "I do know it." He set his glass down, ran a thumb along the rim as he watched her, his dark eyes on hers. "I enjoy you so much."

She felt warmed all over, at his words, his tone. He sounded perfectly serious. She didn't know what to say.

Didn't know how to respond when it wasn't purely about sex.

She sipped her drink, the gin going down her throat in a smooth burn. She sipped again, wanting it: the burn, the resulting loosening of her limbs, her mind. She leaned forward, saw Gideon's eyes flick briefly to her cleavage. "Take me home and fuck me, Gideon."

He grinned. "Say please."

"Please." Then lower, "Oh, please."

He laughed once more, threw back his scotch on the rocks. "Drink up, then, darlin'."

Why did that make her shiver? It was just one little word. She smiled, sipped her martini, set it down. "I'm ready now."

He helped her from her stool and led her to the front of the hotel, had the valet bring his car. She sank deep into the heavy black leather seat as he drove into the night, the lights of the city spread below them as they made their way down from the top of Geary Street.

"I love these old muscle cars," she said. "Have I ever told you that?"

"No, you never have. I thought you only loved to feel the metal of the hood up against your naked skin."

She laughed. "Well, yes. But growing up in the Midwest, these were the dream cars. The cars that were completely unobtainable. Oh, some of the guys would buy old junkers, try to fix them up. But in the town I lived in, anyway, they were mostly held together with baling wire and covered in Bondo."

"So was this one, at one time."

"And you had it restored?"

"I did most of the work myself."

"You're kidding."

"Why would I be kidding?"

She studied his profile for a moment, the strong jaw, the chiseled cheekbones, the elegant bit of gray at his temples.

"You don't strike me as the sort of man who would work on his own car."

"You don't think I like to get dirty?" He cast a quick grin at her before turning back to the road.

"Oh, I know you like dirty."

"So do you."

Gideon reached over and slid a hand up her thigh, pulling up the hem of her dress until it was bunched around her waist. She was bare underneath. He glanced over, grinned at her once more. "Spread for me."

She did, and he slipped a hand into her wet heat.

"Ah . . . Gideon, you're driving."

"I'm quite good at multitasking." He pushed two fingers inside her.

"Jesus. I'm going to come again," she groaned through gritted teeth.

"I should hope so."

She closed her eyes and let her head fall back against the headrest, inhaling deeply of the scent of leather and Gideon's cologne, that sophisticated, smoky scent. He was working her with his fingers. Quickly. Expertly. The heel of his hand ground onto the tight nub of her clit while his fingers pushed in and out of her. She bore down onto his hand, pleasure shafting through her, making her shiver again. And the vibration of the engine rumbled through her body, making it all more intense.

She let her eyes flutter open, watching Gideon's profile as he drove, a look of concentration on his face. He was so damn handsome. Beyond him the lights of the city flashed past in a blur.

He kept at it, his fingers in her sex, rubbing, pushing, pulling at her insides. And very quickly she was coming, a pure, stabbing pleasure rolling over her, the motion of the car rocking her. This time she cried out loud, gripping the edge of the leather seat with her fingertips.

"Jesus, Gideon!"

He smiled at her again, his eyes dark and glittering, kept his fingers inside her for a few moments more as the last waves subsided. Then he pulled them from her body, carefully put them in his mouth one by one and licked them.

"Beautiful," he murmured.

She was still trembling. Her head was spinning. Was it just the sex that made her feel as though she would do anything for him?

Anything.

The idea of it made her feel weak. But she knew she wasn't thinking clearly. No, better to stand back and allow things to happen, wait to see where it went. Gideon didn't seem in any more rush to be in a relationship than she was, so why was she worried?

Maybe because you do want more.

She shook the thought away. Impossible.

Wasn't it?

They pulled up in front of her house, and he helped her from the car, took her house keys, and unlocked the door, guided her inside.

Ever the gentleman.

She'd left one low lamp on in the living room. He was moving toward her already, taking off his jacket. Underneath it he wore a classic, starched white shirt, so pristine against his tanned skin. He rolled up his sleeves as he moved in closer, kept his eyes on hers as he backed her right up against the arm of the couch. With one hand on her shoulder, the other at her waist, he sat her on the edge. She could feel the heat of his body, his hard cock through the fabric of his charcoal slacks pressing against her thigh. He bent and kissed her neck, trailed his tongue over her skin, paused to bite her.

"Fuck, Gideon, that hurt!"

"Yes," he murmured.

But she was going warm all over again, her sex lighting up, needing him.

He pushed her down, until she lay on the sofa cushions, her hips raised still on the arm, her legs hanging over. A rather inglorious position. But she hardly had time to think about it. Gideon slid her dress up, spread her thighs with his hands, and bent in, planting his wet, sucking mouth over her cleft.

"Ah, Gideon..."

He went right to work, as he always did, running his tongue up and down her slit, pushing in between the plump lips, holding her legs wide open with rough hands. And licking her, licking her hard clit, then delving into her waiting hole. Everything so fast, so hard, it made her head spin. She was nothing but this sensation. His mouth on her. The heat. The wet. His soft, slippery tongue.

Pleasure shimmered through her, into her sex, up into her belly. She threw her hands over her head, giving herself up to him, to the sensations, to that sense of utter helplessness beneath his hands, his mouth, his presence.

His tongue stabbed into her savagely, and he pressed on her clitoris with his thumb. And she came once more, crying out, writhing, barely able to breathe.

She shook with the force of it, her legs quivering. Gideon pulled back, stood staring at her in the half-lit room, her thighs still spread, her hips raised on the arm of the couch, her sex naked and open to his gaze.

There was fever in his eyes. She saw his cock, hard and ready, beneath the wool trousers. And no matter how many times she'd come tonight already, she wanted him.

His cock, yes. But something else? Something more? Too hard to think right now. She was too listless, her body spent. She moved to pull her thighs together, but he said sharply, "No." She left them spread, felt the gentle, weightless pull of her legs dangling over the edge of the couch. Felt her wanton nakedness like a hand caressing her swollen sex.

He paced a little, rubbing the back of his neck, watching her. She'd never been looked at in quite this way before. She loved it.

Gideon moved in closer, stroked a finger over her cleft, dipped inside. Sensation shivered through her system, her stomach clenching.

"You are so responsive, Karalee. To every single thing I do. To everything I say. Fucking amazing, really." He spoke so quietly, almost as though he were alone, speaking to himself. "I don't know what the hell to do with you any longer."

"Fuck me, Gideon," she said, her voice low, breathless.

"Yes, that's not a problem. I could fuck you all night."

She started to sit up, wondering what was going on with him, but he quickly came to stand next to her, pushed her back down, leaving his splayed hand between her breasts. She would have been frightened if there was anything at all menacing about his voice, but there wasn't. He sounded a little vague, in fact.

"I can fuck you, Karalee, but then what? I can fuck you some more. Make you come over and over, which you do all too easily. Oh, I don't mean that as any kind of insult. Just the opposite. I can't get enough of that, of making you come. Watching your face."

She looked up at him, saw the way his eyes roved her body. And then he reached down and untied her dress, pushed the folds apart with his hands, baring her breasts. He caressed them, making her sigh. Yet a part of her mind was on edge, hyperaware of his shifting mood.

"Yes, see?" he said. "I touch you and your body responds instantly. And you're willing to do anything, aren't you?"

"Yes," she said, her throat inexplicably dry. "Yes, I am. Whatever you want."

She was shaking now, her insides trembling, but it wasn't about sex anymore. Where was he going with this line of conversation?

"The perfect woman. A woman any man would want. Why do I want more from you?"

"I'll give you more," she answered, her throat dryer than ever. Her pulse was racing.

Yes, this was exactly what she wanted. But more what? She couldn't figure it out.

He shook his head, moved away from her, pacing her living room again, his back to her. She sat up and pulled her dress together, moved down to sit on the edge of the sofa cushions.

"Gideon? Tell me what's going on. What exactly are we talking about?"

He paused, standing in front of a small antique bureau, laid his fingers on the old wood surface. He shook his head. "Nothing."

"It's not 'nothing.' I can see that. Please talk to me."

"We've never been very good at talking, have we?"

"What? Of course we have. We've talked about our pasts . . . all sorts of things."

"Have we really?"

She had to stop and think about it a moment, struggling to get her thoughts organized. She'd talked about her own childhood, but he'd been rather vague about the details of his past, his life. He'd merely skimmed the surface. There were enormous chunks missing from what she knew about him, what he'd shown her about who he was. He remained, for the most part, inscrutable.

She asked quietly, "Why have you never taken me to your house, Gideon?"

She knew even before she saw his shoulders tense that she'd said the wrong thing. She didn't understand why the answer to her question felt so important.

There was a long pause. Long enough to make her squirm on the edge of the sofa. Then he said quietly, "I'm going to go now."

"What?"

But he didn't say any more. He picked up his discarded jacket. His face looked as though it were carved from stone.

"Gideon, you can't just... leave like this. What did I do? What did I say? Tell me. This isn't making any sense."

"I don't want to have this discussion, Karalee."

"So, you're just going to leave? To walk out of here leaving me wondering what the hell is going on? That's not fair."

"Life isn't fair, Karalee."

"Jesus, just stop it." She was angry now, the heat of it lending her strength. "Just stop, Gideon, with all the secrecy, and talk to me. Or am I just your fuck buddy, so you don't think we need to have conversations of any substance? Is that it?"

There was anger in his tone now. "If that were it, I wouldn't be here. There would be no conversation at all. I would have fucked you in the janitors' closet and that would have been the end. I wouldn't have come back over and over again."

"But you did."

He paused, rubbed at the back of his neck. "Yes, I did. Christ, Karalee."

He sat on the arm of the sofa, where only moments before he'd been going down on her. She couldn't get over how strange the whole thing was. How had the evening turned into such a mess?

"Tell me what's going on," she said quietly, demanding for once.

He shook his head again. "I don't take anyone there. To my house. I can't do it."

"Why not?"

"Because that was her house. My wife's. She lived in that house. And she died there."

She was too stunned to answer for several moments.

"Jesus, Gideon. I . . . I'm so sorry."

He shrugged, but his whole posture was as ramrod stiff as steel. When she put a hand on his arm, he didn't move. But there was the slightest loosening, the smallest signal of acceptance of her touch.

He kept his eyes on the floor. "I married Alicia right out of college. We had a good life. A great life. We wanted all of the same things, the same lifestyle. It was a ridiculously ideal marriage, if you want to know the truth. We traveled every summer, spent a lot of time with her family." He paused, rubbed a hand over his jaw. "We were in Italy with her parents when she got sick, had to come home. It was pancreatic cancer, so it happened fast. One minute we were trekking through Europe, and the next she was . . . gone. That's when I moved to Santa Barbara. I couldn't stay."

Karalee's chest was so tight she could barely breathe. Tight and warm with sympathy, and with something else . . . She couldn't take it all in. And she could see the struggle in the tight lines around his mouth.

"You don't have to say anything more, Gideon. I'm sorry I forced you into telling me this way."

"You would have had to know eventually, if I were going to continue seeing you."

"And were you? Going to continue seeing me, I mean?"

He turned to her then. She couldn't read his expression. "Yes."

Her entire body went warm and loose, as though she'd been holding her breath for a very long time. Maybe she had.

She ran a hand over his forearm, over the soft, dark hair, the smooth, corded muscle. "Come to bed with me, Gideon."

He ran both his hands over his hair, blew out a breath. "Alright."

Standing, he dropped his coat on the sofa and helped her to her feet. He led her down the hall to her bedroom, silently undressed her, then himself. Her body was responding to him as it always did: her nipples hard, her sex damp and needy. But she wasn't sure where his head was right now.

They got into her big bed, and he pulled her body in close to his. She breathed him in, that scent of elegance, of sex, of her own juices still on his skin. She wanted him. No doubt about it. Enough that it nearly hurt. But she was also so full of emotion she couldn't really think about anything. All she could do was feel.

His body was warm, his skin soft and hard at the same time in the way only a man's skin could be. He felt good, every plane and angle, every strong rise of muscle. They'd never had this sort of quiet moment together for her to simply focus on the feel of his body against hers. No, it had always been fucking like mad, then collapsing in exhaustion. This was lovely. Confusing. She didn't know how the hell to feel, what to think. She focused on his breathing, on matching the rhythm of her breath to his.

After a while he turned her to face him, pulled her up so that her mouth was only inches from his, and he began to kiss her. Slowly, gently, in a way he never had before. His lips, his tongue, were soft, searching. Her arms wound around his neck, and he moved her, laid her body over his, her breasts crushed against his chest.

His cock was soft beneath her. She felt disappointed. Selfish. But in only moments it came to life, hardening at the apex of her thighs. She rubbed her body against his, her mound back and forth over his hardening cock, her breasts against his chest, excitement building, coursing through her.

He was still kissing her, his tongue thrusting gently into her mouth, his lips lush against hers. And she was melting all over, in a soft, warm rush. Everything was so different suddenly. But she didn't want to think about it.

She broke away long enough to lean over him and pull a condom from her nightstand drawer. Straddling his body, she tore the packet open, reached down between them, and rolled the condom over his rigid shaft. He moaned, held her hips in his hands, and guided her onto his cock, slipped the tip inside her.

She held perfectly still, poised, with just the head of his cock inside her body. Sensation washed through her, small ripples that became more intense somehow, even while they held perfectly still, the only movement her breath and his. In the half-dark she could make out the outline of his face, his fine jaw, the way his dark hair fell away from his forehead. And for some reason, she smiled.

He lifted her then, just the slightest inch, and settled her again onto his cock, driving a little deeper this time, driving pleasure into her body. She rocked against him, aware of every warm shiver of desire, of the heat of their bodies pressed together, of the cool night air on her skin. And the strange sense of familiarity, mixed with the utter strangeness of the tenderness running like a cord between them.

Even as the heat rose in her body, pleasure swarming her in soft, rippling waves, tears stung the back of her eyes. Dazed, she rocked against him harder, her mound pressing down on his pubic bone with every thrust, taking her higher and higher.

As her climax shuddered through her system, she grabbed his shoulders, held on tight, and his hands went around her wrists, holding her to him. His eyes met hers, and she watched the exquisite agony on his face as he came, felt him tense and shiver. He groaned, and she groaned with him. Together they shook, their eyes locked. And for the first time, she understood the meaning of intimacy.

chapter ✍ thirteen

JAGGER HAD WAITED THREE DAYS TO TALK TO HER. HE'D
skipped school Wednesday night. It was too hard to see her.
He hadn't been ready to sit in class, to watch her lecture,
without touching her, talking to her. It was torture to even
think about it. He'd needed distance. Perspective.

It hadn't helped.

Tonight had been hard, even sitting in the back of the
room where he could avoid her eyes. Those green eyes, like
dark moss. Beautiful. He'd sat in his seat, forcing himself to
hold still, pretending to take notes, to be focused on his pad
of legal paper when all he'd wanted to do was watch her
every move, her mouth as she talked.

The lecture had covered some of the darker fetish practices:
amputee fetish, scat play, bloodletting, bestiality, things he

found repulsive. It didn't matter. He'd been hard as iron the whole damn time just hearing her voice.

He'd taken off the moment class was over, while everyone else was still gathering their books. Pushing through the heavy double doors of the building, he'd stepped out into the cold evening air. He'd needed it, needed that cool rush against his skin. He'd pulled in breath after breath, just so he could wait a few minutes to call her, to give her time to wrap things up, pack up her notes, talk to other students.

He walked the campus for fifteen minutes in long strides, circling the big building where Mia's class took place twice, three times. He knew she needed some time; the students always had questions for the professors on Fridays, before doing homework and writing papers over the weekend. Finally he pulled his cell from his pocket, dialed, waited for her to pick up.

"Hey there, Mia Rose."

"Hi." She sounded breathless. Sexy.

He was still half hard.

"What are you doing? Are you still in your classroom?"

"I'm just leaving the building. Where are you?"

"Do you need to go to your office, to do anything else before you leave?" Why was his heart hammering, waiting for her to answer?

"No, I was going straight to my car. I was just going home."

"Come with me, Mia Rose."

He rounded the corner of the building, saw her standing there by the doorway, the fluorescent lights from inside making her hair burn with blue highlights. She looked so professional, in her narrow black skirt, her cream-colored sweater.

But her heels were just a little too high, making her legs look long and lean.

She looked up as he approached, smiled, lowering her cell phone into her purse. That smile was so open, so purely happy to see him. Surprising. Beautiful.

"Mia Rose. Hi."

"Hi." She glanced down for a moment, looked back up, her eyes searching his face.

"I should have called you," he started.

"No, I haven't called, either. I was . . . I don't know. I had to think."

He nodded. "Yeah."

"Thanks for giving me some space." She stopped, shifted her briefcase from one hand to the other, laughed a little. "God, that sounds so stupid."

"No it doesn't. I know what you mean. I can't think when I'm around you at all." It was true. He didn't mind saying it to her. "Come with me," he said again.

"Where?"

"Anywhere. To a café. We can have a glass of wine, talk."

She nodded her head. "Okay."

Almost too easy. But he needed that, needed not to have to think too hard about it. He just needed to see her, talk to her. *Be* with her. He didn't want to know what it was all about. There would be time for that later. Right now she was only inches away. He could smell that vanilla scent on her skin, in her hair. He would be able to touch her soon. Anything else could wait.

🍂

The little café was warm, the windows fogged so that, from the inside, Mia could barely see the people moving down the sidewalk outside. The streetlights, the pink neon glow from a sign across the street, were blurred streaks of translucence coming through the glass.

They sat at a table in a corner of the front window, on velvet-covered wingback chairs, a small, round marble-topped table between them. Around them the walls were covered in shelves full of books. If she looked past Jagger's head, she saw Goethe, Virginia Woolf, Hemingway, volumes of poetry.

"This really is one of those places for the local intelligentsia, isn't it? Where the literary crowd hangs out," she said, tracing her fingers over the rim of her wineglass. The dark Cabernet looked like liquid rubies. She was trying hard not to remember Jagger pouring wine over her skin, her breasts, licking it off . . .

"I suppose. Or at least, they like to look literary. I don't know if anyone actually reads here."

He was watching her, his eyes a dark, smoky gray. Why did it make her feel as though he were touching her, running his hands over her skin? She shivered.

Looking away, she sipped her wine, glanced back at him, caught his gaze. Then he reached out, laid a hand over hers, and there it was, that now-familiar electric current running like molten heat through her system whenever he touched her, looked at her a certain way.

"Jagger . . ." But suddenly her throat was too dry to speak.

He nodded, licked his lips. "Yeah. I thought we'd sit here and talk. Have some wine. Just talk."

"I know."

"I don't want to come off like I'm not interested in talking with you. In what you have to say."

"No, no, of course not."

They stared at each other for a moment, her pulse hammering, hot.

"Let's get out of here, Mia Rose." His voice was low, urgent. "Let's just go."

She nodded. They stood, and he helped her shrug into her coat, lifted her purse from the back of the chair and handed it to her, and they went out into the night. Her car was parked close by; he held the door for her while she got in, went around and settled into the passenger seat. They were quiet on the drive to his place, some classic rock playing on the radio the only backdrop to the sounds of the city at night: other cars moving by, the occasional rumbling of one of the big buses. She glanced at him once; he smiled, and she felt everything in that smile. All the heat between them, the exquisite tension. Her breasts filled, tightened. She had to force her attention back to the road.

She found parking on Sixth Street, only a few doors down from his building. Jagger helped her out from the car with the same care with which he'd handed her in. And even that small touch, his hand on her elbow, made her shiver with need.

They went inside, waited for the big freight elevator. Jagger slipped an arm around her waist, pulling her closer into his side, until she could feel the heat of his body through her clothes. He bent and brushed a kiss across her hair, murmured, "I can't wait to get you alone."

Her sex gave one hard pulse at his words. It couldn't be soon enough.

She turned to look up at him. His eyes were gleaming, dark, full of smoke. She couldn't look away. He held her tighter, until she could feel the imprint of his hand on her waist.

The elevator came and he pulled her in. Yanked her in, really, right into his body, one hand going into her hair. Then he was kissing her, hard, bruising kisses. He opened her lips, dove in with his tongue, hot and wet and making her crazy with need right away.

She could smell him, that lovely, unique scent, mixed with the old wood and metal of the elevator.

She was panting into his mouth, couldn't catch her breath, as his hands roamed her body beneath her coat. And then her coat was coming off, and his, and his hands were under her sweater, cupping her breasts, thumbing her nipples beneath her bra.

She slid her hands around his waist, down over his tight buttocks, and he tilted his hips, the surge of the elevator rocking them, making the ridge of his erection press into her belly. But she wanted to feel him inside her, *needed* to.

"Jagger..."

"Yeah, baby..."

He reached out and punched a button, and the elevator came to a grinding stop. His mouth was back on hers in seconds, his tongue driving between her lips. She didn't stop to question him, just went for his belt, struggled with it until he helped her. Then he slid her sweater up, unsnapped the front clasp on her bra, filled his palms with her bare breasts, making her flesh sting with desire.

"Ah, Jagger."

She reached down and ran her fingertips over the bulge

beneath his jeans. A small groan from him, then she unzipped him and pulled his cock out. It was heavy in her
hands, warm, solid. She squeezed and he moaned once
more.

There was an edge of desperation to everything: to the
way he kissed her, the way he touched her. And she was no
less frenzied herself, needing to touch him, taste him.
Needing him inside her body. She could hardly stand it.

Jagger pulled her skirt up around her waist, slipped her
panties down, and she stepped out of them. His mouth
never left hers as he backed her into one wall of the old elevator. He pressed her up hard against it, her sweater bunch-
ing behind her back. She wrapped one leg around his hip,
held on to his shoulders as he snaked a hand under her naked
bottom. With the other hand he reached down and swept
his fingers across her soaking-wet sex. She groaned into his
mouth as he used his fingers to part those swollen lips, and
slid his cock inside her.

Sensation drove deep into her body, then deeper still with
every rough stroke. It was all so wet: his cock sliding in and
out, his lovely mouth on hers. She was shaking with it. And
then he pulled his lips away, whispered, "Mia Rose, here,
open your mouth."

"What? Jagger . . ."

His fingers slid between her lips, and he pushed a small
object into her mouth. It was only a moment before she realized it was chocolate, melting like pure sin on her tongue.
Pleasure surged, hot and strong, and he drove his cock
harder into her body.

Her head was spinning. And when he reached down between them and rubbed her clit with his fingers she came,

exploding, her mind blank, while he rammed into her, and the chocolate disappeared like a mirage in her mouth.

A few more thrusts and he groaned, tensed, shuddered, one hand pulling her face in to kiss her over and over, his goatee rough against her skin. And she loved it: him coming inside her, the taste of chocolate and *him* on her tongue.

Finally they both stopped shaking and he pulled out of her. Quietly, he helped her back into her clothes. He was smiling at her, tender. Such a lovely contrast after the rough sex. He hit a button and the elevator started again with a loud sigh. They didn't speak as they surged upward, but he kept his arm looped around her waist until they were in his apartment.

He took her coat from her hands and threw it with his own brown leather jacket over the back of one of the bar stools at the kitchen counter. He took her hand, led her around the counter into the kitchen. Then he pulled his sweater off, swept hers over her head, removed her bra. He slipped her skirt off next, his hands gentle, reverent.

"Mia Rose, stay here."

Her eyes followed him as he opened his refrigerator, pulled a few items out and set them on the counter.

"What are you doing, Jagger?"

"You'll see."

But she could see already. He had a squeeze bottle of chocolate syrup in his hand, something else in a glass jar. She was beginning to shake again already, guessing what he might do with these things.

Quickly, he put the items one by one into the microwave, the bell going off a few moments later like a small shock of desire lighting up her system. She was acutely aware of standing nearly naked in his kitchen, the scent of melted chocolate in the air. She couldn't have moved if she wanted to.

He turned back to her, too beautiful in his faded jeans, his heavy black boots. His tattoos stood out against his biceps, marking the curve of muscle there. Her sex gave a squeeze. She needed him to touch her. Why was he waiting? Excruciating.

He paused, smiled at her. "One last thing. Don't move."

He turned to the counter behind him and she couldn't see what he was doing, but she could smell it: the sharp tang of fresh citrus. He came back to her then, laid out a small row of items. He leaned in, brushed his lips across hers, whispered, "I think you're going to like this. I think I'm going to like this."

He knelt then, at her feet, and slipped her damp panties down over her legs, slowly. Almost painful, how many moments it took for her to be completely naked before him. He stayed on his knees, his breath hot on the narrow strip of curls between her thighs. She shifted her weight, her sex swelling beneath his gaze.

"Can you stand here, Mia Rose?"

"Yes."

He ran a hand over her body: her belly, her thighs, and a trail of pure pleasure followed his touch.

"Please, Jagger."

"Right here, baby," he said quietly. "I'm right here."

He reached behind her and in his hand was a lemon, cut in half. He squeezed it and the strong scent of citrus filled the air once more.

"What . . . what are you going to do with that?"

"Shh. Here, part your legs for me. Yeah, that's it."

She did as he asked, trembling all over. And then he rubbed the juicy lemon over her lower belly. A shock went through her, a shock of pure lust.

"God, Jagger." Her fingers gripped the edge of the counter.

He was quiet, moving the lemon lower, using his fingers to hold the lips of her sex open and running the lemon over her cleft, her hardening clitoris. She'd never felt anything like it. Slippery, stinging just a little, and the scent of it in her nostrils made it better, somehow. Simply knowing that he was touching her with it. And the fact that it was him.

Jagger.

She looked down at his broad, brown shoulders and a new shiver ran through her. He was so goddamned beautiful. And he was giving her exactly what she wanted. Needed. Had needed for years.

Her head was reeling.

He ran the fruit over her sex, and she went wet in a rush of heat and need. She cried out, her entire body pulsing, ready to come already.

He stopped.

"No, Jagger, please. God, please . . ."

"I'm right here."

She knew what he meant. But it was hard to wait even a moment while he stood and picked up the glass jar of what she realized was caramel syrup. He held it over her, watching her, his beautiful face intent. And then he drizzled the warm syrup onto her breasts.

She gasped as it hit her skin, slid over the curve of flesh, dripped down onto her nipples. It was almost too hot, the scent of sugar strong in the air. She gasped again when he bent to lick it off. His tongue swept over her in long strokes as he gathered her breasts in both hands, slippery with the syrup. She'd never felt anything so good in her life.

Her breasts ached, her nipples so hard they hurt. And then he took one into his mouth. And once more she immediately thought she might come just from that wet sucking. He paused, moved his mouth to the other side, sucked on her rigid flesh again, until she was squirming, pleasure washing over her in heated waves until she didn't think she could stand it anymore.

Her hands went into his hair. And she was shaking harder than ever, trying not to come so soon.

"Yeah, that's it, baby. Let's slow down a minute." He pulled back, stared at her. "You are so beautiful, baby girl, do you know that? I can't look at you and not touch you. Kiss you."

He leaned in and pressed his mouth to hers, his full of caramel the color of his skin. He pulled back, a fraction of an inch, and whispered, "You make me crazy, Mia Rose."

Then he was stripping his jeans off, and his boots, until he was as naked as she was. He picked up the plastic bottle of chocolate syrup this time and squeezed it over her breasts, over his own chest. He pressed against her, pushing her back into the counter. And he was all slippery sweetness, the hard planes of his chest up against her breasts, the chocolate making an unbelievable texture between their bodies, the taste of the warm caramel lingering on her tongue.

He squeezed more of the stuff into his hands and began to rub it all over her: her sides, her hips, her buttocks. She was absolutely overwhelmed by sensation, shaking so hard she could barely stand.

"Jagger . . ."

"Hmmm, what is it, baby?"

"I never . . ." She was panting, her breath tight in her throat. "I never knew it would be this good."

He smiled down at her, their eyes meeting, and something passed between them, some sort of understanding that ran deeper than any connection she'd felt with anyone before.

And still, lust raged in her body. She was as ready to come as ever.

Jagger bent his head, ran his tongue over her breasts, down between them, while she shivered and moaned. Then he moved lower, kissing her stomach, then lower still, his slippery hands parting her thighs, the lips of her sex. And he went in with his mouth, kissing the swollen folds softly, driving her crazy, pleasure moving through her like fire. Burning hot, engulfing her.

When he sucked her clitoris into his mouth she couldn't hold back. She fell over that edge, fell apart. She cried out, her fingers digging into his shoulders.

"Jagger! God, God, God . . ."

It wouldn't stop: his sucking mouth on her, the chocolate melting all over her skin. She was coming and coming, so damn hard.

And then she was falling into his arms. He caught her, lifted her up. Her body still shook with the last trembling waves of orgasm.

He carried her into the big bathroom, set her on her feet, and steadied her as he reached in and turned on the shower. He pulled a white T-shirt from a hook on the back of the door.

"Mia Rose, will you put this on for me?"

"I'll do whatever you want."

Was that her own voice, so weak, so shaky? Hell, she felt shaky. Small tremors still ran through her sex, her entire body.

He smiled, flipped the T-shirt over the shower door. She didn't understand. She could not get her brain to work. Then he pulled her into the shower, and they stood together under the water. He took the hand sprayer and wet her all over, washing the chocolate and the caramel from her skin. Then he grabbed the shirt and slipped it over her head. She caught his scent in the shirt before he sprayed it down, until the white cotton clung to her body.

"Oh, yeah, baby, that's it. That's what I love. Jesus."

Jagger ran his hands over her, loving every curve beneath the soaking wet fabric. Even better that it was his own T-shirt on her. His cock was full to bursting, so damn hard. Some kind of fantastic torture that he wasn't inside her yet.

She was unbelievable, the way her body looked, the fabric plastered over her breasts, her nipples hard and red through the water-sheered cotton. He squeezed her breasts, pinched at her nipples. Then he pulled her hard up against him, rubbing his body against hers.

"You feel so damn good, Mia Rose."

She was so warm, yielding to whatever he wanted to do, like some kind of wild doll. Yet she was all flesh, hot, human flesh.

He reached down and guided his cock between her thighs, slid in between them.

"Ah, Jagger. Yes . . ."

She spread her legs for him, wrapped one around his waist.

He found her opening, buried his cock in her, running his hands over her skin, the sight and the feel of the wet cotton working like a conduit, driving pleasure deeper into his body.

He was going to take it slow, enjoy the moment. But she felt too good, so hot and tight inside. He lifted her, until both of her legs were wrapped around his waist. And he pushed into her, deeper, deeper. Faster. Harder. The water fell all around them, slid over his skin, over hers, over the wet, white cotton that seemed almost to have become a part of her flesh.

"Jagger, harder. I need it tonight. Please."

"Anything, baby."

He backed her up against the wall, really slamming into her. Every thrust sent a jolt of pleasure deep into his belly. Like electricity. Like a shock.

She was moaning, writhing. Wet. Pleasure built, made him shiver. And just as her hot little pussy clenched around his cock, he was coming, yelling her name, gripping her naked ass in his hands. He couldn't stop fucking her.

Making love to her.

"Mia Rose . . . baby, baby."

He fell against the tiled wall with her in his arms, his still-hard cock inside her. And together they slid to the floor of the shower. The water fell, warm and soothing, over their bodies. Her head fell onto his chest. He pulled her in closer, held on tight. His breath was coming in ragged pants. And she felt so damn good in his arms.

How could he ever let this woman go?

Too much to think about. Too much to feel. But there was no running from it anymore.

He was in love with her. He was in love with Mia Rose Curry.

chapter ⌒ fourteen

MIA OPENED HER EYES, HER BODY COMING OUT OF A REST-less sleep. It was very late Sunday night, or early Monday, really. And she could barely stand the idea of having to leave him in the morning.

She lay in the comfort of Jagger's big bed, the scent of him, of them both, all over the sheets. He used white sheets on his bed, just as she did. She loved the clean feel of them. White sheets had always felt clean to her. She'd almost begun to take for granted that they had so many small, insignificant details in common.

They'd spent the weekend in bed. Or rather, in the kitchen, the shower, on Jagger's living room floor. They went by Mia's house at one point to collect a change of clothes, which she'd barely used.

Then back to his place, where they spent hours playing

with food, different textures, tastes, sensations. He fed her crêpes expertly cooked at midnight, pasta with fresh pesto, some of the spiciest hot wings she'd ever tasted with a tangy barbecue sauce he made himself, then rubbed all over her in the big shower. He covered her skin in the chocolate again, because it was simply too good not to: the flavor, the feel of it. And that led to chocolate pudding, which Mia really loved, cold from the refrigerator, adding another dimension to their sensual exploration.

Jagger put her in the shower at least once a day, in one of his crisp cotton, button-up shirts, in his blue-and-white-striped pajama bottoms, in his T-shirts. And he put her into his big slate bathtub in her silk camisole and tap pants.

She adored it when he did these things, loved to see what it did for him, did *to* him. Loved to see how his face just fell apart, seeing the wet fabric plastered to her skin, how he lost all control.

And after, he was so gentle with her. So caring. She'd been trying hard not to think about it, about how that fed a part of her she hadn't even known was there until now.

The apartment was dark, but there was always the comforting glow of streetlights, the hint of color from neon signs, seeping through the windows from the street below.

She loved it there, she realized. Just over this weekend, she'd developed a sort of easy comfort being in his apartment.

She felt at home.

It was because of Jagger. Turning her head, she listened to his soft, shallow breath as he slept. He lay on his stomach, as he often did, one arm thrown over her body. She could make out his dark silhouette, that lovely curve of lean muscle. His skin was warm, fragrant.

She could lie there and watch him forever. Except that a part of her wanted him to wake up. To be with her before the alarm went off and they both had to start their day, their week. The rest of their lives.

What did that all mean, anyway?

Her chest tightened. She slid her hand over his arm, needing to touch him.

She'd been trying so hard all weekend not to analyze what was happening between them. What was happening to her. There was a sort of softening going on inside her. A letting go. It had seemed so easy. Until she thought of being outside of this time and place, the safe cocoon of his apartment, of the weekend, where the real world didn't intrude.

But outside was the real world. And in that world, their relationship was forbidden. In that world, she was not the kind of woman who was willing to risk falling for a man only to lose him in some terrible way. Not ever again.

Her hand tightened on his arm and he shifted, resettled.

She bit down hard on her lip, the pain distracting her from the tears gathering in her eyes.

She would not do this. She knew all too well what could happen when she let herself love someone. And she was not willing to go through that again. It was too hard.

But being with him was so easy.

God damn it!

Her fingers flexed once more, and this time Jagger muttered, shifted again, pulling her into his arms. And the tears came, unbidden. Hot, resentful tears.

She did not want to feel this!

Grinding her jaw, she swallowed the sobs that wanted to

come pouring from her body. What the hell was wrong with her?

But she couldn't stop it. The tears slid over her cheeks, burning a trail of old pain, the anticipation of new pain. And soon she could barely breathe, her throat tying itself into a hard knot from holding the flood of emotion inside.

Finally, a sob slipped out. Nothing she could do about it. *Damn it!*

"Mia Rose? Baby, what is it?"

His voice was thick with sleep. So concerned. She couldn't stand it. She tried to sit up, to get away, but he only held her tighter.

"Baby, shh. Tell me what's wrong."

She shook her head in the dark. Croaked out, "No."

He let her cry it out then. Just held her in a way no one ever had, except twice in her life. Her grandmother had held her the morning after her mother had left her. And again the day Ben had died.

She hadn't allowed anyone to do that for her since.

"Jagger," she finally gasped. "I don't . . . I don't need this. From anyone."

But she was shaking in his arms even as she said it.

"Don't be afraid," he said, his voice soft.

"I'm not. I'm not!"

"Tell me what's going on with you, baby girl."

"Oh, God, don't call me that now. Please."

"I thought you liked it."

"I do." She sobbed harder.

"Okay, okay." He smoothed her hair, wiped her cheek with his thumb.

"I don't want to do this with you, Jagger."

"Who else are you going to do it with?"

Her throat was really going to close up. "I don't have anyone else."

"I'm sorry, Mia Rose. And it's not pity. I'm just sorry, okay?"

"Okay." The heat of his body was almost too much, but she couldn't pull away. She nodded her head, as though reassuring herself. Of what, she wasn't certain. Her head was spinning with emotion. "Okay."

They lay together for a while, until her tears calmed, until she was able to take in air without her breath hitching. After a while Jagger asked her, "Tell me what's going on."

"I . . . it's not you. I mean, being with you has . . . made me remember things I need to forget."

"What do you need to forget, baby?"

She had to stop, her throat constricting once more. She pulled in a deep breath, fought down a wave of panic.

Just say it.

"I need to forget what it feels like to . . . to care for someone. To care for someone and lose them. Being with you these last weeks has made me . . . it's brought it all up for me again. I thought I'd dealt with it. I thought I had my life all planned out. And that plan didn't include . . . you."

"I'm not understanding this, Mia Rose."

"I'm sorry. I know I'm not making much sense." She paused, drew in another deep breath, said very quietly, "I loved someone once. His name was Ben. He was . . . he was so good to me. So careful of me, in a way no one but my grandmother had ever been. More than I'd ever been led to think I could expect from anyone."

"He sounds like a good person."

"He was." She could picture him now, his curly brown hair, his blue eyes, his tall, lanky frame. He'd had big hands, long, graceful fingers, like Jagger. "He's the reason why I . . . he was the one who got me into the food thing. God, I don't want to say it like that. It cheapens it, somehow. But it wasn't like that. It was all beautiful with him, you know?"

Jagger stroked her face. "Yeah. Yeah, I do."

"I got out of high school early. I wasn't into it. After living practically on the streets with my mom, I couldn't relate to those kids. So I took the state proficiency exam at sixteen and started college that same year. That's where I met Ben. He was eighteen. My first real boyfriend. He was the kindest person I'd ever known. We dated for a long time before he'd do more than kiss me. I was too young, he kept saying. I guess I was. But he wouldn't sleep with me. No matter how badly I wanted to. He wouldn't do it. But we . . . God, I don't know if you want to hear this stuff."

"I want to hear whatever you want to tell me. Whatever you need to get out of your system. Because I think you've left some pretty heavy shit locked up for a long time."

"Okay. Okay." She paused, curled her hand around his wrist and held on, needing that point of contact to ground her. "Ben was . . . he was creative at finding ways to please me without ever crossing that one line. One night he pulled out a can of whipped cream. That instant stuff you spray on. And he covered me in it. Just my breasts. And he . . . he licked it off my skin . . . God, just the way you do sometimes, Jagger. And I had my first orgasm that night. Do you understand? That one night completely sexualized food for me. And I've spent years studying fetishes, trying to figure it all out. Because I never got to explore it more with him. And I've never gone there with anyone else. Until now."

"What happened? You broke up?"

She started to tremble all over; the only thing grounding her was her head on Jagger's chest, that sensation of strong muscle, holding her together. "No. He . . . a few days later he was in an accident. He had a motorcycle. I was always reminding him to wear his helmet, but he hated the thing. Said it took away the sense of freedom that made him love his bike. So . . . he had an accident." She had to stop for a moment, to pull in a breath. She couldn't stop shaking. "And he . . . he died, Jagger."

She could see in her head her grandmother standing in the doorway of her bedroom, that look on her face. She'd known there was bad news, had sensed disaster. She'd begged her grandmother not to tell her. But of course she had. Her chest tightened, but with Jagger's arms around her, she was still able to breathe somehow.

"Jesus, Mia Rose. I'm so sorry, baby. So sorry for everything you've been through."

"The worst part of it is that it was his own fault. If only he'd worn the damn helmet. If only he'd made the right decision that day. But he didn't."

"The worst part of it is that you've lived with the loss all these years," Jagger said quietly.

"Yes. Maybe."

A bus rumbled by on the street below, drawing her eyes to the tall bank of windows. Outside, the moon cast silver across the cloudy sky. And she had that frightening sense she'd had so many times before in her life of how small she was in the universe, how insignificant. Yet, for the first time, she felt safe. Safe with Jagger: in his home, in his arms.

"I've had this weird life, Jagger. I know that. I'm very well aware of how it's damaged me. But until now, I've simply accepted that about myself. I've had to. I grew up with a drug addict for a mother. Spent years living in our car. Went hungry more times than I really want to remember. And then she abandoned me. My father abandoned me before I was even born. I understand how that screwed me up. So why do I feel the need to dig deeper suddenly? And I'm telling you, I do not want to do it. But I feel compelled. And it's because of you, I think.

"I've just realized that the main reason I haven't explored that side of myself that has to do with food and sex, that part of me which originated with Ben, is because somehow in my mind I've connected my desires with loss. That's why it's been too frightening for me to even approach it. But you've made it okay. Not just okay to try it, but to think about it. To question my motives. Because of how you make me feel. And I don't want to feel this way. I don't want to do this."

"Just stop fighting it, Mia Rose."

"I'm trying. I really am."

His arms tightened around her. "I can't ask for any more than that. Can I? I would if I could."

They were quiet for a long time, their breathing falling into sync. Eventually her body relaxed, went loose. She wove her legs through Jagger's, needing to feel the solid weight of him.

She felt self-indulgent, simply taking from him what she wanted, what she needed. It seemed wrong, somehow. And a little scary. Because whatever he gave to her could so easily be taken away.

But she didn't want to think about consequences anymore tonight. She'd done enough of that her entire life. Tonight, she wanted to simply be with him, soak up whatever comfort he offered. And pretend she didn't realize what that meant to her.

Karalee sat in Gideon's car, hyperaware of her bare legs against the cool leather seat, of her naked sex beneath her wool skirt. She had left her panties at home, which was exactly the way he liked her. She was just as aware of Gideon beside her, of his strong hands on the wheel as they pulled out of the parking lot of the Cliff House. The old restaurant had been a part of San Francisco history since the late nineteenth century. They'd had a wonderful dinner there at a window table overlooking the dark, crashing Pacific, followed by drinks while he brought her to a bone-melting climax using the cool bowl of a soup spoon under the table.

Gideon turned onto the Great Highway and followed the curving road, drove up Point Lobos Avenue, away from the ocean. She had no idea where they were going. It didn't matter. He often liked to go for a drive, pulling over so he could fuck her in his car, or on it.

"Karalee."

"Yes?"

A shiver of anticipation at hearing her name on his lips, his voice deep, sexy.

"Suck me."

She smiled, leaned over, and undid his dark slacks, pulled

his gorgeous cock out. He was half hard already, and she'd barely touched him. She bent over, inhaled the musky scent of him, flicked her tongue at the swelling head.

"No teasing. Just suck it. Hard."

"Yes, sir."

He grabbed the back of her hair, digging his fingers into her scalp. "Just do it."

She swallowed him, the length of his flesh hardening even as it slipped between her lips. She loved the taste of him, loved the way he filled her, whether it was her mouth, her sex, her ass.

She pulled him in deeper, until his cock hit the back of her throat. She took in a deep breath through her nose, silently commanded her throat to open up, then she really went to work on him. Moving her head, she slid her mouth up and down his shaft, squeezing the base of it with her fingers, using them along with her lips, her tongue, to vary the texture. And pleasure rose in her own body as he grew harder, as the muscles of his thighs tensed beneath her.

"Fuck, Karalee," Gideon muttered, pulling the car over to the curb, and she knew she had him. She melted a little all over.

Yes, there was power in allowing him to take her over in this way, to command her. To bring a man like Gideon to his knees, even for a few moments, was as thrilling as letting him fuck her in public.

"Just have to fuck you, Karalee. Just fuck your lovely mouth ... and fuck you." His fingers dug into her hair, held on. "Only you, Karalee."

Yes ...

She shivered, her sex pounding like the pulse of the

ocean. And that sense of being entirely possessed by him made it even better. Knowing that he wanted her in this way.

She needed to tell him. He was still thrusting hard into her mouth; she was still trembling with the desire coursing through her body, her sex. She pulled her lips from his cock long enough to whisper, "Gideon . . . I'm yours. Yours . . ."

"Yes. Mine . . . ah, God. I'm going to come."

She took him into her mouth again, sucked him deep into her throat. He groaned, rammed into her, his hips pumping. His fingers moved down to grip her shoulder, his short nails digging in.

Yours.

She smiled to herself. Belonging felt better than she ever could have imagined.

He let her go, pulled her up to face him, and kissed her, his mouth soft on hers. She loved his mouth when he was like this, all plush and loose from coming. There was almost a helplessness about him at these moments.

Almost.

His tongue slid between her lips, tangled with hers, and she could still taste the salt of his come heavy on her tongue. His hand went into her hair once more, pulled tight, making her gasp. Dragging her head back, he kissed her throat, small, gentle kisses. Ah yes, she loved this, this combination of brutality and tenderness. It made her want to sink to her knees, to promise this man anything.

He pulled back, his eyes glittering in the dim streetlights.

"Come with me, Karalee. Come back to my house."

Her heart stuttered in her chest.

"Are you sure?"

He was quiet a moment, looking at her. The sound of the

ocean a few blocks away was a heavy throb in her ears. The scent of it was everywhere, tangy and sharp.

"Yes. I'm sure."

She stroked his cheek, something she'd never have dared to do before. Not with him. But suddenly, everything had changed. Her stomach fluttered.

Everything had changed.

But she was ready for it. Finally.

Not the usual kind of romance, that was for sure. But the usual romance would never have worked with her. No, she'd needed someone as powerful as Gideon. Someone who was strong enough to take her over in the way he did. Sexually, yes, but there was more to it than that. Something more cerebral. More emotional.

She reached down, threaded her fingers through his. "Let's go."

It took only a few moments for Gideon to zip up, to pull back onto the road. He seemed intent on driving. And she didn't want to talk, didn't want to risk breaking this spell. She was afraid he might change his mind.

She knew what this meant for him, taking her to his home. And as he turned up Fulton Street and drove along the edge of Golden Gate Park, her stomach began to knot up. Was she ready for this? A few moments ago she'd thought so. But now . . .

She turned to look at him. His profile was so strong, even softened by the night. He glanced at her, smiled, reached over, and took her hand in his. And she knew everything would be okay.

Settling into the leather seat, her hand warmed by his, she drove with him across town. Up Fulton and around the end of the park, then down Fell Street. They passed rows of Victorians, some in a state of disrepair, some restored to their original beauty. And she thought how these houses were like people. How sometimes you were sort of left in a state of neglect, even if it was your own doing. And all it took was the right person to come along, to breathe life back into you.

Into *her.*

Her heart was racing. But she wanted to do this, to be with him.

Soon they were moving through the wide streets of the Potrero District, and Gideon made a right turn, downshifted as they climbed a hill. He pulled up in front of a three-story brown shingle.

"This is it."

He turned to her, and his face was as somber as she'd ever seen it. She smiled at him even though her stomach was a tight ball of nerves, and after a moment his features relaxed and he smiled back.

He helped her from the car, ever the gentleman, and led her up the narrow brick walkway. Tall banana plants flanked the front door, their big leaves dark and silky in the dim porch light. Gideon opened the door and led her inside.

His home was almost exactly as she'd pictured it. The room was all tall windows with wooden shutters pulled back to let in the view of the city and the San Francisco Bay below, the lights of the Bay Bridge twinkling through the fog. Dark wood floors, with a few woven rugs in rich neutral tones, bookcases flanking the fireplace. A large brown leather sofa dominated the space, and a red leather chair sat beside the hearth. But what really surprised her was the art on the walls.

Bold colors and shapes, paintings she recognized with breathless awe.

She moved to one piece, put her fingers out to touch it, then pulled back.

"This is a Miró," she breathed.

"Yes."

"And that one; it looks like Kandinsky."

Gideon nodded.

"My God, Gideon, do you know what these pieces are worth? How difficult they are to acquire? Of course you do, stupid question. I didn't know you collect."

"I didn't used to. I bought the Miró very recently."

"They're beautiful. Stark." She shook her head, trying to absorb this new bit of information about him. "I didn't expect this of you."

He moved closer, wrapped an arm around her waist.

"Why? Because I have such depraved sexual tastes?"

His hand crept up and cupped her breast, squeezed and kneaded. Her nipples came up hard beneath his probing fingers.

"Ah, Gideon, you know just how to shut me up."

He leaned in and nuzzled her neck, bit into the tender flesh there. "On the contrary. I plan to make you scream, Karalee."

She laughed, the tension in her body melting away in the heat of his touch, his mouth on her skin.

He brought his lips to hers and kissed her hard, his tongue driving into her mouth. Then it was all wet, breathless heat, the need for him building until it hurt. She pressed her body closer, felt the solid ridge of his arousal against her belly. His thigh slid between hers, and she ground her mound into him, needing relief.

His hands were everywhere: slipping beneath her shirt, tugging her skirt down over her thighs. She was soaking wet.

She pulled her mouth away. They were both panting. She whispered, "I need you to fuck me, Gideon."

"I intend to." His voice was a deep growl, heavy with lust.

He paused long enough to pull his slacks off, his shirt, then hers, leaving her in her lacy bra. His hands on her again, he backed her up until she felt the edge of the leather sofa behind her, and he tipped her back onto the pillows, going down with her, his body covering hers. Her legs wrapped around his strong back, her fingernails scratching into his skin. He groaned, pressing his cock against her aching sex.

"You are so damn wet, Karalee."

"I need you." She arched her hips, grinding her pelvis into him. "Take me to your bed, Gideon. I want you to fuck me in your bed."

His hands went lax on her as the rest of his body tensed. He sat up abruptly.

"Gideon? What . . . ?"

He sat on the edge of the sofa, rubbed his hands over his face, his hair. He said in a low, hard voice, "Christ, Karalee."

"What is it?" But she knew. Her heart was hammering so hard she could almost hear it.

He was quiet for a long time. Too long. And she felt too naked, sitting on the sofa in nothing but her bra, the leather warming beneath her bare thighs. She almost wanted to cover herself, naked and vulnerable in a way she'd never felt before.

Why didn't he say something?

Finally he said quietly, "I can't do this, Karalee."

That was it. No apology. No explanation. Just one simple statement, spoken through clenched teeth, that made her heart twist up in her chest.

"Look, I need to take you home."

He stood up and dressed, keeping his back to her. Her head felt hot and tight; her entire body felt tight, as though each muscle were tensed and pulled to the breaking point.

Breaking. Yes, that was it exactly. She was breaking.

It didn't occur to her to cry. That was something she simply never did. Not as she quietly got dressed, not when he gestured her out the door, refusing to look at her. She could not believe this was happening.

On the front step she turned to him and said, "Gideon? Can't we talk? Just sit and talk about...this. About what's happening here."

He shook his head. His face was absolutely shut down. Dark, a storm brewing behind the flatness in his eyes.

She took in a sighing breath, stood watching him for a few moments, waiting for that shift in his features that would tell her everything was okay again. But she knew it wasn't going to happen.

"Maybe I should call a cab?" she suggested.

"Don't be silly. I'll take you home."

Painful, how cold his voice was.

She nodded, followed him to his car. He opened her door, moved to help her in, but she turned away from his arm. She couldn't stand it if he touched her right now.

The ride to her place seemed to go on forever. The city was dark around them, too quiet. There was nothing to get her out of her own head. And inside it was an unbearable pressure, as though a vise were bearing down on her, crushing her skull bit by bit. She didn't quite understand what was happening to her; the sensation was so physical.

By the time they reached her neighborhood she had a pounding headache. Her whole head was hot, burning. And that tight feeling would not go away. It had spread down to her chest, like a thickness clogging her lungs, her throat. She imagined it like black tar, choking her.

Gideon pulled up in front of her house, not even into her driveway. He came around and held the door for her. Again she avoided his hand, using the car door for leverage. Once on her feet, she realized how weak her legs were, took a few deep breaths to steady herself. It didn't help.

Gideon slammed the door closed, and without another word, another look, he got back into the driver's seat, started the engine, and drove off, leaving her standing on the curb.

A wind came up, whipping the edges of her coat, her hair. She watched his taillights disappearing down the street. Kept staring even after she could no longer see his car. And it was only then the tightness expanded and broke apart.

One long sob welled up, choking her as it poured out. Horrified, she clamped a hand over her mouth, but it was too late.

Too late!

Oh, God.

She clutched her purse to her chest, trying to make herself stop, but another sob came, this one harder, a long, keening cry.

She buried her face in her hands, barely able to stay on her feet.

How had this happened? To her, of all people!

She shook her head, unbelieving still, even as pain wracked her body. Her heart.

Finally she was able to tear herself away, to stumble to her front door, to find her keys and go inside. She got as far as shutting the door behind her before her legs gave way and she crumpled in a heap on the floor, the door at her back the only thing in the entire world that felt solid.

chapter ✐ fifteen

JAGGER PULLED MIA INTO HIS APARTMENT, ONE ARM AROUND her slim waist. Getting through class tonight had been agony. Hell, it had been painful letting her out of his bed that morning so she could go to work. He'd known Monday was coming; he hadn't had any way of knowing how difficult it was going to be to let her go after their weekend together. After she'd finally opened herself to him.

He'd been thinking about her all day. Preparing for this evening. He had no idea what he would have done if she'd turned down his invitation. But he didn't need to worry about that now. She was here.

He closed the door, backed her up against it, his hands on her hips.

"Hey, beautiful."

"Hey."

She smiled, that devastating smile. So natural, something so pure about it. She wasn't the type of woman to smile unless she really meant it. No artifice with her.

He pushed up against her, just to feel the soft curves of her body against his. He was getting hard already, being this close to her, her scent as soft as her flesh. He leaned in and brushed a kiss across her mouth, those succulent red lips. Felt her go loose all over. Yeah.

"I have something special planned for you," he told her.

"What is it?"

"It's a surprise. Why don't you go take a long, hot shower while I get everything ready?" He stepped back, gently propelled her toward the bathroom.

She grabbed his hand, tugged on it. "You're not coming with me? Come on, Jagger."

Oh, that sultry, pleading tone. Almost too much to resist. "Not now. I'll come in and get you when I'm ready."

"Mysterious tonight, aren't we?"

He lifted her hand, kissed it. "Don't worry, you'll like what I have in mind. Don't come out until I come and get you."

She shrugged, her breasts rising beneath the fabric of her pristine white cotton blouse. "Okay."

She turned and moved toward the bathroom. He stayed where he was for a moment, until he was sure she'd gone in and shut the door behind her. Then he went to the kitchen.

He pulled platters from the refrigerator he'd prepared earlier in the day, jars from the cupboard, and carried several loads into the dining area. There, he set everything down on the big table, and went around the room, lighting the dozens of candles he'd arranged that afternoon.

He could barely stand to think of her naked in the

shower, the water sluicing over her pale skin. He could go in there right now, strip down, and get in the shower with her, both of them wet and slippery. He could picture how her skin looked, with the water spilling in glistening drops over her breasts, her stomach. How it clung to that narrow path of dark hair between her thighs. The steam all around them as he went down on her, tasting her . . .

Lord.

He had to get hold of himself. There would be time enough for that later. For that, and more. Right now he had to focus on his task. Tonight was for her.

Turning the lights down low, he prepared his scenario for the evening. He wanted to do this for her. Wanted to do everything for her.

Some small, mean voice in the back of his mind told him it wouldn't work on her. Not in the long run. She was too afraid, still too closed up. And he was wearing his heart on his sleeve like some high school kid crazy over a girl for the first time.

It fucking felt like the first time.

But he couldn't stay away from Mia Rose. Couldn't stand not to touch her, to be with her. And the way he felt about her . . . he had to hope the feelings that had been growing, expanding every day, meant that he could do this. That *she* could do this. That he could show her how.

Not now, not now.

No, now he needed to be in the moment, to savor what was about to happen.

A thrill ran up his spine as he began to arrange the food on the table. Oh yeah, she was going to love this. She'd go right out of her head. And he would love it, too. Love watching her pleasure. He'd always been aware of a woman's pleasure, but never more so than with her. It was almost all that mattered to him lately.

He stopped what he was doing, glanced toward the bathroom, heard the muted sound of the shower running. Yeah, he had it bad.

He loved the girl.

It was a physical sensation, loving her. Like a warm wave, washing over his body, only it came from the inside. And suddenly, he knew he had to tell her. Maybe not at this moment. Maybe not tonight. But soon.

He went to the sideboard and poured himself a glass of Cabernet, took a sip. He had no idea how she would take it. She wasn't the usual woman. Not the kind to let herself really fall for a guy. He understood that. But he knew she felt something for him. How far those feelings went remained to be seen. He could be patient. Mia Rose Curry was a woman worth waiting for. She was worth everything, anything.

Anything.

If only she would have him, really have him. He knew she had history, that she'd been through some pretty rough shit. He understood why she kept that emotional side of herself locked down so tight. But he'd had a few glimpses, and that side of her, that history, that pain, was every bit as beautiful to him as the rest of her.

Don't do it. Don't go there. Not again.

Yeah, that ugly voice in the back of his mind would have to be silenced. Because he was goddamned sick and tired of buckling under to his past, allowing that to dictate how he felt about women, relationships, about emotional connections. He'd had it with that whole thing: being the victim, licking his wounds. Hell, the wounds were gone, healed. The rest was just leftover crap. He didn't need it anymore. All he wanted was *her*. And if she let him love her for a while before she took off and left him in the dust, so be it.

He moved toward the bathroom, his glass of wine in his hand, sipping as he went. When he opened the door, steam came wafting out, carrying the scent of soap, the damp heat of the shower he loved so much. He set the glass down on the counter and said, "Mia Rose. It's time."

He'd dried her with tender care, wrapped her in his own white terry robe, given her some wine to drink, then led her from the womblike heat and steam of the bathroom. His hand was warm on hers.

There was something lovely about the anticipation, about wondering what he was up to, what he was going to do with her.

"Where are we going, Jagger?"

"Shh. You'll see."

He smiled at her, took the wine out of her hand, drew her toward the dining room.

Her breath caught. There were candles everywhere, tall candelabra standing on the wood floors, pillar candles covering the surface of the sideboard, the wine cabinet. But it was the sight of the dining table that made her dizzy. Absolutely breathless.

He'd laid the table out like a giant platter. In the center was what appeared to be foil. All around the edges fruit was piled artfully: pineapple, strawberries, sliced melon, with smaller berries scattered here and there. Chocolate sauce was drizzled in decorative swirls over the fruit, dark brown and white. At the very outer edges were tiny pyramids of truffles. And here and there, among the fruit and the candy, were flowers: pansies, nasturtiums, lovely edible blossoms.

"Oh, God, Jagger..." But she couldn't catch enough breath to say more. She was going weak all over, damp and aching and *needing*.

She could not believe he'd done this. And she knew exactly what he was going to do next. She was shaking just thinking about what was to come.

Jagger pulled the robe from her shoulders, let it fall to the floor, leaving her naked.

"I...I don't know if I can do this," she said, but it came out as a whisper.

"Sure you can."

She shook her head. "Do you know what it's like to have your darkest, deepest dreams come true?"

"A little overwhelming, I imagine."

She looked up at him, at his beautiful face, at his gentle eyes. She nodded, her throat dry.

"Come on, you can do this, Mia Rose," he said quietly. "You know you want to."

She swallowed hard, lust and emotion running through her body, making it burn, making it thrum. "More than anything."

He took her arm then, helped her onto a chair, then to step onto the table, over the piled fruit, the chocolate.

"Lie down, baby."

"God, Jagger."

He was still holding on to her hand. He lifted it to his lips, kissed it softly. "It's okay. I'm here. It'll be good, so good."

It was good already. She went down on her knees,

uncurled, and lay on her back. The foil was cool against her skin, the table hard beneath her. But it all added to what was happening somehow. The scent of the fruit, of the candy, was filling her senses, making her even dizzier. And she was as wet as she'd ever been in her life, trembling with desire so strong she could barely think.

"Just let it go," Jagger told her. "I'll do it all. Give yourself over to me, Mia Rose."

Yes, it was happening already. That inevitable letting go, that loosening inside herself, the one thing in her life she was completely unable to control with Jagger.

Let it happen.

Not that she had any choice. Her body was speaking for her, and every word was *yes*.

She watched as Jagger pulled his shirt off, loved the sight of his lean torso, his glorious brown skin, his strong chest, the dark tribal bands tattooed around his arms. Loved that it was *this* man who was doing these things with her, taking her into the heart of her fantasies.

He leaned over her, brushed a kiss across her lips. She shivered, the heat of his mouth running like a cord to her breasts, her sex. Then his hands were on her, smoothing over the skin of her belly, her thighs. Oh yes, too good, his hands on her, while she lay there like some sort of perverted buffet.

Perverted, yes, but lovely. Fucking exquisite, this feeling of being laid out, helpless, surrounded by the objects of her obsession.

Jagger lifted a glass jar, and she smelled the earthy scent of honey even before he began to ladle it onto her skin. It was warm as he drizzled it over her body: her shoulders first, then he turned her palms upward and let the thick amber liquid drip onto that sensitive flesh on her inner arms, into the palms themselves. An incredible sensation; she couldn't believe how erotic it was, that warm liquid in her hands.

By the time he got to her breasts she was aching with desire, her sex plump and needy. They'd barely started and already she didn't know how much more she could take.

"Jagger . . ."

"Yeah, it's good, baby, isn't it?" he murmured.

He was so intent on what he was doing, taking a large ramekin of warm chocolate sauce and spilling it onto her stomach, her thighs. Then using his hands to part her legs. When the fragrant liquid hit her cleft she cried out, her hips arching. The scent of honey and chocolate was everywhere.

"God, Jagger, touch me."

He smiled, swiped one finger over her chocolate-covered slit.

"Ah!"

But that was all she got before he moved on, drizzling the chocolate over her calves, her feet.

"Caramel is next, baby girl."

Another ramekin of warm, sticky liquid, the sharp scent of burned sugar in the air. Lovely. The caramel felt like pure sex on her skin, the sensation of it sensual in itself, sexual. She was burning with desire, her nipples hard and aching, her sex swollen and hot. She could barely hold still.

"Jagger, please. Please . . ."

"I have one last thing for you, Mia Rose."

He lifted a can of whipped cream, and she nearly lost her mind.

"Yes . . . Ah, God."

He sprayed a small amount onto his fingers, put them to

her lips. And she opened right up for him, licked them off, sucked on them. So damned sweet, but more than that. Her body remembered all too well. Heat lashed through her, and she was shaking all over, panting.

Jagger leaned over her. "Do you know how beautiful you are right now? Your eyes are enormous. Dark. So full of wanting. And your mouth...Lord, I can barely stand to look at your mouth. I'm so hard for you, baby. But this is all for you. That's what gets me off."

He sprayed more of the whipped cream onto his fingers, let her suck them once more. And she trembled as she did it, with desire, with the need to please him, with the need to feel him in her body somehow.

He drew his hand back and said very quietly, "And now we begin."

She drew in a sharp breath, her heart thundering in her chest. Those words meant so much more than this one experience, in a way she couldn't figure out. Her mind was going blank, her body melting into that sea of scents and flavors as yet untasted.

Soon.

Now.

He bent over her, his dark eyes gleaming in the shifting candlelight. He stopped a few inches from her face, whispered, "This is going to be every single thing you've ever wanted, Mia Rose."

A long tremor ran through her. Then his lips were on hers, and she could taste the faint flavor of the whipped cream again. But his tongue in her mouth was even sweeter. Just *him.* Jagger.

He pulled away, reached out with one finger, and drew it

in an achingly slow line down the center of her body, smearing the chocolate, the honey, the caramel, until it all mixed together on her flesh. Leaning over her stomach, his tongue darted out, licking at the sticky sweetness. Desire surged, hot and strong. And as he dragged his tongue down her body, lower and lower, that heat built, flooding her breasts, her sex. She moaned, squirmed.

He used his hands to spread her thighs a bit wider, moved lower, so slowly. Pure torture. But she never wanted it to end. She could not believe this was happening.

He was still holding her thighs apart, and she waited as his tongue moved lower, as he licked at her skin, rubbed his plush lips over her belly. But he didn't do more than hold her thighs in his strong hands, so that she felt open, vulnerable, chocolate dripping down her aching cleft.

"Jagger..."

He lifted his head, smiled at her. Those beautiful white teeth. A bit of chocolate sauce at one corner of his mouth. She wanted to lick it off.

He held the can of whipped cream over her once more, and her sex clenched. Then he sprayed it in delicious coils onto her hardened nipples.

"This is what you want, isn't it, Mia Rose? Just this one thing, more than anything."

"Yes," she breathed.

He touched one snowy mound with a fingertip, brought it to her mouth. And once more she took it between her lips, the sweet creaminess working on her like some kind of wild aphrodisiac.

When he leaned in and drew one cream-covered nipple into his mouth, she groaned, the sensation going through her like a sensual shock. But she never let his finger slide from her mouth; she pulled it in deeper.

His tongue swirled over her nipple, and he sucked harder. Her sex was thrumming with need, hot and aching to be filled. He moved to the other breast, drew her nipple into his mouth, and sensation shot through her, a lightning bolt of pleasure.

His finger slipped from her mouth. "Ah, Jagger! Please . . . God, I can't wait!"

And as he sucked harder, the sweet scent of the whipped cream surrounding her, her head and her body filled with the memory of what this felt like, what this meant to her. She came, exploding, crying out. Pleasure hammered through her veins, hot and sharp. So damn sharp she was yelling now, nearly sobbing, her body convulsing. Pure ecstasy.

She was still shivering with her climax when he pulled away, stood watching her face. She didn't care how she looked at this moment. She didn't care about anything but what was happening to her.

"So beautiful when you come, Mia Rose. This is only the first time tonight. I'm going to make you come over and over. I want to see it, to feel your body tremble. To taste you as you come onto my tongue."

"Ah, God . . ."

He moved down then, ran his tongue in a long line up one thigh, making her squirm. And even though she had climaxed only moments before, she was nearly ready to come again the moment he lapped at her chocolate-covered cleft.

God, it was too good, too much! She arched her hips as pleasure drove into her with every flick of his tongue. The scent of chocolate was strong in her nostrils, sweet and sharp all at the same time. And his lovely, lapping mouth. So good. Then he used his fingers to really open her up, and his wet tongue dove inside, that velvet softness licking at her flesh, making her crazy with need.

She was panting, breathless, another climax building, bit by fiery bit. When he latched on to her clit, it seemed to swell right into his mouth, against his soft tongue.

"Jagger! Please... don't stop. I... I need you. Please... please..."

Some part of her knew she was incoherent. Didn't matter. All that mattered was his wet, sucking mouth on her, his fingers sliding over the stickiness on her skin, that scent of heat and sugar.

Very quickly the tension in her body built, pure ecstasy centered in her core, spreading outward, until she was humming all over with it. And Jagger kept on, sucking, licking, using his fingers now to massage the lips of her sex. To dip inside. Pleasure drove into her, searing her with its heat, arrowing deep down. And she came once more, shattering, her system turning to molten liquid. She was nothing more than sensation, one long, trembling surge of pleasure after another.

"Oh... oh... Yes!"

She was bucking into his mouth, her muscles clenching so damn hard. Tears slid down her cheeks. Tears of joy. Tears of pain for what she'd missed all these years.

When it was over Jagger lifted his head, wiped his face on the back of one arm. When he kissed her she could taste it all: the whipped cream, the chocolate and caramel, and the sharp tang of honey mixed with her own ocean flavor, salty and so sweet.

She was melting, shivering, small frissons of pleasure still shooting through her body.

"Yeah. Fast and furious, baby," Jagger said to her, his voice quiet. "You needed it. Now we can take our time. Now we can really play."

He wiped a finger over her skin, swept it over his own lips, and kissed her. Soft kisses, full of sugar. He pulled back, stood looking at her. She couldn't think straight. She only wanted him to touch her again.

Her mind felt far away, and yet she was as tuned in to her body as she'd ever been in her life. Her limbs were heavy against the wooden table, as though she were grounded there, an organic part of it.

Jagger undressed himself, moving slowly. When he stepped forward and she caught sight of his cock, brown and hard and beautiful, her mouth literally watered.

"I need to touch you," she told him, her voice quavering.

He pulled a chair over, stepped onto it, then onto the table, and knelt over her body. He picked up a ramekin, poured it over his cock. Some of the still-warm liquid dripped onto her stomach. She drew in a deep breath, taking in the sharp, earthy concoction of caramelized sugar, the scent of fruit, the scent of desire.

Jagger picked up a strawberry, ran it over the tip of his caramel-covered cock, and she heard his own sharp indrawn breath, saw his cock pulse. He lifted the berry to her lips, and she opened for him, let him slide the fruit inside. She sucked the caramel off, then bit into it.

"Yeah, that's it, baby."

Shifting, he raised his hips over her, and she lifted her head a little to take his swollen shaft into her mouth.

Inch by sweet inch, she swallowed him. And as she did, she felt almost as though his cock were pushing into her sex. She was wet, clenching, pulsing with pleasure once more, just from the sensation of his flesh in her mouth, the taste of the caramel on his skin. He snaked a hand behind her head, holding her fast to his pumping cock. He was hitting the back of her throat; her eyes were watering. But she wanted all of him, as much as she could get. And the harder he thrust, the harder her sex pulsed, thrummed with need, building and building.

"Ah, Mia Rose, you're too good, baby. I have to stop."

Jagger pulled out of her mouth, leaving her empty.

"Jagger, no . . ."

He smiled, bent down, and kissed her. "We have all night. And I have promises to keep."

He covered her body with his then, the chocolate and caramel and honey making their bodies slide, as though they were beings made entirely of liquid, getting warmer as he moved. He slipped lower, ran his fingers over her belly, her breasts.

He picked up a slice of fresh mango, put it to her lips, and told her, "Just suck on it, Mia Rose, don't bite into it."

She did as he asked, too mindless to do anything else. She opened her lips, and he slipped the fruit in. It was cool and lovely on her tongue before he pulled it out. He did it again, and it was almost like a small cock sliding in and out of her mouth. The sensation, the idea of it, sent shivers racing through her body. Her nipples, her clitoris, were so hard, painful with need. But she concentrated on the fruit sliding in and out of her mouth, sweet and fresh. Like fucking. Like love.

Jagger pulled the fruit from her mouth, bent over her, and kissed her lips.

"So sweet, my Mia Rose," he murmured. He sat back, and she watched his face, saw how his features were loose with desire, his lush lips swollen as he rubbed the mango over them, sucked it into his mouth for a moment.

Using one hand, he reached down and held the lips of her sex open. Then he slid the mango over her aching cleft.

"Oh!"

"It's good, isn't it? I knew you'd like it."

He ran the plump slice of mango over her slit, then, dipping lower, pushed the tip of it right into her.

"Ah, God, Jagger!"

He pulled it out, dipped inside her again, and she was panting, aching, crying once more. And when he slipped the mango out of her, put it to his lips, and ate it, she nearly lost her mind.

He bent over her, rubbing his cock over her sticky belly. And she loved it, loved the way he pushed his hard shaft against her stomach: the slip and slide of flesh against flesh. He moved up, held her breasts together with his hands, and slid his cock in between. And as he pumped between her breasts, he used his thumbs to tease her nipples. Her hips arched up off the table, her sex too empty, wanting, yearning.

"Jagger, I need you inside me. Now. Please," she gasped.

"I need you, too, baby."

He pulled her legs up and apart, until her knees were bent, tight against her shoulders. She was so completely open to him as he knelt between her thighs. There was one brief moment when she was dimly aware of Jagger pulling a condom packet from somewhere on the table, rolling it over his cock. And then he was pushing into her, all the way to the hilt in one long, lovely stroke.

She reached up and held on to his strong shoulders, his skin sticky and slippery all at the same time. All around them was the scent of warm sugar as he drove into her. Long, sweeping strokes of his hips, each one more devastating than the last. And he kept his eyes locked on hers, his expression of pleasure driving into her as deeply as his cock.

Desire swarmed her, taking her higher, and soon she was at that lovely peak once more. Jagger's gray eyes glittered, dark and deep, bottomless. And as he tensed over her, her climax took over her body, drowning her in pleasure, in him.

Surge after surge, like heat, like liquid fire, like sugar melting in her veins. And something inside her broke open, broke apart in a warm rush. She felt it, that opening up. And it was scary for one brief moment before she let the fear go, too.

Jagger's hand was on the back of her neck, his fingers burrowing in her hair as he shivered and groaned. And he kept his gaze locked on hers, so that she saw everything in his eyes. Beautiful. Powerful.

Their bodies were still writhing, sweet flesh sticking together. And there was a new ache in her body, in her chest. She wanted to cry. And yet she'd never felt happier in her life.

"Jagger . . . what is this?"

His gaze still held hers. He lifted her head closer, bent and brushed his shivering lips across hers.

"It's love, Mia Rose. It's love."

chapter ✑ sixteen

MIA BIT DOWN HARD ON THE WAVE OF PANIC RIPPLING OVER her skin like an icy chill.

Love.

God, but hadn't that very idea run through her mind only a few minutes earlier? So naturally she hadn't even questioned it. How could she be so damn scared she was shaking, even as she lay beneath Jagger's warm body? On the table where he had staged her deepest fantasy. He had done this for *her*. No man had ever done anything of this magnitude for her. She'd never even dreamed anyone would. But Jagger was different from anyone she'd ever met.

She was different, with him.

Fear lay like a hard lump in her throat. She couldn't speak. And her head was still spinning, her body buzzing with pleasure.

Jagger was kissing her, tiny kisses over her cheeks, her chin, her closed eyelids. She couldn't bear to look at him now, not into those beautiful gray eyes. She knew she couldn't handle it. Knew she would see too much there. Knew if she opened her eyes and looked into his at this moment, she would fall totally and irrevocably in love with him.

She squeezed her eyes tight. But his lips, so soft against her skin, seemed to be working their way beneath it. His warmth was spreading right into her, into her body, her mind, her heart.

No, no, no!

But when he kissed her lips, so tenderly it made the tears spill over her cheeks, a small torrent of emotion she had absolutely no control over, she knew it was too late.

"God, Jagger," she whispered in awe, unable to control what she was saying any more than she could what she was feeling. "I'm in love with you."

His lips were so close to hers, she could feel his breath warm and fragrant on her face. She opened her eyes and looked at him finally, through the blur of hot tears.

"Baby, don't cry. It's alright. I love you, Mia Rose."

He held her face between his hands, and that touch alone was sweeter than anything she'd felt in her life. That touch, the expression on his beautiful face, the tone of his voice, warm and heavy with love.

She'd never been so scared in her life.

"I...I can't believe this is happening." Was that her voice? So choked, so unsure?

"It's all good, baby." Jagger stroked her cheek with his thumb.

She shook her head. But she let him help her to sit up, to

lead her to the shower, where they stood under the water, quiet together. She leaned her head on his chest, let him wash her. So gently, so tenderly. Then he dried her with a thick, white towel, wrapped her in one of his pajama tops, slipped the bottoms over his own slim hips. Then he took her to his bed, lay down next to her, his arms around her.

She tried to relax, but she couldn't do it. Her mind was whirling.

When he slipped his hand up and cupped her breast, her body responded to his touch as it always did: that immediate fire in her blood, burning through her like some long-lost yearning she'd never been aware of until she met him. But she resisted now, rolled away from his touch.

"Mia Rose, what is it? What's wrong?"

"I don't know how to explain it. I'm just...so damn scared. God, I can't do this. I can't."

"Is it the age thing? The student-teacher thing? I'll quit the class. I can take a summer course. I've been thinking about it all weekend."

"No, you can't do that. This is the last class you need to graduate. You can't screw that up because of me."

"It wouldn't be because of you. It would be because of me. Because I love you, baby. And I'll do whatever I need to so we can be together. I can't pretend it's not happening anymore. Not now. Everything has changed."

He was right. Everything had changed. But she didn't know if she could deal with what was happening between them. It was all so much simpler when they were nothing more than two people who were attracted to each other, exploring a sexual fantasy together. But it had been a while since the dynamic between them was that easy, that basic.

Still, she didn't like that he'd make such a foolish choice about his future. Not when it was based on their relationship, a relationship she wasn't even certain she could handle.

"I think that's a bad idea, Jagger."

"I can still start at Berkeley in the fall."

"That's not the point."

He was quiet a moment, then he turned her body toward him, looked into her eyes.

"What is it, then? What are you saying?"

She bit down on her lip, willing that pain to take away the sharp ache in her chest. "I'm . . . I'm saying that maybe I don't know how to do this. And that I think it's foolish for you to make a choice right now that can influence your future. I don't think you're being entirely rational."

"There's nothing rational about love, Mia Rose."

"Please don't make a joke of this!"

"I'm not. Do you have any idea how real this is for me? Because I'm taking a hell of a chance here, with you. It's like I'm slicing a part of myself open, leaving myself raw. But I have to do it. I've been so damn hurt before. I was never going to chance this again. But I can't not love you. Even if it tears me apart all over again."

"That makes it even worse!" Her heart was hammering, her whole body hurt.

"Worse?" He lifted himself up so he was braced on one elbow, looking down at her. He ran a hand through his hair. "What's so bad about loving each other?"

But she saw something flash in his eyes. He was feeling it, too. That uncertainty.

She said quietly, "I think you have some idea of what the problem is, Jagger. I'm . . . I'm deficient when it comes to

relationships. I don't really let anyone in. Oh, I've been trying. With Karalee. With you. But it's not nearly good
enough. And you have your issues, too, obviously. Old baggage. And I'm exactly the sort of woman who could hurt you
in the worst way possible. Because I don't . . . I don't really
know how to love. Not anymore."

"I thought I didn't, either. And then I met you. I had to
ask myself if all that shit was just a cop-out. And you know
what? It is. I'm coming to understand that on some level I
thought my past relationships falling apart was my fault.
Maybe it was. Who knows? I'm beyond wasting time dissect-
ing it now. Now I think I can do it right, with you. Don't let
your fears mess it up, Mia Rose."

Her face went hot with anger. "I'm not the only one who's
afraid."

"No. But you're the only one who's willing to walk away."

"I can't talk about this now."

"You can't just pretend you don't love me."

She shook her head, tears welling in her eyes once more.
"No. But I can take some time to decide what to do
about it."

"Fuck." He flopped onto his back on the bed, leaving a
cold distance between them.

"I think I should go home."

He was quiet for a long time. She watched him, his jaw
working as he squeezed his eyes shut for a moment, rubbed a
hand over them. "Yeah. Okay. Maybe you should."

The knot in her stomach pulled tight; it seemed to weigh
a thousand pounds. A thousand pounds of pain. But she
didn't know what else to do. She had to think, to figure out
what loving this man might mean for her, for him.

"Jagger . . ." She put a hand out, touched his arm, felt him flinch. She dropped her hand, a new surge of pain stabbing into her belly. "Okay. Okay. I just wanted to say . . . this doesn't mean . . . this doesn't mean I don't want to be with you. I just don't know. I don't know what it means."

He turned to look at her. His eyes were dark, full of emotion. She felt like a complete bitch for doing this to him.

"Let me know when you figure it out."

There was anger in his voice. She didn't blame him.

The wood floor was cold beneath her bare feet as, slipping out of bed she found her clothes and got dressed in the dim neon light filtering through the windows. Picking up her purse, she paused, thought of going back to where Jagger lay quietly in the big, soft bed, but she had no idea what she should say to him. She supposed she'd already said everything she needed to for tonight. Too much, probably. Instead, she opened the heavy door and slipped out of the apartment, feeling as though she were stealing away. She felt like a coward. But she had to go.

By the time she got into her car, the tears were coming hot and fast. She had to keep blinking them away so she could see to drive, the city lights like watercolors bleeding into the night outside the windows. Her mind was spinning, her body strung tight with nerves, with adrenaline.

She could not believe she was in love with him.

She could not believe she loved him, and had left him behind.

The city seemed all too quiet as she drove over the hills, her heart pounding in her ears the only sound she heard; that and her own gasping breath as she struggled to hold the anguish inside.

More tears came, until she had to give up and pull over, yanking a little too hard on the parking brake, hurting her hand. She didn't know where she was, exactly. She didn't care.

You have lost your mind.

No, you've lost your heart.

Damn it!

The tight, heavy ball in her chest expanded, filled her so completely she couldn't breathe. Her head was spinning, so full of information, emotion, she was blinded, deafened, by it all.

She bent over the steering wheel, curling as much into a ball as she could manage in the cramped car seat. She was shaking. The tears still fell silently. The enormous sob that had been building in her throat since the moment Jagger told her he loved her was like some solid thing. She almost expected to see it swell, to rise from her body, to choke her. To kill her.

How could she survive feeling like this? So fucking awful. It hurt too much.

The sob welled up, and for several seconds she truly could not breathe. A ragged heat built in her chest, scalded her, made her head feel as though it were being crushed. And then the sob broke out, like shards of glass coming out of her throat. And she was making noises like some injured animal, a long, raspy keening that seemed to go on forever. She was horrified. In pain. So much pain. Her body ached, screamed with it. And she was shaking so damn hard her teeth were chattering.

Images of Ben, her mother, her grandmother, flashed through her mind, a series of incoherent ideas and memories. And she saw Jagger's face there, too.

"Oh, God . . ." It came out in a choked whisper. "I've lost him already."

◈

Karalee groaned as she sat up. She'd fallen asleep on the sofa at some point. Now she was stiff and cold. Pulling a throw blanket from the arm of the couch, she slid it around her shoulders. It must be early; it was still half dark. As her mind cleared, she remembered what she was doing there, everything that had happened the night before.

She took in a deep breath, the cool morning air calming her. Rising on stiff legs, she went to look out the living room window. She didn't know what she was looking for. She just needed to move.

It was a classic foggy San Francisco morning outside. She'd always loved the fog in some strange way. It was one reason why she'd moved to this neighborhood, so close to the ocean. But this morning she'd never seen anything more bleak.

She knew it was because of how she felt inside. Because of how Gideon had made her feel. *Made* her feel. She'd allowed it to happen, yes, but he had been the one to bring her to this bleak place.

Suddenly the grief was overshadowed by anger, burning bright, burning through the morning fog, through the hurt.

How dare he do this to her? Lead her on, let her see his emotions finally, admit his pain, his secrets, then dump her?

How dare he make her feel something for him? How dare he make her open her heart, then walk all over it?

She tossed the blanket to the floor. She was not having this; oh no. She was going back to Gideon's house and giving him the reaming he so richly deserved. No man played with her emotions this way. She'd spent a lifetime happily avoiding it. Look what had happened when she'd finally let someone in!

She stalked down the hallway to her bedroom, quickly changed out of her skirt and into a pair of jeans and a sweater. Gideon loved her in a skirt. But she wasn't dressing for him this time.

Grabbing her keys, she flung the front door back, stalked to her car, and drove across town through the quiet, gray morning.

Gideon's neighborhood was even more quiet. But she really didn't notice anything around her; she was too focused on reaching his front door. She lifted her hand and gave it a hard rap, the anger still burning through her.

He pulled the door open, looking rumpled and half asleep, and still dressed in his clothes from the night before.

"Christ, Karalee. What are you doing here?"

"I had to talk to you."

"I want to talk to you, too." His voice was rough. Sexy.

Fuck.

She was not going to notice that.

"You had your say last night. Or rather, you didn't fucking say anything. Except good-bye, in the most abbreviated way."

"I know." He rubbed a hand over his unshaven jaw. "Here, come inside."

The anger was still trying to boil as she brushed past him. But beneath it was an enormous surge of wanting she couldn't deny. When he turned to look at her she took a step back, forcing her hands to stay still at her sides when all she wanted was to touch him.

"Okay."

Gideon moved past her and went to stand by the bank of windows in the living room, started to pace. She didn't step away from the entryway by the door.

He paused in his pacing. "Karalee, will you sit down?" Then, when she refused to move, "Please?"

She crossed her arms, shook her head, but she went to sit on the brown leather couch.

"Okay, Gideon. Talk. Say whatever it is you wanted to say." The anger was draining away, no matter how hard she tried to hang on to it.

He ran a hand over his jaw once more, and she saw the stubble there, how tired he looked. His eyes were red, his features soft. He was pacing again, his bare feet scuffing over the wood floor. She hated that seeing him like this made her melt a little inside. She bit down on her lip, trying to brace herself against the emotions flooding through her.

Finally he stopped and looked right at her.

"I'm sorry, Karalee."

"That's a good start. Tell me what you're sorry for."

"For hurting you."

Lord, too much emotion in his voice, too much sincerity. She couldn't stand it. Her fingers twisted together in her lap. "Go on."

"You have to understand, Karalee. Last night was the first time I've had a woman in my house since . . . since my wife died."

"I do understand that. But I assumed you bringing me

here meant you were ready for . . . for more. With me." She pushed her hair away from her face, blew out a short breath. "Don't make me be the one to say it, Gideon."

He looked at her, his dark eyes glittering in the way they often did. But this time it wasn't about sex at all.

He took two long strides, and then he was standing right before her. "I thought I was ready. I thought I'd put it all behind me. But the thing is, Karalee, you can't lose someone like that and ever really get over it. Not entirely. It'll always be a part of me, that loss. You'll have to accept that about me. And to do that, you'll have to be willing to let me in. I don't know if you are."

She wrapped her arms around her body, held on tight. "I know you've done this once and lost. I've never done this . . . this relationship thing. I'm fucking floundering here. I don't know what I'm doing. We both know this is not a natural state of events for me. You'll have to accept that about me, Gideon, that this . . . that what I'm feeling for you goes beyond my basic belief system. I *want* to let you in. But I don't have any idea what I'm capable of and what I'm not."

"Any relationship is about taking a risk."

"Is that what this is, a relationship?"

"Isn't it? Would we be here now if it weren't?"

"You tell me, Gideon. I need you to tell me what this is." She was shivering all over. "I need you to say the words."

He nodded, stepped closer, and pulled her to her feet, so that they were eye-to-eye.

His hands on her were warm, even through her sweater. She could smell him now, that night-dark scent that was all him.

"Karalee." His voice was rough, as dark as his scent. Every bit as intoxicating. "I'm falling in love with you."

The warmth from his hands spread as his words sank in, as she accepted the truth of them. She nodded her head, her throat tight.

"Do you love me, Karalee?"

She nodded. "Yes. I love you."

How alien those words felt, coming from her mouth. *Hers!* But it was the truth. And she couldn't deny it anymore, no matter how jaded she liked to think she was.

His eyes roved over her face, and then his hands. And he moved in and kissed her, a kiss rough with emotion. It couldn't be any other way for them. His tongue slipped between her lips, as demanding as ever. Her arms slid around his neck, held on tight.

She wanted to cry. But she was done crying.

When they broke apart she asked him, "What happens now?"

"Now we figure it out. Take each day as it comes. Learn to love each other. Flounder our way through."

She nodded her head once more. "I need it to be that simple."

"Yes. So do I."

He was watching her again, trying to see through her with those deep brown eyes of his. He was so damn beautiful to her. In every way, even that darkest part of him. And she was heating up all over just looking at him, his hands on her face. She reached up and grabbed them both, slid them down over her shoulders, her breasts.

"Make love to me, Gideon."

He didn't say a word as he undressed her. And when she stood naked, he took his own clothes off, picked her up, and carried her up the stairs to his bed.

He laid her down on the soft suede duvet, covered her body with his. She blinked up at the skylights in the vaulted ceiling overhead. Beautiful. And she took a moment to simply breathe him in, to revel in the weight of him.

Safe.

Yes, as safe as she'd ever felt. There were still issues to be worked out. Hers. His. But she'd never felt anything so right, just being with him. And for the first time, she needed this. Needed someone. Needed *him.*

He began to kiss his way down her body; his breath, his lips, warm on her skin. She couldn't get enough of him, the soft feel of his mouth on her. His mouth, his hands, all of him. She wanted it all.

Desperate suddenly, she pulled him closer, spread her thighs, and reached down to guide his cock into her wet and waiting sex.

"I need you inside me, Gideon."

"Yes . . ."

"No, you don't understand. I *need* you . . ."

He paused, looked hard into her eyes. His voice was rough. "I understand exactly what you mean, Karalee. I understand."

He angled his hips, slipped inside, an inch at a time. Pleasure washed over her like a warm wave. And the weight of his body was like the soft, quiet weight of water on hers.

When he was deep inside her he held still for a moment, raised himself on his elbows, and gazed into her eyes once more. And she felt a rush of exquisite emotion that left her breathless.

No man had ever looked into her eyes this way while making love to her.

No man had ever truly made love to her before.

So this is what it's like.

Need.

Lovely. So good it almost hurt, to feel so much, to have him deep in her body, melded together in some inexplicable way. In some way which was not explainable by the mere physical act. She couldn't wrap her mind around it. And so she let it go, while Gideon kissed her lips, slid in and out of her body, touched her all over. And pleasure became some warm current she floated on, that they floated on together.

His panting breath matched hers as the intensity built low in her belly, as his sliding cock pushed the sensation deeper and deeper. And his lips on hers, his wet tongue in her mouth, felt so damn good, as though his mouth were somehow between her thighs even as his cock was. Sensation spread, crested, and she began to shake. Her body poised on that lovely edge, and she held it there, loath to let it go just yet.

"Gideon . . . Gideon . . ."

She twisted her fingers into his short hair, inhaled the scent of him, filling her lungs with him.

Their legs were a tangle of muscle and skin; desire a coil running through her body, into his and back again. Pulsing, aching. And he kept his gaze on hers, dark and powerful, reaching inside her.

He drove into her, her arms and legs locked around his

body. And when she came, it was in a long undulating current. Like a river. Like clouds thundering down on the earth. Pleasure so exquisite, so intense, her mind went entirely blank. And all she saw were his dark eyes, the beauty of his mouth as he came inside her, calling out her name.

She understood now that she'd wanted this all her life; she'd simply never dared to hope it could ever be real, had rejected the idea as mere fantasy. Now that she'd known this state of love, there was no turning back. And for once, she didn't want to.

chapter ✿ seventeen

MIA PULLED THE HEAVY DOWN QUILT OVER HER SHIVERING body, burrowing deeper into her pillow. It was damp with her tears. Had she slept at all?

She glanced at the clock on her nightstand. It was five in the afternoon already. After her long night, she'd called the school and canceled her office hours. Then she'd crawled into bed, her body aching, and had tried to sleep. But she wasn't certain her mind had ever really stopped turning, spinning, grieving.

She couldn't seem to get warm, even beneath the layers of flannel sheets, blankets, the big quilt. Maybe a hot shower, a cup of tea, would help?

Nothing is going to help.

But she got out of bed anyway, slipping into her thick velour robe, padded in her slippers over the wood floors and into the kitchen. She went through the motions of filling the kettle, setting it on the stove, finding a cup, the box of tea, like a blind woman. She wasn't seeing anything, wasn't able to think or feel anything but the pain that still racked her body, flooded her mind, her heart.

Yet despite the need to bury herself behind a wall, to hide away from any sense of vulnerability, she wanted— needed—to talk to someone. To talk to a friend, a confidante.

She fought it off while the water boiled and the kettle whistled, the sound like some lonely keening in her quiet kitchen. Pouring a spoonful of honey into her tea, she let it steep for a moment before grabbing the phone from the counter and taking it with her to the kitchen table.

Looking out the window, she tried to focus on her grandmother's roses, but the afternoon was too gray outside. She couldn't stand to think of her grandmother right now. She looked away, dialed the phone.

"Hello?"

"Karalee, it's Mia."

"Mia, you sound awful. Are you sick?"

"No, not sick. I'm . . . I'm not so good, Karalee. I'm . . . God, I can't even talk. Can you come over to my place? Please?"

"Of course. I'll be there as soon as I can. Um, I need your address. I've never been to your house before."

"Oh, of course. I'm at 1135 Sloat. Right across from Stern Grove, up the street from the zoo."

"I'll find it. Just hang on."

"Okay. Okay."

She hung up the phone, numb all over. Sipping her tea, she waited, trying not to count the minutes until Karalee would arrive. Now that she'd admitted to herself the need to talk to someone, that need was overwhelming.

Time seemed to stretch out, so that she had absolutely no sense of how long it was before Karalee knocked at her door. She opened it, and felt an enormous sense of relief at seeing her friend standing there.

Her *friend*.

"Jesus, Mia." Karalee pushed her way in, taking Mia by the arm and shutting the door behind her. "You need to sit down."

She led her into the kitchen, seeming to know somehow that it was Mia's favorite room, a place of comfort.

They sat at her little kitchen table, and Mia wrapped her fingers around her now-empty tea mug.

"So," Karalee said. "What's going on? Talk to me."

Mia shook her head, staring at the mug in her hands. "I don't know where to start. I'm . . . I'm so glad to see you—" She broke off, a sob welling in her throat. "I'm no good at this stuff, Karalee. I don't know how to do any of this."

"It's okay." Karalee laid a hand on her arm. "It's Jagger, isn't it?"

Mia nodded her head. She could barely stand to see the sympathy in Karalee's eyes. "I fucked up. I was . . . too scared. And I ran away. And I'm still too scared to go back. I can't do it."

"Why not?"

"You know my father left when I was a baby. I never even knew him. Do you know what that's like? To be completely devoid of any memory of the person who created you? It's like this empty place inside that will never, ever be filled. It's an anger that will never go away. A sense of utter betrayal. And then when my mother left me here, it just confirmed every fear I'd ever had. I'd always known she'd leave me someday, too. That I'd chase her away."

"Mia, didn't you tell me your mother was into drugs? How was that your fault?"

"I don't know! I've just realized that I blamed myself for my parents abandoning me. This very moment. I mean, I've always understood it in some vague way, on an intellectual level. But understanding on an emotional level...that's something completely different. And it's just now really hitting me. God."

She buried her face in her hands. How had she failed to understand that this was as much the basis of her fears as the experience of being abandoned was?

"Oh, honey."

Karalee squeezed her arm. And that warmth, that sympathy, reminded her of her grandmother. No one else had ever cared for her this way. No one except Jagger. And Ben. She knew she had to let him go, finally. But there was still so much wreckage to deal with.

Mia lifted her head, looked at Karalee. The sun was going down outside the fogged windows. "I feel like I'm in this bizarre state, where my brain's not really working, yet all of these things are happening in there. Thoughts, ideas. Epiphanies. And some of it is about you, and being friends with you, learning how to really do that. And a huge part of it is about Jagger."

"I can understand why that would be scary, Mia. I've

been through some of that with Gideon. And he has with me. But we're working it all out. You can, too."

"I don't know if I'm brave enough. Some part of me is still convinced I'll drive him away, too. That sounds stupid..."

"No. You're just afraid. I don't blame you."

"I just...I don't even know if I'm even capable of being the person I'd have to be in order to have a healthy relationship, Karalee. To be what he deserves."

"And so you ran away from him."

"Yes." The pain was back, constricting her throat.

"You can decide to go back, you know."

"Yes." It came out on a whisper.

"It's all about choices, Mia. You have to choose to be vulnerable. To be open to being hurt. Or you'll miss out on everything. I'm learning that myself. That's what it comes down to for all of us, in the end. I guess the question you have to ask yourself is, would it be worth it? That risk? Because honestly, you look like you've been through hell already. I don't think it could get any worse. And you may feel like shit, but you're still breathing. Isn't it worth trying?"

"Yes!" Tears gathered in her eyes. "Except that I'm afraid I've completely screwed this up. I've hurt him. I don't know if he even wants to see me."

"Come on, Mia. You'll only really know if you talk to him. But don't call him. You need to go to him. See him in person."

"You're right. I know you're right. I think part of why I needed you here was to tell me that. To tell me what I already knew." She was shaking. With certainty, with fear.

"Just take a deep breath. You can do it. Why don't you take a shower first? Try to calm down a little."

"Okay. Okay. I will. Karalee, thank you. For coming here. For being my friend even though I'm lousy at it."

"Actually, for someone with so little experience, you're pretty damn good. Come here."

Karalee stood and put out her arms. And Mia went into them, let herself be hugged, comforted.

Maybe if she could learn to be a friend, to have a friend, she could learn to love Jagger, too. To accept that from him.

She was going to find out. She knew she'd done some damage. But she was beginning to heal on the inside. Jagger was a big part of that. Maybe she could find a way to heal things between them, too. If only he would let her.

Jagger answered the sharp knock on his door; he pulled it open and stepped back to let Jean in.

"Where's Leilani? I thought she was coming up, too."

"She's taking a nap. You could use one. You look like shit." Jean swept past him into the apartment, all tough-girl swagger in her black jeans and heavy boots. "Close the door, Jagger."

"What? Oh, yeah."

He shut the door and followed Jean into his kitchen, where she reached into a cupboard for a wineglass, poured from the bottle of Cabernet he kept on the counter, and handed it to him.

"Aren't you having any?"

"Maybe later. You're the one who needs it, Jagger."

"Yeah. Maybe I do."

"Come on, let's sit down and you can tell me what's going on. You sounded really strange on the phone." Jean settled down on the big green couch, leaning back, her long legs stretched out before her. He sat down next to her. "So, talk to me."

He took a slow sip of the wine, cradled the glass in his hand. "Things are really screwed up."

"With Mia? What did you do?"

"I didn't do anything! Fuck, I'm sorry. I didn't... I don't think I did anything." He took a swig of the wine, swallowed, took another. "I told her I loved her last night. And she freaked. She tried to hide it for a while, but it all came out... Christ, I don't get it. I knew she had some issues. But don't we all? Aren't we all just as fucked up, deep down, in our own way?"

"Sure. But for some people, that's hard to hear. Love."

"Yeah. It was hard for her to hear." He took another sip of the wine, needing its warmth to fight the stark cold that hovered in his chest ever since Mia Rose had left the night before. "So, what do I do now?"

Jean grabbed his wineglass, drank, handed it back to him. "If you want the soft, pretty version, you'd better wait until Leilani wakes up."

"I can take it. Straight-out. Say whatever needs to be said." His fingers tightened around the stem of the glass.

"Go after her. Don't let it wait. Don't let it simmer. She's scared. Some insane shit is going through her head. Don't sit back and let her do that, think like that. Go talk to her. Now."

"Right now? Tonight?"

"Yes, tonight. You have to understand a few things about women, Jagger. We don't like to be kept waiting. And the longer we wait, the crazier the shit that goes through our minds. Just do it. Don't waste time talking to me."

"It's not a waste of time, Jean."

She lowered her voice. "Come on. You know exactly what I mean. Why are you stalling?"

He shook his head. Why *was* he stalling? He looked past the pale blond spikes of Jean's hair and through the windows, into the night. The familiar neon glow from the streets below normally comforted him, made the apartment seem womblike. But tonight, the pink and gold light only seemed to illuminate more clearly how empty his home felt without Mia Rose in it.

He handed Jean his wineglass and stood up. "I'm going."

"Good. Don't lose her, Jagger."

"I'm not going to. I am damn well not going to. Thanks, Jean."

She shrugged. "I didn't really do anything. Except tell you what you already knew."

"Thanks anyway."

"Just go. Find her. Talk to her."

He nodded as he grabbed his jacket and his keys. Adrenaline pumped through his veins. He couldn't get to Mia Rose soon enough, suddenly.

Jean was right: He had to talk to her. Make her face the fact that he loved her. And even more, that she loved him back.

Mia blotted the water from her hair with a thick towel, dried her body, then slipped into her robe. Karalee was right; the shower had helped to warm her, soothe her. Her pulse was still racing, but she could take a breath now without feeling as though her chest were about to cave in.

A knock at the door startled her; Karalee must have forgotten something. She moved down the hall, pulled the door open.

Jagger stood there, as beautiful as ever. She had to pull in a sharp, gasping breath. Fresh grief washed over her, grief and love and a need so strong she could barely breathe.

"Mia Rose."

He stepped inside, kicked the door shut behind him, and pulled her into his arms.

"God, Jagger."

"Baby, baby," he whispered before lowering his mouth to hers. Just a sweet brushing of his lips, over and over, making her weak with desire. Making her heart ache.

He kissed her harder, pressing his lips down on hers until it hurt. The need for him welled up inside her, a powerful tide, and yet at the back of her mind, she knew certain things needed to be said before they went any further.

She pulled away, panting for breath. "Jagger, we need to talk."

"Now?"

"Yes, now."

"All I want is to be with you." He put a hand out to stroke her hair, and she backed up a step.

She saw the hurt on his face, knew it was her fault. "I'm sorry. I know I'm not doing this right, any of it. But there are some things you have to understand."

"I love you, Mia Rose. What else do I have to know?"

"That I'm . . . I understand I screwed up. And I'll probably do it again. There are reasons why I'm this way. Reasons

I'm trying to work through, but I know I have a long road ahead. And I don't know if it's fair to you to drag you along."

"We all have baggage."

"I have more baggage than most people." Her hands twisted together at her waist. She wanted so badly to touch him. "Being with you has made me see things about myself, about my life, I didn't see before. And it's not only about the food fetish, although that's part of it. Facing that part of myself has forced me to face other things about my past, about who I am. It's as though being with you has opened up my Pandora's box. But not everything inside there is pretty."

"It doesn't have to be. None of us are all pretty on the inside. All that twisted crap I've been carrying around about my past relationships. About not being able to love you because of what another woman did to my heart. But I understand now I don't have to allow that to determine whether or not I let myself love you. I was on autopilot, operating on an outdated idea about what I had to do. I had to meet you, to fall in love with you, to fight it."

"I don't know if I'm strong enough. I don't know if I can trust myself enough. I want to be with you. You know I do. But there are other issues involved."

"Issues like our age difference?"

"No. I've hardly thought of that since I first met you."

"It's about the school thing, then."

"Jagger, I just don't think you should quit with only this one semester to go! You're too close to your degree. I can't let you do that."

"It's my decision." He took her hands in his, held on

tight. "There's no way I can wait for the end of the semester to be with you. I'm going to do it. I'm dropping the class tomorrow morning. I'll take a summer class to make it up."

"I think it's a foolish decision."

"You think I'm foolish?"

He dropped her hands, and the loss of his warmth cut into her like a knife.

"No. That's not what I'm saying."

"What are you saying, then?" His voice was stark, cold.

"I'm just . . . I don't . . ." She shook her head. She couldn't find the right way to say it.

"You don't trust me to make a good decision for myself, do you?" he asked quietly. "Because of Ben. Because he decided to ride without a helmet, and he died because of that choice."

"Please, don't bring Ben into this."

"Ben will always be a part of you, Mia Rose." He paused, ran a hand over his hair. "You lost Ben because he made a stupid choice. But I'm not him."

"I know that. I understand it's not about you. But that's what I mean about my baggage." The more she tried to explain, the harder the knot in her stomach twisted, grew. The worse she felt about hurting him. And she didn't even know anymore if her own rationalizations made sense. She was so tired. So sad. She was losing him. And it was her own damn fault. "God, I don't mean to hurt you, Jagger. I don't. How can you even love me?"

The tears came again, hot on her cheeks. The sense of impending loss felt like drowning, like suffocating. She couldn't breathe, couldn't stand on her own feet. And she just collapsed, her legs going out from under her. Jagger caught her in his arms, held her up, held her tight. Held her while she cried.

"Shh, baby. That's what this is all about, isn't it? You think you're not lovable? You think that's why the people you love have left you? But it's not true. I love you. And I'm not going anywhere. You just need to let it be okay. Be with me. Love me. Let me love you."

"I don't want to do it wrong."

His arms tightened around her even more, crushing her to his chest. "You won't. We'll figure things out together. And it'll work. Because we love each other."

"I do. I love you."

He cradled her face in his hands, wiped her tears away with his thumbs. "That makes everything okay."

A warm flood of relief was seeping through her body, like a current of honey: that sweet, that slow. And with it was pure love. Powerful. Intoxicating.

Jagger leaned in and kissed her forehead, her cheek. And when she turned her face up to his, he kissed her mouth.

His lips were soft and sweet at first, but in moments he was kissing her hard, parting her lips with his tongue. And she felt that same urgency she sensed from him, a small trembling vibration just beneath his skin.

Her own skin was heating up as she pressed closer. And as she slipped her tongue into his mouth, wet heat against wet heat, he groaned, grabbed her around the waist, yanked her hard up against him.

Then all tenderness was gone. All that was left was a greedy hunger, a driving need that hummed in the air all around them, between them. His mouth was hard on hers, his hands everywhere at once, pulling her robe off, gliding over her skin.

"Ah, Jagger. I can't wait. I can't wait one more moment. Please."

He took her hand and moved toward the doorway leading to the kitchen, but she stopped him.

"No. I don't need that now."

"Are you sure?" His voice was raw with desire.

"Yes, I'm sure. I'll want it again sometimes. But right now all I need is you."

He nodded, smiled. Kissed her as he backed her up to the sofa, sat her down, and pushed her onto the pillows. It took him only moments to strip his clothes off. Then he was kneeling over her, parting her thighs with rough hands. But she needed that from him, needed him not to tease, not to seduce. She was right there already, waiting, eager. She was soaking wet.

"Lord, Mia Rose, I need to be inside you now. Right now, baby."

"Yes..."

He cupped the back of her head in one hand, and with the other he guided his cock into her body. Pleasure knifed into her, hot and sharp. And when he drove home in one long thrust, she cried out.

Her arms went around his neck, her legs around his back. She couldn't get close enough.

"More," she whispered.

"There's always more for you." His voice was a low rasp. "Always, baby. *My* baby."

He slid out, then back in, each devastating arc of his hips driving pleasure deeper and deeper into her body. Sensation built on sensation: sensation and scent and her heart nearly bursting with emotion.

"More," she begged again.

He slid his hand over her cheek, her jaw, his fingertips brushing her lips as he drove harder, hammering into her. Desire built, crested, and it was too lovely. She forced herself to hover there, to draw it out.

"I'm . . . oh God, I'm going to come, Jagger."

"Love you, Mia Rose." Harder and harder. "Love you, love you . . . ah!"

He tensed, and she let it go, let her body tumble over the edge and into that exquisite darkness. Her heart followed. Pleasure roared through her, drowning her. She was pulsing, hot, raw. Blind with pleasure, blind with love. And as wide open as she'd ever been to another human being.

They were still moving together, all damp skin and a tangle of arms and legs. Panting, sighing, as though with one breath.

"I love you, Jagger," she whispered, and felt the gentle brush of his lips on her hair.

She had never felt anything like this. So much more than she'd ever expected to have. He'd opened her up, and no matter what he'd found inside, the fear, the ugliness, he thought she was beautiful. Worthy of love. Like so few others in her life ever had.

"Jagger . . ."

"Yeah, baby."

"Have I ever told you about my grandmother?"

"No, not much. But we have all the time in the world. You can tell me anything you want."

It was true. They did have all the time in the world, if she would let it happen. If she could let them love each other. She was learning. And Jagger was teaching her.

Impossible. Yet here they were, together. Somehow she'd found him. Found release. Found joy.

Found love.

Hungry for more?
Turn over for a tantalising preview of
THE DARK GARDEN
Also by Eden Bradley

ONE

Rowan ran her hand over the cool metal of the chain suspended from the ceiling, drawing her fingers along the sleek, steely surface, one link, then the next. She curled her fingers around the length of it, slid her hand down until she felt the soft touch of leather against her skin, moving her fingers absently over the buckles of the cuffs.

She breathed in the familiar, earthy scent of leather. Club Privé. The most exclusive BDSM club on the West Coast. Rowan's second home.

She surveyed the space where her friends and acquaintances were preparing for the play party tonight. The room was, as always, womblike, with its dark red walls and dim purple and amber lights. The mesmerizing, tantric cadence of a Gregorian chant filled the air. She crossed the expanse of wood floor to find a seat on one of the red velvet couches that edged the play area, nodding quietly to those she knew, careful not to intrude as they cleaned and prepared their equipment and set the mood with their partners.

The familiar faint buzz of sensual anticipation that was

always present at a play party was heavy in the air, a palpable shared energy that built up as the evening wore on. And as had happened all too often lately, a surge of disappointment rose up in her at the emptiness inside that this place had once filled so beautifully.

When had it all begun to mean so little, when at one time it had been everything to her?

She watched as more people filtered into the room and willed herself not to fidget. Why was she even here? She had no intention of playing tonight; she wasn't in the mood. She was far too edgy, and dominating even the most beautiful boys at the club, the most obedient, was no longer satisfying. She'd been like this for months, and nothing seemed to help. Yet at the same time, her writing, her dark secret writing, was going better than ever. Words seemed to flow out of her fingertips effortlessly in a tide of language and emotion. It should have been a release, yet she never came out of it feeling sated anymore.

The music changed to the familiar trancelike tones that signaled the official beginning of the evening. Submissive men and women were bound to the large wooden crosses, the spanking benches, the racks. They were beautiful, all of them, regardless of their shape or size. She had always thought so. There was beauty in the act of submission itself, something which never failed to amaze her.

She had talked about it at the discussion group she ran one Tuesday night each month for those new to the lifestyle. They talked a lot about the psychology of BDSM, of the rituals and symbols that were the basis of it all. She was glad she was able to help people make the transition into accepting this secret side of themselves. But in the five years she herself had been involved, there was a part of her that never quite felt whole.

Don't think about it now, don't think about why.

One of the male submissives she often played with approached her with a smile of greeting, knelt on the floor before her. He was one of her favorites. Blond, with soft, curling hair and a cherubic face, he had a sweet temperament and the stamina of a racehorse. She shook her head, letting him know she wasn't prepared to play.

"Are you sure, Mistress?"

"Not tonight, Eric. But don't worry, you're sure to catch somebody's eye." She reached out and stroked a finger over his shoulder with a sigh.

"May I serve you, Mistress? A drink, maybe?"

"Thank you, no. Go play. Enjoy your evening. I'm going to observe tonight."

"As you wish." He boldly took her hand and brushed a kiss over her skin.

Rowan smiled. "Off with you, now."

"Yes, Ma'am."

She forced her focus back to the floor. The club was crowded tonight. Almost every play station was in use. Groups lounged on the couches, as she did, or sat at the small café tables placed here and there, the submissives, or bottoms, serving food and drinks to their Masters and Mistresses, or kneeling on the floor at their feet. A small group of new submissives were huddled against one wall like a bunch of teenage girls at their first dance, waiting to be noticed. All wore the white leather protective collar of the club along with their scanty lingerie, signaling their availability and their status as bottoms. Rowan was glad that as a dominant at the club, she'd never had to go through those first excruciating experiences, that waiting to be chosen. *She* chose her partners. It would never be any other way for her. Controlling her sensuality was key. She had allowed herself to be controlled by another once and had paid far too high a price.

She shivered, pushing away the memories, down deep where they belonged, where she had kept them locked away for so long.

When she glanced up, a shining cascade of strawberry blond hair caught her eye and April, a new friend from the monthly discussion group, came to sit on the floor near her feet.

"Good evening, Mistress Rowan." The pretty young woman's voice was light, lilting. Her warm smile reached her round, cornflower blue eyes.

Rowan laughed. "Don't be silly. I'm not your Mistress, no need for such formalities." She patted the seat next to her. "Come, sit with me."

April smiled, tugged at the hem of her short baby pink leather skirt, and settled onto the cushions close to Rowan.

"How are you, April?"

Her lashes fluttered as she looked away. "Nervous. Yearning."

"Ah. Who is he?"

April gestured with her chin toward a large man with close-cut dark hair and a goatee, dressed in the standard Dom attire: black jeans, a black T-shirt, a black leather vest. He was strapping a naked woman to a St. Andrew's cross, a large wooden X on a platform with hooks to which he attached the girl's leather wrist and ankle cuffs.

Rowan nodded. "Decker. He's Irish, but he's been here in the States for a while, and he's been at the club at least as long as I have. Does something in the music industry; a sound engineer, I think. He's very experienced, has great technique. You could do worse. He plays with all the girls here, and they're all half in love with him. But he's never stuck with one woman. He won't scene with anyone for more than one night at a time. He's not the commitment type. You should know that."

April sighed softly. "I know. They never are."

"Not true. Most of the members of the club are part of a couple."

"But not you."

"No, not me," she answered quietly.

"I'm sorry, Rowan. I shouldn't have said that. It's none of my business."

"No, it's alright. I just ... don't know what to say."

"You don't seem yourself tonight. And you look tired."

"I haven't been sleeping well," Rowan admitted.

"I'm sorry. Is there anything I can do to help?" April's eyes were full of sincerity. She was a lovely girl, sweet, innocent in her desire to please. The man she ended up serving would be very lucky.

"No, nothing. Thank you, though." She squeezed April's hand.

There was nothing anyone could do to help her. She didn't know herself what this inner restlessness was about.

A cool rush of night air caught her attention as the door opened for a late arrival. An unfamiliar figure stood for a moment in the doorway, surveying the room. He was tall, well over six feet, with broad shoulders and a tapering waist. There was something elegant in his stance. As he turned to survey the room, she could see his long, pale blond hair was pulled back into a narrow leather thong. He had noble, chiseled features. And even from across the half-dark room, she could see his wide, lush mouth.

A small shiver went through her.

He is not for you.

She could see instantly that this man was a top. Dominance radiated from him like heat. Not one of her pretty boys to play with. But then, she wasn't in the mood to play, was she?

Still, she couldn't take her eyes from him, this stranger dressed all in black. And then he looked at her, locking gazes from across the room. Her stomach tightened beneath the dark blue leather corset she wore.

She forced herself to blink, to look away. Why should this man have such an effect on her?

April leaned over and whispered, "He was looking right at you, Rowan. Through you, almost. Did you see that?"

See it? She'd felt it all the way down to her bones.

"He's a Dom."

"Yes, but still..."

Rowan shook her head. "It's impossible."

"But you find him as beautiful as he obviously finds you."

Rowan was surprised to feel heat flare in her cheeks. She didn't bother to deny it.

April, seeming to sense her discomfort, stood. "Why don't I fetch you a drink? San Pellegrino with a squeeze of lime, yes?"

"Thank you, yes." Good girl, remembering her drink of choice.

She bent her head and rubbed her temples with her fingers as April walked away. What was wrong with her?

When she glanced up again, he was moving across the room in long strides; graceful, predatory. She had no idea why his presence here made her so uncomfortable, so hyper-aware of her own skin, her own breath.

He stopped to talk to Master Hawke, the owner of the club, an enormous man with a full brown beard. They both turned to look at the group of bottoms. Yes, he would choose one of the new girls. What would it be like to watch him play?

Again her stomach quivered. What was going on with her?

She turned away once more, focusing her attention on a triad playing at a spanking bench. The bottom, a lovely young woman, was bound to it, facedown, the arch of her smooth, bare buttocks high in the air. The tops, a man and a woman, were taking turns applying tiny plastic clothespins to her flesh. The bottom remained obediently still, until the man began to use a crop to knock the pins off. The girl squealed, squirmed, then moaned as the evil little pins flew onto the floor.

Rowan smiled. She had played that game before, knew how the blood rushed painfully back into the skin after being pinched away by the pins. It always gave the bottom an exquisite rush of endorphins. She'd watched it happen, that glazing of the eyes, the Mona Lisa smiles.

She was still smiling when a light touch on her arm brought her head up. Master Hawke stood over her with the new Dom at his side. God, he was even more gorgeous up close. His face was a symphony of fine planes and angles, his mouth even darker and more sensual. But it was his eyes that started a warm knot that began in her stomach and spread outward until her limbs went weak. Eyes that were a startling shade of turquoise and jade that shifted like the ocean at twilight.

Control, Rowan.

Master Hawke leaned over her. "I'd like you to meet Master Christian Thorne, just back from Berlin. He's an old member at Privé. Thorne, this is Mistress Rowan."

Before she had a chance to respond, the stranger leaned in, took her hand, bent over it, and brushed a kiss across her knuckles. She felt his touch as though it were made of fire, those lush lips against her skin. But she forced herself not to react, her racing pulse to still. Reminded herself that he was just a man, like any other.

Why did that feel like a lie?

"It's very nice to meet you, Rowan."

She'd expected a German accent, but he appeared to be as American as she was. His voice was deep, smooth, elegant.

She nodded to him, cleared her throat. "Yes, it's nice to meet you, too. I hope you'll enjoy our club."

"I'm enjoying it immensely already."

Was that a wicked gleam in his eye? Suddenly her corset was too tight against her ribs.

Get ahold of yourself, Rowan.

"Thorne, let me introduce you to some of the others."

Master Hawke led him away and she could finally take a breath.

April arrived with her drink. She handed it to her as she took her seat once more. "I saw you talking to him. Who is he? What is he like?"

"Christian Thorne." Rowan wasn't likely to forget that name anytime soon. "He's arrogant, cool, sophisticated. And utterly self-confident." She paused to sip her drink, watching him.

She'd sensed immediately that he was the kind of man those in her group would call a true Dom, someone who was so naturally dominant that everyone—waiters, sales clerks—automatically deferred to him without being aware of it or knowing why.

And Lord help her, he was as beautiful a man as she had ever seen. His face was flawless. Strong, proud, beautifully made. He had one of those mouths that made a woman want to kiss him, to feel his lips on her flesh.

"He's gorgeous." April was smiling at her.

"He's a dominant, April. Any connection between us, other than being friends, is impossible. And I don't know that he's the kind of man I'd want to be friends with."

"But is he the kind of man you . . . want?"

The girl had a habit of asking the most revealing questions. But Rowan wasn't interested in pursuing the answer.

"I need to find a playmate for the evening."

She patted April's hand and rose from her couch. She still wasn't very much in the mood, but she obviously needed some distraction from her wandering mind, from the lust still singing in her veins from that momentary contact of his lips on the back of her hand.

Ridiculous. Ironic. But there it was.

Christian Thorne was the first man who had excited her in a long time. And she could never have him.

∽

It was well after midnight when Rowan let herself into her nineteenth-floor apartment in Century City. She paused at the wide expanse of windows overlooking the city. Los Angeles sparkled like a blanket of diamonds in the dark, illuminated by a brilliant, almost full moon. She loved this view; it had been the main reason why she'd bought this place. But tonight it did nothing to soothe her.

Neither had paddling Jeffrey, one of her usual boys. He was very pretty, with the kind of youthful, androgynous features she liked in her playmates. He was an experienced submissive. Experienced enough to know her heart wasn't in her play tonight. Finally, he'd called an end to the scene and asked her if she was alright. Of course she wasn't. She'd left him with a brief hug and an apology.

She pulled the sheer drapes closed and went to her small granite-and-brushed-steel kitchen to pour herself a glass of wine. The aromatic scent of the fine cabernet hit her nostrils as she opened the bottle.

She carried the glass into her bedroom, set it down on the dresser, and removed her corset, her black pencil skirt, her stiletto-heeled shoes. She placed the shoes into their cubbyhole in her custom-built closet, hung up her skirt, and carefully laid the leather corset in a drawer, comforted somehow by the small ritual of organization. Naked, she carried her glass into the slate-tiled bathroom, sipping as she went, and turned on the water in the tub. A hot bath would relax her, help her to free her mind from the nagging images of this annoyingly fascinating stranger.

While the tub filled she caught her reflection in the enormous bronze-framed vanity mirror. She pulled the pins from her hair and it fell in coal black waves around her shoulders. The dark smudges beneath her blue eyes were a stark contrast against her pale skin. She was bone-tired, and she looked it. Of course, it was late, but there was more to it than that. She hadn't been sleeping well lately. The edginess she'd felt at the dungeon tonight was nothing new.

She ran her hands over the red marks left on her white skin by the boning in the corset, over her ribs, her full breasts. Her nipples peaked at the touch of her own soft fingertips. Yes, it had been far too long since she had enjoyed a man.

She never had sex with the submissive men she played with. Oh, her boys would service her when she allowed them to, but it wasn't quite the same, was it? She'd dated several men out of the lifestyle, had slept with a few, but it never seemed to work for her, and none of those relationships had lasted more than a month or two. She was much more intimate with the small collection of vibrators in her nightstand drawer.

Her muscles tensed at the thought, and she turned off the now full tub, then went back into her bedroom, thinking of the new waterproof toy she'd bought recently. She needed it tonight, needed some release, some relief.

The small, textured lavender vibrator in hand, she returned to the bathroom and slid into the steaming water. It moved like silk against her skin as she sat back, leaning her head against the edge of the tub.

Oh, yes, she was sensitive tonight, every nerve in her body on alert. And all because of him.

Christian Thorne.

She turned the vibrator on high and lowered it beneath

the surface of the water. It wouldn't hurt to think of him, to imagine it was his hands on her body. When she touched the tip of the vibe to her clit a shiver of pleasure ran through her.

She was so sensitive tonight she could probably come in a minute flat. But she wanted to draw it out, to make it last. She closed her eyes, allowed herself to see his face; that beautiful, lush mouth, those mysterious ocean eyes. His hands were big, she'd noticed. What would they feel like on her skin?

She ran one hand over her breasts, caressing them as she imagined he would. But no, he would be cruel about it, wouldn't he? She pinched one of her nipples, hard, and felt the shock of painful pleasure course through her. Yes, that was more like it.

She lowered the vibe once more, let it slide over the lips of her sex. They filled with need as she teased herself. She spread her thighs apart so she could push the tip of the phallic-shaped vibrator inside.

Oh, God, it felt good. And it was his face in her mind, his fingers pushing into her. And then his beautifully masculine face lowering between her legs, that gorgeous, hot mouth on her sex. His tongue flicking over her tight, hard clit.

Her hips bucked, moving into the vibrator as she rubbed it over her cleft, over the slick lips of her sex, dipped inside, then out again, still teasing herself.

His mouth would be warm and wet. *God, yes.* She was so close. She pressed the vibe over her hard little nub, reached down and slid two fingers into her tight, aching hole, pumped them, imagining it was Christian's cock inside her.

He would be thick and heavy, filling her. She added one more finger, moved her hips against her hand, against the trilling buzz of the vibrator, saw his face.

The first wave of her orgasm rolled over her, a stinging wave of pure pleasure. And as her climax gathered in intensity, turned into a sharp, stabbing pulse beat that reverberated through her entire body, the image of Christian in her mind changed, and he was pulling her naked body over his lap, his hand coming down in a stinging slap on her ass. She came harder, moaned aloud. Her legs tensed against the onslaught of sensation, the vibe held firmly as she shook and shuddered. And in her mind's eye, Christian Thorne gave her the spanking of her life.

৩৩

It was after four A.M. when she finally slept that night. Her dreams were dark, veiled in a chiaroscuro cloud, as though she could never quite see what was going on. But she could feel his presence. Christian. He was strong, dynamic. She could feel him, even though she couldn't quite see his face. It was frustrating. Tantalizing.

She woke in the lonely predawn light in a sweat of need and reached into her nightstand drawer, pulling out a small hand-held bullet. She switched it on and slid it down between her trembling thighs, letting the buzzing tremors sweep through her, pressing down hard. She came fast, furiously. Her climax left her shaking and weak. And again, it was his face in her mind. He was all she could see. She fell immediately back into a deep, dreamless sleep.

In the morning she felt as though she had a hangover.

And she cursed herself for her new obsession. She really had to get it under control.

Sunday stretched interminably before her, with little to keep her occupied. A good day to write, perhaps.

Still in her favorite sapphire silk robe, she sat down at the desk in her bedroom with a fragrant cup of Earl Grey tea and flipped open her laptop. She always took a few minutes to read whatever she had written last to get her in the mood, to set the tone in her head.

Ashlyn stared at Gabriel. What had he just offered? A chance to experience the things she had only ever dreamed about, had never dared to discuss with anyone until now. All of those strange yearnings that had pulled at her for years, for as long as she could remember having sexual feelings in her body, sexual thoughts in her mind.

He had offered to give it all to her, if only she was brave enough . . .

Was she?

Images of Gabriel standing over her while she lay tied to a big, four-post bed, his dark golden eyes shining, that evil-looking goatee that she loved, a flogger in his hand. Oh, yes, she knew what it was called. She'd read her secret books, those dark stories of pain and pleasure, of dominance and submission. This was exactly what she wanted. If only it didn't frighten her so much.

Before she could allow her fears to force her to protest, to lose it all, she murmured, "Yes."

Rowan found herself getting wet just reading this simple scene. There wasn't even any sex, just that moment of submission, of giving in. It was that yielding that was the turn-on. She remembered what it had been like for her, all those years ago, that first moment. She didn't want to think now about how horribly wrong it had gone after that. No; now she wanted to feel again that excruciating, exquisite thrill.

She typed furiously for the next hour, as though she burned with fever. She was hot, and everything seemed hazy. Everything except this driving need to put words on paper. To purge some of the confusion and lust from her body.

Yes, let her character experience these things, so she wouldn't have to.

Ashlyn looked up from her kneeling position on the floor at the man who would be the first she would call Master. His dark eyes were unreadable. Was he pleased with her?

The wool rug was scratchy beneath her bare knees, but she didn't care. All she wanted now was to make him happy, to have him touch her, hurt her. It was still strange to her, that she craved the pain. But right now she didn't want to think too much about it.

How surprised she'd been when he'd first turned her over his knee and spanked her last night. His hand had been fire to her flesh, pain and pleasure coursing through her, uniting, becoming one. By the time he had finished she would have done anything for him.

She wanted him to do it again. A titillating bolt of anticipation shot through her. She knew he would. And much more. He had promised to do things to her she had never imagined. She trembled at the idea.

*Despite her inner struggle to accept this side of herself,
she was half in love with him already.*

Rowan shifted in her seat. She was wet again, soaked, in
fact, her sex pulsing. Images of her dream last night flashed
in her mind. Christian's hand coming down hard on her
bare flesh. *Yes.* But how many times in a twenty-four-hour
period could she bring herself to orgasm? She pushed back
her chair and stood. Perhaps just once more.

☞☜

Christian stalked the length of his third-floor studio in his
house on the Venice Canals, that section just off Venice
Beach that was loosely modeled on the canals of Venice,
Italy, with meandering waterways lined with houses of
every description. As he moved past the windows he could
see the small blue and white beach cottage next door, the
contemporary two-story brown shingle next to it, and beyond, the enormous stucco-and-tile structure that made
him think of an old Italian palazzo.

He was restless, couldn't seem to settle anywhere.
There was plenty to do, but he couldn't focus on any one
task. He'd hardly had time to unpack since his arrival in
L.A., except for his studio; it was the first area of the house
he'd set up. His tools were in order on his high workbench:
chisels, planes, buffers. Except he hadn't touched his tools
since he'd arrived back in the States, had he? Or for months
before he'd left Berlin. Work had grown stale for him. He
hadn't found a subject that interested him in far too long.

He was bored with it all, bored with the work. Bored with himself, perhaps. It was one reason why he'd come home to the States. Europe no longer held any inspiration for him. The women who posed for him all seemed the same after a while. Sleeping with them hadn't helped. He'd been telling himself it was about the art, but that was a lie. He hadn't met a woman in a long time who challenged him, who made him think. They were all too easy. Too easy to figure out. Too easy to get into his bed.

He sat down on an antique chaise longue covered in decaying gold velvet that was piled with pillows and several old quilts at one end of the enormous room. He'd picked up the old chaise at an antiques market in London and it had traveled with him all through Europe. He sometimes slept there after working through the night, which he did fairly often, not even bothering to cross the floor to where his big bed stood against the only solid wall on this level of the house. Pulling an all-nighter made him feel achy and edgy, but he did some of his best work in the early hours before dawn. Lately, though, even that almost hypnotic state brought on by lack of sleep had left him empty of inspiration.

Too on edge to sit, he rose and went to smooth his hand over a large piece of raw marble he'd acquired recently, nearly five feet of gorgeous white stone. Normally the stone spoke to him, and he would buy a piece knowing exactly what he intended to do with it, but this one piece remained a mystery to him. Yet he'd had to have it.

He had that same feeling about the glorious Mistress Rowan.

Mistress. He didn't think so. And he was rarely wrong about such things. But he had to admit the magnetic pull he felt for this woman may have obscured his thinking.

He'd immediately seen the strength in her delicate frame, in the dark blue fire burning in her eyes. Lord, she was beautiful. He'd never been so attracted to any woman before in his life.

He'd spent the last number of years in Europe, moving from London to Spain, Italy to France, and finally to Berlin. He'd seen some of the most beautiful women in the world. But none compared to this little beauty.

He had to sculpt her. Had to have her.

And he was pretty damn sure the feeling had been mutual.

He sipped his black coffee and looked out the long bank of windows at the view of the ocean in the distance. To the north lay Santa Monica, to the south Marina del Rey. The coast, only a few blocks away, was still fogged in, obscuring the point at which ocean met sky on the horizon. He loved the ocean, had always found it soothing. But his nerves were stretched tight as piano wire today and even the somnolent gray sea did nothing to calm him.

He'd been wound up tight ever since meeting Rowan at the club last night. Master Hawke had generously gifted him with his own pair of female submissives and Christian had played them well into the night. But he'd been distracted the entire time. He'd been able to see Rowan playing with a male sub out of the corner of one eye. Her scene hadn't lasted long and she'd left. She'd also left him with the impression of her beautiful, regal face imprinted on his mind.

Despite her claim to dominance, he was convinced there was more beneath the surface. But how to convince her? There had to be a way.

He knew he wouldn't see her again until the next play party at the club, which was next weekend. But what then? And meanwhile, he had to concentrate, had to get some work done.

He turned back to the five-foot-tall expanse of untapped marble. It reminded him of Rowan's pale skin. He ran his palm once more over the sleek surface. Lord, she would feel just like this beneath his hands. Silky, cool.

Maybe that was what he found so incredibly attractive about her. That cool control, that composed detachment. And she really was regal; elegant and lovely. She would be a perfect model for him, with her flawless skin and her long, delicate bones...

Frustrated, he grabbed a sketchbook from his workbench and flopped down on the ancient lounge, quickly drawing her face. Yes, that was it, the strong yet fragile-looking jaw, the generous mouth. The mouth of a prostitute really; lush and forbidden. Pure sex. He quickly added the high, rounded cheekbones and the slight tilt to her eyes. He sketched the long, narrow column of her neck, the slope of her shoulders, shaded in her collarbones. But when he tried to imagine her bare breasts it was too much for him and he flung the sketchpad to the wood floor and muttered, "Damn it."

He had to see her again. Had to find out if his instincts were right. Had to find out what it was about this woman that made him doubt himself, that challenged his self-control.

And meanwhile, he had better find a way to distract himself or he was going to lose his mind. He jumped up, determined to put his house in order. The physical activity of moving furniture, hanging his paintings, would work some of this energy off. And seeing the artwork he'd collected over the years always gave him pleasure; surely a good distraction. Then maybe he could manage to concentrate on his work. He had a show coming up in a few weeks and he still had to crate up several small pieces to ship to the gallery. That would keep him busy for a while. But he had a feeling that nothing would keep the mysterious Mistress Rowan out of his mind.

℘

The discussion group at Club Privé began at eight o'clock, but Rowan always tried to arrive a few minutes early, work allowing. Her job as a freelance corporate analyst was all-consuming while she was working on a project, and incredibly detail-oriented. The perfect job for the utter perfectionist she freely admitted to being. And for the control freak she knew she was on some level, even if she didn't like to think about herself in those terms. But today, even though she had really applied herself, even working right through lunch, she'd been distracted by random thoughts of *him*.

Being here at the club wasn't helping. As she set up the circle of chairs around the main staging area, all she could think of was his face in the dim, colored lights, the hot brush of his lips on her hand when he'd kissed it.

Would she ever be able to be here again and think of anything else?

People began to filter in and Rowan greeted them as they took their seats. April ran in, flushed and breathless, her long strawberry hair flying, just as the meeting was about to begin. Rowan smiled at her.

"Welcome, everyone," she began. "Tonight we're going to talk about making the transition into the BDSM lifestyle. Few of us can do this without questioning ourselves; who we are, what we want, why we want it. And if what we're doing, what we crave, is wrong, dirty somehow."

There was a flurry of agreeable nods. Rowan continued. "In the past there have been those in the psychology community who have looked at our fetish as a kind of sickness, but more modern thinkers have come to understand that it can be a healthy expression of our desires, even a constructive way to work through painful experiences in our pasts."

It had helped her, hadn't it? But she had to concentrate on what she was saying.

"Still, there tends to be a lot of shame accompanying the pleasure and relief we find in this sort of play. I'm sure some of you have felt it."

Again, a round of nods. April raised her hand.

"Yes, April?"

"Does it ever go away?"

"For most of us, I think it does. But it's something you have to recognize and work through. And it's a bit different for the tops than it is for the bottoms. The tops, the sadists, have to stop and wonder why they enjoy being in command, why they gain pleasure from 'hurting' people. And the bottoms, the masochists, why they enjoy being ordered around, why they crave pain."

A short, dark-haired woman raised her hand.

"Patricia?"

"How do you know if you're a top or a bottom?"

Rowan shifted in her chair. "Ah . . . I think that answer may be different for everyone. Is this something you're questioning?"

The woman nodded. "I've been playing as a submissive for the last few months, but I don't think I really like being told what to do. And I don't like any of the humiliation stuff."

"These are things you can negotiate with the top you're playing with, Patricia. Not every bottom is a submissive, necessarily. Many enjoy the sensation play, but aren't truly submissive inside."

"I think that describes me. But I also have these thoughts . . ."

"Go on," Rowan encouraged her.

"Well, I've seen some of the sub boys here, and . . . I've often wondered what it would be like to administer a spanking, to have them at my beck and call . . ." She blushed a bright red.

"There's no need to be embarrassed, Patricia. You may be a switch; one of those people who enjoys playing both sides. And they do say those who have experienced bottoming make the best tops. I think if you really have that urge, you should allow yourself to explore it."

April spoke up. "Have you ever bottomed, Rowan?"

"Me? No." She laughed, trying to cover the lie that had come out of her mouth so automatically. She had conditioned herself not to think about that episode in her life. But it wasn't fair for her to be so scornful of the idea. Especially when she had just recommended it to everyone in the room. Especially when she'd been fantasizing about nothing else for two days. Her cheeks burned, and once again Christian's features flooded her mind. And then a brief, unwelcome flash from long ago. The experience she never talked about, dwelled on . . . Why was this coming up lately, over and over again? She had spent a number of years trying very hard to put that year of her life behind her. And she'd been successful. Until she'd met Christian.

How was it this one man was so easily undoing all the years of work she'd put into gathering her strength? Why was she so full of questions, confusion? And the sudden yearning to experience sensation, to submit.

She had an uneasy feeling that this was only the beginning of a complicated issue she would have to face at some point, and perhaps that point was now. Her insane attraction to Christian Thorne, a thoroughly dominant man, was already something she was unable to dismiss. Could she handle it? She wanted the answer to be a quick "Yes!" but she was no longer entirely sure of herself. And she felt on some deep level that Christian's introduction into her life was going to force the issue to the surface. Could it be that somehow this one man was going to change her life forever?

Want more sexy fiction?

September 2012 saw the re-launch of the iconic erotic fiction series *Black Lace* with a brand new look and even steamier fiction. We're also re-visiting some of our most popular titles in our *Black Lace Classics* series.

First launched in 1993, *Black Lace* was the first erotic fiction imprint written by women for women and quickly became the most popular erotica imprint in the world.

To find out more, visit us at:
www.blacklacebooks.co.uk

And join the *Black Lace* community:

🐦 @blacklacebooks

🅵 BlackLaceBooks

BLACK
LACE

The leading imprint of women's sexy fiction is
back – and it's better than ever!

Also available from Black Lace:

The Dark Garden
Eden Bradley

Surrender has its own rewards...

Rowan Cassidy likes to be in charge – especially in her personal life. At Club Privé, the most exclusive S&M club on the West Coast, she can live out her dominant fantasies safely, and with complete control.

Then she meets Christian Thorne. Self-confidant and sophisticated, he's a natural dominant and makes it clear he wants to be Rowan's master. He makes Rowan a daring proposition: she must give herself over to him for thirty days and discover her true nature...

Praise for *The Dark Garden*

'Bradley's well-crafted descriptions help you to visualize the edgy and erotic scenes...strong characters surround the main couple, and a deftly handled subplot rounds out this amazing novel'
Romantic Times

'a masterpiece' Larissa Ione

'People are constantly looking for books similar to *Fifty* ... well look no further, I have what you need! ...Eden Bradley writes the most sensual books I have ever read'
My Secret Romance Reviews

Also available from Black Lace:

Wedding Games
Karen S Smith

Emma is not looking forward to her cousin's wedding: the usual awkward guests, the endless small talk, the bad dancing... But a chance encounter with Kit, a very sexy stranger, leaves her breathless.

Without a chance to say goodbye, Emma resigns herself to the fact their incredibly hot encounter will be just sexy memory, but then she meets Kit at another wedding...

Also available from Black Lace:

Honeymoon Games
Karen S Smith

When newlyweds Emma and Kit speed away on their matching Ducati motorbikes, Emma knows not to expect a conventional honeymoon. From the moment they meet a biker gang and the leader takes a shine to Emma, events take a turn for the bizarre.

With hard-drinking rock bands, hunky stuntmen, booze-fuelled biker festivals and a whole lot of kinky behaviour on the agenda, Emma's taste for adventure is tested to the max – and Kit's not about to step in and save her from the wild bunch as he's having too much fun himself...

**A wild, leather-clad, biker orgy,
this high-octane spin across the continent
is set to send the blood racing.**

Also available from Black Lace:

In Too Deep
Portia Da Costa

Lust among the stacks...

Librarian Gwendolyne Price starts finding indecent proposals and sexy stories in her suggestion box. Shocked that they seem to be tailored specifically to her own deepest sexual fantasies, she begins a tantalising relationship with a man she's never met.

But pretty soon, erotic letters and toe-curlingly sensual emails just aren't enough. She has to meet her mysterious correspondent in the flesh...

Praise for Portia Da Costa

'Imaginative, playful and a lot of fun'
For Women

Also available from Black Lace:

On Demand
Justine Elyot

I have always been drawn to hotels.
I love their anonymity. The hotel does not care
what you do, or with whom.

The Hotel Luxe Noir is a haven for hedonistic liaisons. From brief encounters in the bar to ménages in the elevator, young Sophie Martin has seen it all since she started on reception. But as she witnesses the dark erotic secrets of the staff and guests can she also master her own desires…?

Welcome to the Hotel Luxe Noir – discretion assured, satisfaction guaranteed.

Praise for *On Demand*

'Indulgent and titillating, On Demand is like a tonic for your imagination. The writing is witty, the personal and sexual quirks of the characters entertaining'
Lara Kairos

'Did I mention that every chapter is highly charged with eroticism, BDSM, D/S, and almost every fantasy you can imagine? If you don't get turned on by at least one of these fantasies, here is no hope for you'
Manic Readers

Also available from Black Lace:

The Ninety Days of Genevieve
Lucinda Carrington

He is an arrogant, worldly entrepreneur who always gets what he wants.

And what he wants is for Genevieve to spend the next ninety days submitting to his every desire...

A dark, sensual tale of love and obsession, featuring a very steamy relationship between an inexperienced heroine and a masterful and rich older man.

Praise for *The Ninety Days of Genevieve*

'This month's essential reading...For fans of the renaissance of erotic fiction comes Lucinda Carrington's tale of love and obsession'
Stylist

'sizzling ...It's full of expertly written sex scenes that will appeal to any woman who has ever fantasised about bondage, lust, exhibitionism and voyeurism!...an excellent plot, well written characters and heaps of charm'
Handbag.com

Also available from Black Lace:

Hot Ménage
Edited by Lori Perkins

A super-hot short story collection about threesomes.

In this delightfully wicked anthology, you'll find threesomes of all types ranging from historical to contemporary, with even a touch of the paranormal. Whether it's two men and a woman, two women and a man, or same-sex threesomes, these groups find interesting and inspiring ways to get it on. From sexed-up cowboys to an all male medieval threesome, hot vintage Hollywood to a triple lesbian story right out of *Mad Men*, *Hot Ménage* has a story for everyone.

Contributors include: Jen Bluekissed, Kristabel Reed, Em Brown, K.T. Grant, Janet Post, Jo Atkinson, Courtney Sheets, Cathleen Ross, Rebecca Leigh, Melanie Thompson, Elizabeth Coldwell, Cynthia Gentry, Mercy Loomis, Laura Neilsen, Reno Lark and Brit M.

Also available from Black Lace:

All You Can Eat
Emma Holly

Sex, lies and murder…

Frankie Smith is having a bad day: her boyfriend has just dumped her and she's just found a dead body behind her café.

Still, things look up when sexy local detective, Jack West, turns up to investigate. And when a stranger turns up at the diner looking for work, Frankie soon finds herself juggling two men and an increasingly kinky sex life…

Explicit, erotic fiction from the bestselling author of Ménage

Also available from Black Lace:

The Stranger
Portia Da Costa

Once she had got over the initial shock of the young man's nudity, Claudia allowed herself to breathe properly again...

When Claudia finds a sexy stranger on the beach near her home she discovers that he has lost his memory along with his clothes.

Having turned her back on relationships since the death of her husband, Claudia finds herself scandalising her friends by inviting the stranger into her home and into her bed...

Black Lace Classics – **our best erotic fiction ever from our leading authors**

Also available from Black Lace:

I Kissed a Girl
Edited by Regina Perry

*Everyone's heard the Katy Perry song, but have you
ever been tempted...?*

If so, you're not alone: most heterosexual women have had
same-sex fantasies, and this diverse collection of short
erotic fiction takes us way beyond kissing.

An anthology featuring kinky girl stories from around the
globe and women from every walk of life and culture who
are curious and eager to explore their full sexuality...with
each other.

Black Lace Books: the leading imprint of erotic fiction
by women for women